T0116876

James Wollrab

Perturbation Theory

iUniverse, Inc.
Bloomington

iUniverse books may be ordered through booksellers or by contacting:

iUniverse
1663 Liberty Drive
Bloomington, IN 47403
www.iuniverse.com
1-800-Authors (1-800-288-4677)

ISBN: 978-1-4620-0913-8 (sc)
ISBN: 978-1-4620-0914-5 (ebook)

Printed in the United States of America

iUniverse rev. date: 4/1/2011

Epigraph

Before the beginning,
after the great war between heaven and hell,
God created the earth
and gave dominion over it to the crafty ape He called 'man'.
To each generation was born
a creature of light and a creature of darkness.
The great armies would clash by night
in the ancient war between good and evil.
It was magic then, nobility and unimaginable cruelty.
So it was until the day
that a false sun exploded over Trinity,
and man forever traded away
wonder for reason.

Carnivale-Home Box Office

Cover Graphic Created by Mads Buus Jacobsen

Definitions

Perturbation is a disturbance of the regular elliptic or other motion of a celestial body produced by some force additional to that which causes its regular motion.

Webster's Collegiate Dictionary

Perturbation theory comprises mathematical methods that are used to find an approximate solution to a problem which cannot be solved exactly, by starting from the exact solution of a related problem. Perturbation theory is applicable if the problem at hand can be formulated by adding a "small" term to the mathematical description of the exactly solvable problem.

Wikipedia

Other Books by James Wollrab

Rotational Spectra and Molecular Structure
Shadows in the Caribbean
Match Penalty
Graveyard Train
Malfeasance
Murder at the Palais-Royal
The Malediction
Honor and Vengeance
Russian Winter
Hey, Joe

1

Post Mortem

The lunatic is in my head.
Raise the blade, make the change.
Re-arrange me 'til I'm sane.
Lock the door, throw away the key.
Someone's in my head, but it's not me!

Brain Damage
Pink Floyd

Russian Institute for Biological Sciences
Saint Petersburg, Russia

Sometime in the near future.

He wasn't a big man, especially for a Russian, just under six feet tall and fairly thin. His brown curly hairline was receding slightly, but he wasn't worried about that just now. It was the recent great difficulty he had sleeping that concerned him the most ever since the weird event that happened just over the last week. The whole thing was a blur that his mind couldn't resolve, and it was affecting his behavior. And to top it off, his brother was missing! Not that he had any great love for Tomas, but, after all, he was his brother.

And now they…his military superiors, wanted to meet with him in the strangest of places. Why here in the middle of nowhere? Had they found Tomas? Was he alive or was the news bad?

It was dark and cold, typical of an early winter's evening in Saint Petersburg. Despite his warm coat, he shivered noticeably as his eyes scanned the dark sky searching for anything to take his gaze off of the full moon. He knew it was that very moon that was keeping him awake at night even when he couldn't see it with his eyes. It was talking to him in a low whisper only he could hear. How could that be?

Help me! Help me! were the words his mind could understand. When he looked directly at the moon, the words became louder and more rapid. It was as if the moon could see him the same as he could see the moon! The voice sounded exactly like that of his missing brother. Tomas had a unique way of clearing his throat while he spoke and that sound punctuated the voice that he heard.

Or, he wondered whether he was just losing his mind? Once again he had begun to question his own sanity. He had recently taken influenza shots, but that couldn't be the reason…could it? He was completely lost as his mind searched for acceptable answers to his many questions.

Suddenly, through the icy darkness he heard the sound of approaching footsteps. Soon he realized that the military boots crushing the newly fallen snow were those of Captain Kulikov and one of his aides. They greeted him as friends would greet a friend, so the man relaxed.

But before he could extend his hand in greeting, there was a sound behind him and suddenly all went black!

The dark main hallway leading to the seldom used north wing of the old building suddenly came to life with the clatter of a mobile hospital bed being pushed by two men in military garb. The passageway was more like a tunnel than anything else, and there were no windows or electric lights. It was buried almost two floors below the surface of the City of Saint Petersburg, and the high percentage of water in the surrounding earth pushed the humidity in this labyrinth to almost unbearable levels. Luckily, the mobile bed was equipped with two sturdy flashlights anchored by several strands of duct tape, and the two Russian soldiers, having been on this duty station for quite some time, were very familiar with the path they had to follow.

The passageway floor was composed of ancient earthen bricks that had settled and cracked over the years while the walls and the stone-imbedded ceiling formed an arch that was consistently almost ten feet from the floor at its apex. The annoying clatter of the old iron bed was significantly amplified by echoes bouncing off the musty walls, but, again, the two men guiding it were more than used to these unusual sounds which might have caused even the bravest of warriors to turn back and never return.

The man lying on his back on the mobile bed had his face covered by a thick black cloth. Rumor had it that he was Armenian by birth, but his name did not appear on the medical form attached to the base of the bed. He was clearly unconscious, and his breathing was quite labored. Not that they were necessary, but eight heavy-duty leather straps restrained his arms and legs presumably to prevent his escape. Several cylindrical chemical flasks were securely attached to the metal of the front bedposts. Each flask contained some sort of medical solution, and each was connected through regulators by plastic tubing to the patient's left arm and right leg. The small monitor located above the patient's head showed evidence of what was at best a weak heartbeat.

Eventually, the military men and their cargo reached a fairly modern steel security door. After a special code was entered and a fingerprint analyzed, the door shook and then slowly slid open accompanied by an ominously grinding rattle, thus permitting them to pass farther into the bowels of the underground structure. Once they cleared the security area and the door closed behind them, the same drab tunnel structure lay dead ahead. This section of the passageway seemed to be darker yet, if that was possible.

"I hate this godforsaken place, Oleg!" whispered the shorter of the two soldiers to his compatriot in a depressed tone. "This dump should have been condemned centuries ago, but then, where would the ghosts from that era live? Maybe *live* isn't the right word? And without the ghosts and demons roaming these premises, how would our fat and lazy and stupid bosses justify their own existence? I guess the Americans could use it at one of their theme parks for Halloween! It's said that the avatar of Josef Stalin lurks down here waiting to swallow up souls. The same goes for the infamous revolutionary, Isreal Lezarevich Gelfand...or should I just call him Parvus? Of course, he's much more fun than Stalin because he always brings good-looking females with him. Too bad they're dead, too!"

Dimitri paused as the duo negotiated some rather deep bumps in their path while trying to keep their unidentified cargo undisturbed. Once they had cleared the array of obstacles, Dimitri continued his analysis.

"I would almost bet a month's pay and my vodka rations to boot that this building is so old that Peter the Great himself must have roamed these halls. I feel that his ghost is watching us even now and that he disagrees with most of everything we are doing down here. Maybe I should say *they* are doing here! Unlike our so-called leaders, he was a man of principle...a man of the people! If we are ever able to bring humans back from the dead instead of just sending them there, he should definitely be the first to return. It would be so pleasant for a change to work for someone who knew what he was doing at least part of the time!"

Dimitri paused to wipe the sweat from his brow one more time. No matter what the weather was outside, these passageways were always very warm and the air was extremely humid. Because of all the surrounding water on the surface of the city, it was like walking through a rain forest in the Amazon but without the cackle of wild parrots to entertain you. Again, he continued not really caring whether his partner was listening.

"It's as if we are entering Frankenstein's laboratory. These poor bastards, whoever they are…whoever they were, stretched out on these slabs, go into this mausoleum but never come out again, not alive at least! By all that is holy, we should have taken this fellow to the city hospital for treatment. And by that I mean the civilian hospital, not the military facility he probably came from, but then one of us would have to take his place on this plastic slab. Better him than me…or you, Oleg! That's for certain.

"You've heard the rumors making the rounds at the barracks, I'm sure. Everyone in our unit agrees. These are mad, egotistical, self-centered so-called scientists we're dealing with here…completely and totally mad! They are feasting on the souls of these poor bastards. To call them vampires would be a compliment!"

There was another moment of silence punctuated only by the rattle of the old cart on the brick floor. Oleg stopped for a moment and uncovered the man's face.

"And, then what, Dimitri?" responded Oleg pensively as he watched a small rat scurry away into the protective darkness. "From the looks of this man and you know that he does look familiar somehow, he will probably die soon enough anyway, and we would be target practice for a firing squad at the least! Your rumor mill says this fellow and the previous two were what…spies? Our spies! Russian spies! What do you think of that? We are experimenting on our own people! First, they risk their lives for our beloved Mother Russia and then they are used as lab rats! It's a sickness, Dimitri. We are sick, too. We turned our heads the other way. We are expediting pure evil with no resistance! I'll bet that rat that just ran past me into the darkness was once one of us! We will pay for our sins soon enough."

Oleg paused for a second to wipe the sweat from his forehead.

"And, if we let this fellow reach a public place where others can see him…it's treason! No trial. No excuses. We're dead! We are guilty of betraying our country Mother Russia by trying to save the life and maybe the soul of a fellow human being. Our relatives will be forced to commit suicide en masse. School children will spit and defecate on our graves…if they give us graves?"

Both men paused as an unusually large rat scampered up in front of the cart, hesitated, twitched its nose, and then hurried past them into the darkness not showing any fear of the humans. It was almost as if the rodent had been listening to the conversation.

"We're no better off than these poor bastards that ride on this cart. At least they got a little foreign travel and maybe some women for their trouble. But, then again, look at this guy; he's not that old. He's probably younger than either of us. The same goes for most of the others we've brought down into this cave. Too young to die in such a pathetic way! Promising lives snuffed out by ridiculous bureaucrats and mad scientists.

"And better yet, supposedly, their bodies are now inhabited by demons, spirits that cause a plague in the brain's intelligence operatives. The walls tell me that these demons are created right here in this underground laboratory…by our fellow humans. Do you see the strange glow above his head? The evil demon is coming out for us. First, it draws itself together as an avatar…a spiritual form of the man himself. Somehow, it knows we are doing him wrong. Is that not obvious? Next, his eyes begin to glow… first blue and then red. Once you see the red glow, your brain is infected, and you are ready for the long and painful journey to hell down this same hole in the earth!"

Oleg really enjoyed kidding his partner, a habit that wasn't much appreciated by Dimitri, although Dimitri did marvel at his friend's ability to make up exotic tales that always seemed to fit the situation. Witchcraft was his favorite paradigm.

"Luckily, peons like you and I have nothing upstairs in our brains worth knowing or stealing. Now I finally realize that being an idiot has its advantages, especially around here. No evil spirit worth its salt would dare waste its time invading our brains. They have much more interesting places to be and way more important work to do. Ah, there, I knew it. I feel better already about skipping classes back of school!"

Oleg paused for effect, letting his story capture Dimitri's imagination, which wasn't hard to do in this environment.

"Anyway, I'm sure that I'm…we're on the right track for once. We are probably dealing with treason here in its highest form. But, whom were they actually spying for? Who knows? Double agents? Triple agents? Actually, I really don't want to know. I'll live a lot longer that way, and maybe even enjoy my retirement in Paris or Prague rather than Siberia like our friend Koslov? I don't have to remind you how he pulled that duty, do I? Take my advice, Dimitri…keep your head down and your eyes closed if you're smart! No news is good news."

Dimitri thought for a moment before responding.

"What makes you think Siberia's such a bad place? Clean air! Vladimir Iliyich…Lenin met his wife there. Stalin went there six times…vacationed there six times at government expense! As long as Koslov has his vodka, he's probably in seventh heaven…whatever that is? I'll bet he gets more vodka than we do…combined!

"And you know how he loves playing with those electronic spy gadgets of his. He even told me once that he built a small robot all by himself. Now, accomplishing that takes some serious brain-power. He said he could tell it to fetch a beer for him from the refrigerator. I find it hard to believe that, but he swore by the little monster! It would even open the can or bottle for him. How's that?"

The interchange of words was enough to silence both men for a moment as they proceeded down the dark, damp tunnel. Soon, the soldiers and their human cargo reached what appeared to be a dead end in the seemingly never-ending main hallway. A decision on direction had to be made at this point. There were three smaller tunnels intersecting at this juncture. Oleg eventually signaled a right turn after checking a sheet of paper attached to a clipboard hooked to the gurney. Dimitri was throwing some light down the dreary passageway with the help of a third small flashlight. As usual, the smell of mold became more intense with each step forward. At least the smaller tunnel was level, and they weren't descending ever deeper into the unforgiving earth.

"Animism! That's it!" whispered Dimitri a little too loudly. "I've been racking my pea brain for that word. We should…could use incantations, mystical chants and prescriptions, and sorcery to drive the evil one from this man's brain. I've got to try it just once…please. Humor me! There's no surveillance at this point in this tunnel. I've got to know if it will work."

Dimitri always fancied himself as an amateur sorcerer and was often found reading up on subjects like witchcraft when he was off duty. Oleg remembered suggesting Tarot card reading to Dimitri, more or less as a joke, and sure enough, in a short time Dimitri was reading Oleg's future in the cards. Oleg liked the colorful Tarot cards because they kept him entertained during the long, boring parts of their duty.

"The main laboratory for this fine fellow," Oleg finally whispered in response, seemingly ignoring Dimitri's request. "As you can see, his face has been covered by central processing, and he has no name. He must be someone important...someone we would recognize! May God, if there is one, have mercy on his poor, tortured soul. He certainly won't see the light of day again."

Oleg hesitated for a moment after rethinking the situation and covering the man's face again.

"Could he...might he be the missing cosmonaut? His brother is...was a cosmonaut, too. You know...they were twins, weren't they? He must have a name. I will call him Leon after the cosmonaut...okay?"

Dimitri just shrugged his shoulders at his partner's comments.

"Ahhh, go ahead with your chant. It can't hurt anything...except the imaginary demons and avatars. But keep it down, and keep it short, if you can? If our transport time is outside Command's parameters, they'll have us for lunch...I mean we'll be the lunch! And remember, no matter what happens, you are not authorized to be *my* witchdoctor under any circumstances or any situation!"

Dimitri slowly and purposefully waved his arms over the patient's body and then muttered a string of unintelligible sounds. It was all Oleg could do to keep from laughing aloud, but he didn't want to ruin his friend's fun. Soon, the brief ceremony was over as Dimitri stared at the musty ceiling above him looking for evidence of each demon's escape from Leon's body. Then, after about a minute, he just shrugged his shoulders and dropped his head.

"I did my best for the poor soul. The vapors have risen to the ceiling! I have cast the demons out, but was it soon enough to save him? For his sake, let's hope it worked and that they don't return or come back and invade us!"

At that very moment the patient began to show signs of life much to Dimitri's great surprise. His fists clenched several times and his eyelids fluttered. Suddenly, despite his deep-seated disbelief, Oleg was interested, too. He again flipped back Leon's head covering to expose his face.

"What's happening, Dimitri? Your incantation seems to have had an effect! He's moving his extremities."

"He's trying to talk," whispered Dimitri with all the calm he could muster. There was a look of surprise and amazement on his face, too. "Look at his lips...they're moving as if he's trying to form words. Whatever demon had his soul has released it for now. Unbelievable!"

Leon was indeed trying his best to utter coherent sounds. In spite of the darkness he seemed to sense the presence of his guards. Both men quickly leaned down close to the front of the mobile bed so as to detect any words from their prisoner. Slowly, but surely, they came out of his mouth!

"Trebor...Trebor Yrtsov is my contact! Warn him...in Houston... America! They know who he is! He is in great danger! The earth is in great danger! They are coming for me...coming for us!"

Slowly, Leon fell back into a state of passive unconsciousness. The guards waited patiently, but Leon was out cold. After about a minute of silence, Oleg grabbed Dimitri by the shoulders and hit him with some serious advice.

"We heard nothing, Dimitri! Do you understand me? He never gained consciousness in our presence...never! We didn't know his name or see his face! I know you will want to tell people about this...about your ritual and how it worked. But, I want to live to see Paris before I die!"

After a few seconds of thought, Dimitri nodded his head in agreement.

"He was never conscious, Oleg. I didn't conjure up any spirits. Let's go and complete our delivery."

After the soldiers turned another corner and proceeded a short distance down another dark but even narrower hallway, a man in a white lab coat suddenly appeared before them with his hands raised in the air. For an instant Dimitri thought it was some sort of demon he had conjured coming back for revenge against him. Quickly, he changed his mind.

"I'll take our visitor the rest of the way to his assigned stateroom, gentlemen. Remember your oath of absolute silence. This man's identity and his presence here are top secret! Forget everything you know about our guest. Forget his face and his name and his condition. I shouldn't have to tell you this, but... Where is the security sheet for this patient?"

"Here you are, Doctor Karpov," Oleg replied, as he saluted and handed the doctor the clipboard and flashlight.

"He's still with us, I presume," mumbled Karpov, not really expecting an answer. It was the same thing he said by force of habit each time he received a new subject into his laboratory.

"Sir," Oleg responded, "we've been with him...with this patient every minute since the military ambulance arrived, as ordered. He never became conscious and to our knowledge his condition is weak but stable. As far as we can tell, as I said, he's in the same...condition as when we received him. What you see here is what we got from Command. I want to make that fact very clear! And we have already forgotten…never knew who he is…was."

Karpov briefly nodded seemingly accepting the guard's parting summary, then inspected the man on the gurney by lifting the cloth from his head and checking his eyes and probing for his weak pulse. Apparently satisfied with what he found, he signed the top sheet in two places, then removed about ten pieces of paper, and handed the clipboard and top sheet back to Oleg. This was the standard procedure.

"Men, thank you for your service. Have a pleasant day…or life, whichever is longer," uttered Karpov with a smirk on his face as he turned away from the soldiers. The men of the military guard watched with obvious relief as their charge was wheeled off into the darkness to meet what would probably be his ultimate fate. Dimitri made a sign of the cross with his right hand.

"At least he still has a sense of humor," mumbled Oleg under his breath as a grin broke out on his face. "What a relief! Yet, I'd really like to see what happens to these poor bastards like Leon, but…not enough to risk my own skin. But, you know, after spending time with him, it's hard not to get emotionally attached, especially…never mind. I wasn't here, and I didn't say that!"

Dimitri was all too familiar with Oleg's sense of humor so he didn't respond. It was clearly time to move out of harm's way!

As the soldiers finally made their way back through the murky darkness toward the surface and their normal duty stations, both obviously relieved by the end of their mission, Dimitri looked over his shoulder for a final brief moment, then turned to whisper to Oleg.

"I hope these crazy bastards never get the idea of using us for their weird, demented experiments. Of course, I was joking about the demons running around in his body, but after seeing the way Karpov looked at him and touched him, I don't know any more. He was acting as though our cargo was carrying something lethal somewhere in his body. I wouldn't trade places with that poor bastard Leon for anything. Karpov was treating him as if he wasn't human. If you see me strapped to one of those carts, cut me loose! I'm serious! I'll do the same for you! You can count on that. You have my word, which I rarely give, on that subject. If need be, I'll kill Karpov for you, and we'll bury him down here…never to be found again."

Under the far end of the dark northern wing of the Institute Building, Doctor Karpov gently moved the gurney through two sets of folding doors and past what served as an elevator into a brightly lit laboratory area that was well equipped for neurological studies. Once inside the main room of the laboratory, he was immediately joined by another physician wearing a clean white lab coat. Karpov handed the sheets of paper he had retrieved from the clipboard to Doctor Pavel Malkin.

"Pavel, have you been using the elevator recently?"

Malkin shook his head negatively.

"Why do you ask?"

"The latch was undone as I went past. This is no time for intruders. If Command stumbled across something like this, they'd cut our heads off! They live for security breaches like this."

Malkin walked back into the hallway and secured the elevator. In moments he was back next to the gurney.

"Alexi, we have to…we must make this one count!" said Malkin firmly but in a friendly voice. "Our sources in Houston seem to believe that the Americans have made a major breakthrough on Spacelab, but our people haven't penetrated the space station yet as far as we know. Koslov should give us a heads up as soon as he learns anything. I know he's a bit paranoid, but he's the best we've got. He's meticulous and single-minded if nothing else. Whatever the Americans are doing out there in orbit, he'll figure it out and let us know.

"Still, command's sources believe something major has happened that could alter the course of our research. We have time for no more errors or blind alleys. Command will be very unhappy if we do not deliver the goods…and soon! Our very lives may depend on it."

Alexi Karpov froze for a moment and then turned away throwing his hands up at the same time.

"Don't you see who this is? It's no coincidence. It's the missing cosmonaut's brother! What is he doing here…now? Of all people, why is he our Guinea pig? If you remember anything, remember this. We didn't recognize the man on the slab! We didn't notice his face!"

Without waiting for an answer, Karpov continued.

"The Science Committee seems to believe that we can accomplish more in this dungeon full of vermin and germs and rats than the Americans can in their modern orbital laboratory using robots built from robotic technology they swiped from us. Here in this miserable medieval dungeon, we expose ourselves and our innocent countrymen to this dangerous contamination while the Americans utilize robots in space to do their dirty work. Do you detect a societal pattern at work here? We are still a damn third-world country in moral terms, Pavel! If they...the Americans make a mistake, they blow the thing up in space where presumably it's someone else's problem. If we make a mistake, we all die and take the blame, too! Blame first; then we die.

"Yet, I've seen some of the robots we've produced in the Minsk lab. Milan tells me that we are years ahead of everyone in robotics! Even the Japanese are trying to spy on us if you believe Command. Why don't we use that advantage here...where it really counts? I'm not trying to get us replaced, but it makes complete sense. You know why? They don't trust us, Pavel! When they eliminate us, they'll say that the virus did us in.

"They are paranoid, too. Like I'm going to run off to London or Washington with some of their precious robots and sell them to the west. I don't even know how to turn the damn things on or off, and Command wouldn't let me touch them or operate one myself when I was in Minsk. They treated me like I was a damn spy...for Brazil! That's because I can speak Portuguese. They denied me clearance just because I speak some Portuguese! I have my wife and my dumb-ass mother-in-law to thank for that! But I must admit that Rio is a pretty classy place. But I digress.

"And look what they did to Koslov! Robotics guy indeed...off to Siberia? I've heard all the arguments as to why that's a good place for his talents. It's all a large amount of bull! We're all marked for death."

Alexi paused as images of the beach passed through his memory. He had no idea why he was talking about Siberia and visualizing a sunny beach somewhere in France.

"I've explained the dangers and the negative possibilities to them a million times, but this is what you get when bureaucrats run your science programs. At least they're not religious nutcases, but that doesn't help us now. Our research planning is to the American system what Intelligent Design is to the Theory of Evolution. Not a bad analogy. We have a bunch of dim bulbs telling us how and where to conduct viral research and what the results must be before we do the actual experiments. It's science by wishful mythology."

Alexi paused as he rubbed his chin.

"It's a religion to them! It's like someone telling you about god who doesn't know the earth isn't flat! That's as smart as the Tsar assuming command of the army in World War I. Stupid! Just plain stupid! We're as stupid as the Americans and that's pretty stupid!"

Malkin nodded his head in agreement with some trepidation. He worried that his partner's complaints might be overheard by Command.

"Be careful, Alexi. The Tsar paid for his mistakes...the hard way. He should have learned the lesson from Louis XVI of France, but he didn't. Too much ego and wealth and too little brains in that family tree! That's what happens when the gene pool dries up in a bucket of money. They cut your head off and cut down your family tree!"

Pavel paused and looked around the room. Then, placing his hand over his mouth, he began to whisper.

"The walls often have ears as the English have been heard to say. Remember what I told you about keeping your hand over your mouth when you're talking...especially when you're talking to me! Of course, who else would we be talking to down here? Leon's not saying a word. Still, Central Command has some very skilled lip-readers up there on the surface. How's that for a dumb job. Imagine trying to pick up a girl in a bar and telling her that you read lips for a living. I'll have to try that some time and see if it works.

"And there's more creepy news...about Koslov. I think they injected him with the base virus just before he left for Siberia. I didn't know...I don't know if you knew that? Don't say anything now. Just think about it."

"Okay, okay," muttered Karpov to his friend and associate. He was quite surprised about that last remark. "Let's do our best with what we have. Koslov's on his own, at least for now. First, we prep old Leon here with the radiation profile. Then, we are ready to inject the new generation of the read virus. That would be six hours after the subject is terminal if he goes right away. Once it's in, we wait...three hours this time, I believe, to extract the virus. Then we wait to see if the read virus communicates with its platform counterpart. Wish I could be in the room to watch..."

"You know that's not possible!" said Malkin sternly to his associate. "One little mistake, one little leak and that precious brain of yours will be Swiss cheese on a permanent basis! And you'll spend the rest of your short, miserable life in lockdown as a guinea pig. You know, one of those short-tailed, short-eared rodents we tortured in medical school. And while your brain is probed by one of those bureaucrats you love so much, I'll probably be forced to watch. At that point your only hope would be for a quick death, painless or not. And don't look for me to get you out of it. I'll probably be strapped to the cart next to you or running away as fast as I can!"

Karpov had heard this warning many times before from his friend Malkin and others, and deep inside he knew they were correct in their assessment of the situation. Politics ruled science, as it always had in Russia.

"Pavel, I know you're right. But consider the other side of this question. Should we be creating these dangerous organisms just because we want to read the brains and memory banks of dead people? Do we have the moral right to do that? Should the all-powerful state have unfettered access to our entire being even after we are no longer alive? Will Mother Russia eat its children even after they are dead?"

Karpov scratched his head and went on.

"And worse yet, what comes next? Loosing these monstrous things upon living people? Why am I saying that? We're doing it already! We invent the ultimate truth serum, but who has the right to use it? We once believed that at least our thoughts were safe from the prying eyes and ears of Big Brother. Of course, you had to be able to withstand water-boarding, hot pokers, sleep deprivation and the like. You remember, don't you? They called it the Dick Cheney vacation. At least those Americans still have a sense of humor.

"Western literature got it right some time ago. Big Brother is a perfect name for what we're dealing with here. It just wasn't exactly clear to George Orwell how our humanity would be taken from us. Little did we ever guess in our wildest dreams that it would be a tiny, tiny virus, and that we would willingly do it to ourselves. That's right. There is no God nor is there a Devil. We create and play both roles ourselves, and we do both badly especially when compared to the Greeks. Where is Apollo when we need him?

"But worse yet...ponder this thought for a moment. Realizing that your enemy can download your mind and memory after you are dead, the government invents a new virus that erases your memories while you are still alive! We have nowhere to run and no place to hide. You're wrong if you do and wrong if you don't. You are...become whoever they want you to be.

"I've lost my soul, Pavel. So have you. We aren't scientists; we're slaves and executioners, and the really bad news is that we don't have seventy-two virgins waiting for us after we die either!"

All of a sudden a grin broke out on Karpov's face. It was the last thing his associate expected.

"But, you know...there is still hope. That last briefing of ours seemed to suggest that the Americans were also working on or thinking about an anti-virus. An anti-virus? A defense against this monster we're creating?

How…? Hell, I guess anything's possible. All I can say is more power to them. Do you think either side would mind if we switched sides in the middle of the race?"

Malkin waited a few moments for Karpov to cool down. He couldn't disagree with much of what Alexi had said, and he didn't know whether to laugh or cry right now. But the dangers of such an outspoken opinion were all too clear to both of them. They had to settle down and behave more like the robots they wanted to use to perform these difficult and dangerous experiments that faced them.

"Alexi, I didn't hear a word of what you just said. I wasn't here until just this moment. As usual, you were mumbling to yourself, again. Now, if you can, please join me in focusing on the scientific problem at hand."

Malkin waited for about thirty seconds for Karpov to nod his head. Karpov realized that he had no choice but to proceed with the planned experiment even though he knew that what they were about to do was murder another helpless human being and fellow Russian. It was little consolation that Leon was almost dead already. Karpov glanced at the ceiling for a few moments as if he were asking his God for forgiveness and even more so for His intervention. These thoughts were flashing through his mind despite the fact that he didn't believe in a god until just now!

"What baseline information did Command program our guest with?" asked Malkin as he perused the report sheets. "Never mind. Here it is. He was allowed to watch a movie in English. It says here that he picked the subject himself. It will be the first substantive data the read virus will search for."

"What was it?" asked Karpov with a smirk on his face. "James Bond? These eastern European types can't get enough of the Brits. It must be the sleazy women in those movies. That's what does it for me."

Malkin was shaking his head as a rare smile also flashed across his face. He loved arguing about western art and literature with his partner.

"Much more ironic, if that's possible. *Rosenkrantz and Guildenstern!*"

"Who?" mumbled a confused Karpov.

"Don't you remember your Shakespeare? Your Hamlet? I even saw the play in Riga several years ago when I still had a life. When my wife was still alive, and we were in love, we went on a second honeymoon. It's called *Rosenkrantz and Guildenstern are Dead*! Or was it *Rosenkrantz and Guildenstern Must Die*? Do you think our friend Leon here realized that his end was near as he watched? But then I believe that those two in the story were reported as being dead, but actually escaped with their lives. I believe that their hanging at sea was faked just as if it were a play. Maybe Leon here will be able to tell us? The play is the thing, you know! Maybe he's planning his own escape, and he's asking us for help? I wouldn't put it past him. It's what I would do. I love the ironies built into our research!"

As the two scientists conversed, their patient twitched several times, movements they didn't observe. But they weren't the only ones watching. Soon the phone in the lab buzzed, and Malkin answered the call. The conversation was short, and quickly Malkin and Karpov were hovering over their patient.

"Command claims Leon twitched three times. I told them we were distracted by our discussion of virus implementation. We can't do everything! I told them last week that we need a staff of three technicians and two nurses, but they flatly turned me down again. Security concerns were the excuse, as usual!"

Realizing that they were being watched closely, the two scientists wheeled their silent guest into a radiation chamber where Leon was placed on a special table which itself had robotic features. Once the patient was sealed inside, a radiation sequence was initiated with a scheduled duration of almost three hours. The scientists were not privy to the exact radiation profile being given to their patient. Again, this was explained as a security precaution.

All went well for the first forty minutes. Then, for no apparent reason the device suddenly shut down and the lab phone began ringing. The voice on the other end of the line informed Malkin and Karpov that the experiment was over and that a special military unit would arrive in five minutes to take the subject back to the military medical facility from which he came.

In less than three minutes four armed men entered the lab with a mobile hospital bed and without any words left the lab with the comatose patient less than a minute later.

"Wow," whispered Karpov in a low tone. "When was the last time those bastards admitted a mistake? We are off the hook...for now."

"A mistake?" responded a confused Malkin.

"Yes. I'll bet that they injected the wrong strain of virus into Leon's head. Hopefully, for him, it was a benign strain. That must be why he kept twitching when all the others were already dead at this stage. I'll bet we'll be seeing old Leon again and soon. But next time he'll be stiff as a board."

"What did you do with the counter-viral sample? It was right here on this lab bench a moment ago."

Malkin's only response was the blank look on his face as he searched the area with his eyes.

"I need a glass of vodka!" Malkin shouted, making sure those listening to him could hear his protest.

Unfortunately for Malkin, his expression was interrupted by a systematic vibration that seemed to begin on the ceiling and worked its way down to the floor until the whole laboratory was shaking.

"Earthquake?" mumbled Karpov as he fell to the floor. "I warned them about the new fault line!"

In about thirty seconds the vibration suddenly ceased and all was quiet. Karpov and Malkin dusted themselves off and looked around to assess the damage. By some miracle, there seemed to be no serious physical damage. All of the electronics seemed to be intact and functioning.

"That was no earthquake!" whispered Malkin. "Too steady and too brief. This thing was man-made. Something weird was going on up on the surface. I wonder if it had anything to do with Leon and his captors?"

Karpov shrugged his shoulders.

"Let's forget it," shouted Malkin. "We've got a date with a bottle up on the surface. Someone will let us know what happened up there soon enough. But now...the vodka!"

2
The Incident

Out of the ruins, out from the wreckage.
Can't make the same mistake this time.
We are the children, the ones they left behind.
And I wonder when we are ever gonna change.
Living under the fear till nothing else remains.

Tina Turner
We Don't Need Another Hero

The Houston NASA Space Center

The highly-secured data center was currently occupied by two individuals whose brightly colored badges, hanging prominently from the pockets of their suit coats, verified substantial security clearances. Each man also wore a separate badge hanging like a necklace from around his neck. The unspoken conclusion of an unseen observer could easily have been that their security procedures were more important than solving the scientific and engineering problems that were presented to them.

Their attention was presently focused on an impressive array of twenty-eight solid-state high-resolution monitors that presently displayed real-time visual information issuing from an orbiting NASA space vehicle of considerable size. Surveillance cameras aboard the orbiting American scientific research laboratory, officially designated as the Scientific Laboratory for Orbital Bioscience, covered almost every cubic inch of the spacecraft's interior.

On a digital situation board located above the four rows of screens, several red indicator lights were ominously flashing. The observers immediately realized that something aboard Spacelab, the popular name given to the laboratory by NASA personnel and the press, was amiss. Neither observer had seen an active red caution light on this board since the station's launch over a year ago except when security tests were being run. They were caught completely by surprise.

The information on the data board was instantaneously transmitted to Washington so the men knew that it was just a matter of time before they would be queried by their superiors about the problem and their actions to correct it. It was the type of situation both men were thoroughly trained to handle but which they never wished to experience.

"I have a feeling that we're gonna pay dearly for this little mistake for a long, long time, Phil…for a very long time no matter what the actual cause is," the older man muttered nervously under his breath. "Robotic malfunction, my ass! I'd bet my eyeteeth, if I still had eyeteeth, that it is more like unnecessary and unwarranted human intervention. Those robots up there never make a mistake barring a software glitch. Only a human could cause something like this to occur! The Spacelab is vibrating and experimental samples are flying all over the place. I knew that I should have taken a week of vacation when I had the chance. I could have been in Vegas playing craps where my entire future isn't dependent on a roll of the dice!"

Phil's head was nodding vigorously in obvious agreement with his partner.

"So you actually figured all of that out for yourself, did you, Frank?" Phil finally commented to the other observer in an obviously sarcastic tone. "We didn't propose the mission nor did we program those damn robots either. As a matter of fact, our guidelines…official NASA documentation to be more accurate, state in big bold print that only properly programmed robotic entities are ever…ever to access Spacelab during experimentation periods. And this last week has most certainly been an experimentation period. Those robots have been going 24-7 up there doing their thing just perfectly with those little microbes. It's enough to make a virologist stand on his head and spit wooden nickels. Not a single problem until… Exactly what caused this problem?"

Phil stood up and cleared his throat preparing to do his best Richard Burton imitation. Phil loved old movies, particularly 1984 which was Burton's last film, and on many occasions he would also pull his John Wayne and Boris Karlov imitations out to make a point.

"Even in the event of human intervention, our own rules clearly limit access to the entire lab area and the decontamination chambers to specially trained NASA personnel and then only in a declared emergency. It's harder to gain entry to Spacelab than it is for a Venezulian Communist to get into the White House and steal George Washington's portrait. I'm not taking the blame for this one, security or no security. And neither should you, Frank!"

Phil hesitated to add a dramatic flair to his presentation.

"But somehow, Professor Laurie did it, Frank! I don't see our signatures authorizing his presence aboard Spacelab anywhere on the mission sheet, do you? That arrogant bastard got the top brass to send him up to oversee the results of his little experiments on Spacelab in violation of every principle of common sense. He violated his own inviolate rules! In the unlikely event that there is a god somewhere out there in our universe, I wish he'd dish out a little punishment to the old professor, but not right now. It would do my heart good, and I might then just become a believer."

Phil stepped over to a desk and grabbed another sheet of paper and waved it in the air as if it were the Constitution or the Magna Carta.

"And another thing we'd never get away with. There's no signature verifying the pre-flight physical. You know as well as I do that the exam is necessary one hundred percent of the time. No exceptions! This mark isn't a signature. Mahadavan would have done this one for sure and that scribble certainly isn't his. So, what's going on here? Did they decide to do away with all of the rules and forget to tell us? And then decide to blame us if anything went wrong?"

Frank just shook his head and mumbled something unintelligible under his breath as Phil continued his diatribe. The latter realized that a little humor was in order to lighten the mood. Phil decided to roll out an old joke that was sure to distract his boss.

"You're not serious about blaming Frank Herbert for this whole thing...are you?"

Again Phil paused for effect.

"I always thought you were kidding, Frank. Blaming a science fiction writer of decades ago, who happens to have the same first name...and almost the same last name as you do, is funny at first, but it wears thin, especially if you're trying to convince the Congress that the greatest scientific mind of our era is a lunatic because he has postulated...just what has Laurie postulated anyway?"

Getting no audible response from Frank, Phil went on. What else could he do? The door to Frank's least favorite subject was open, for better or for worse.

"It seems to me that people are putting words into his mouth...into Professor Laurie's mouth. If I were you, I'd lodge a protest with the Patent Office. You...well, your almost namesake was the first to propose folding space as far as I know. Even Einstein didn't go that far...did he? He concluded that space was curved, but he never mentioned folding it back on itself, right? And our earth isn't flat, but our universe sure seems to be, relatively speaking. Is he going to have to fold the entire space-time continuum of our universe to get from here to San Antonio?"

Frank didn't enjoy the humor in Phil's words but instead gritted his teeth and pounded his fist on the table. This was actually what Phil was hoping for, an emotional outburst to release and clear Frank's mind. Finally, Frank burst forth.

"The bastard acts as if we were only one small step away from... traveling through space without moving. I call it *folding space* just like the real author did in his novels. Professor Laurie hasn't gone that far yet...but he will. Mark my words, Phil. He has no soul, no scientific conscience! He will steal the idea and say it was original with him. I remember asking him if he read all the *Dune* novels, and he said he never had looked at the books. He even denied seeing the movies! He's going to try to grab the whole thing for himself. He will, by God, or my name isn't...Frank Hurbert!"

Phil still couldn't fathom his boss's objection to the nebulous relativistic and quantum-mechanical concept of folding space, but he loved the fact that he could divert Frank with the mere mention of a science-fiction author from the past.

"Frank, do you remember that really old sci-fi movie called *Back to the Future*? I think there were three of them. The original and two sequels. They came out almost the same time *Dune* was released. They were about time travel by humans."

Frank groaned as he realized that Phil was about to float one of his really bad science jokes. At least *Back to the Future* and its sequels were among Frank's favorite classic movies. Frank closed his eyes and awaited the inevitable reference to a DeLorean.

"Maybe we could hint to Laurie that we've invented a working prototype of the *flux-capacitor*. All we need is a DeLorean that will go 88 miles an hour, and we could do some serious time travel. We'll show him how to time travel if he shows us how to fold space!

"Wait! Actually, we could go forward in time and see if it can actually be done without even asking Laurie. But where in the hell are we gonna get a DeLorean? That's the hard part. We'll have to travel back in time to get gas, but we need gas to get there. It's definitely a chicken and egg problem."

It was obvious from the frown on Frank's face that he didn't think much of Phil's attempted humor. But it was a benign frown with no long-term malice attached. Frank knew that he needed Phil's technical expertise to get past the current situation and waiting for an updated situation report from Spacelab was trying their nerves.

"Those were turn of the century movies," mumbled Frank under his breath. "I would much rather have lived then, that's for sure. And Dr. Who's telephone callbox would be my preferred mode of travel. The Tardis for sure! No folding of space required. Just get in the callbox and go. And K-9 was a great pet to have."

Phil walked over and reset the scanning sequencer for the decontamination room cameras aboard Spacelab as he continued his discussion of old sci-fi movies.

"Maybe Professor Laurie was looking for the planet *Dune* in his spare time up there in Spacelab…or is it really called *Arrakis*? There is a telescope up there for him to use, isn't there? I've never tasted the spice or even seen any of the worms…except in the movies. Have you?"

Phil stopped short for a second, then slapped the open palm of his left hand against his forehead.

"Whoops…there was that night at O'Shea's Bar in St. Louis. Remember? It was when we saw the owner's son doing a line or was it an eight ball right at the bar in plain view? I actually do often wonder if the spice is more like hash or…cocaine or even…heroin. It's a natural product, right? But, the difference is that it's from an animal instead of a plant. Now, that's an interesting point I haven't heard anyone mention before. Maybe that's the real key to the spice's special powers. It's a natural product from an animal instead of from a plant! We've got to focus on that difference, Frank. There might be some big money to be made here!"

Frank realized that he had never considered that aspect of the spice so he let Phil continue. Frank knew that they should be attending to the problem on Spacelab, but he needed to clear his mind so he let Phil's rant go on.

"But those boys in *The Spacing Guild* didn't ever seem to complain, did they? Why should they? They got all the free drugs they could consume and were literally on a trip all the time. I know that was a bad pun. By the way, your eyes have been looking a little bluer lately, Frank. That's much better than the bloodshot eyes you have after drinking too much! Does the blue in your eyes mean you're on the spice?"

Both men were aware of the fact that Frank had heard these same comments at least a hundred times before, comments that made sense only to those who had read Frank Herbert's sci-fi thrillers about the planet Dune and the spice drug that permitted space travel without actually moving. Usage of the spice turned the user's eyes a bright blue.

Unfortunately, Phil's attempt to lighten the tense atmosphere seemed to have fallen flat again as Frank walked away toward the men's room, his chin buried in his chest. Phil just smiled to himself and went back to the monitors and the pile of papers he had been sifting through. After all, one of his main job responsibilities and Frank's too, was damage control with the public. But primarily and most importantly, he had to try to maintain favor with the United States Congress. And the incident aboard Spacelab this winter evening would undoubtedly hit the papers in the morning meaning that some sort of news conference was a certainty, particularly since Spacelab funding for the next three years was now on the table before said Congress which was also fighting an enormous federal deficit.

As Phil sorted through the files on his desk, he noticed a CIA Intelligence folder marked *Russian Cosmonauts*. He had heard the rumors circulating about a missing Russian spaceman but paid little attention to them. As he opened the file, he came upon several old photographs of the Yengoyan twins. Tomas and Leon were now twenty-five years old, and they possessed the similar look twins would be expected to have. According to what he remembered, Tomas was supposedly the missing man although the Russian government had officially denied the rumor. Phil made a mental note to review the file thoroughly when he had time.

What Phil failed to notice immediately as he checked the monitors one by one was the intermittent flickering and then darkness on monitor 19. This monitor had been displaying the contents of one of the decontamination rooms aboard Spacelab. It wasn't unusual for transmissions to fall out of sync for a few seconds, but monitor 19 was experiencing something more serious.

Phil accessed the data recorder and re-ran several minutes of surveillance data. As he did, he started shaking his head and muttering to himself.

"I didn't notice that before! What's with the vibration? That area was shaking for fifteen or twenty seconds. What in the world would cause that? I've only seen something like this during a docking maneuver when the alignment is off. And the main docking port is stable. The emergency dock is...crap, monitor 19 is still down."

After a few minutes Frank returned and immediately shifted into his public persona. Phil could sense that his boss had caught a second wind so he didn't say anything about the vibration.

"It's interesting that Washington hasn't put their fat noses into our business yet, Phil. They will, so let's get ready for it ahead of time."

Phil nodded his head and cleared his throat waiting for Frank to begin.

"Okay, Dr. Blair, where do things stand now? And kindly start from the beginning as if I'm Senator Jensen from Oklahoma, and I have a pitchfork stuck up my ass. Convince me...convince him that we have everything up in orbit under control, and maybe you get to...keep your meaningless little job a little bit longer!"

Phil could sense that Frank knew more than he was telling even though the Spacelab incident was only a few hours old and even though all the facts weren't in yet. Phil decided he'd play along in this game with his boss. The practice might prove valuable, especially if he wanted to remain a government employee or get a reasonable recommendation toward getting his next job. Besides, with each passing week Phil began to feel more and more like Frank's personal psychiatrist. In Phil's mind, his main job was to keep his boss from blowing his brains out!

Phil pushed his chair back and stood up. Without any words he grabbed his boss by the shoulders and shoved him down into the chair he had just vacated. Then, to set the mood, he moved over to a small table in the corner and retrieved a bottle of water. He carefully uncapped the bottle and took a sip to lubricate his tongue and sharpen his vocal cords. When Frank started to say something, Phil thrust a rigid right hand into Frank's face, which clearly signified that only silence on Frank's part was acceptable.

Phil was a little surprised when Frank immediately complied with his wishes without complaint. It seemed like the right time for Phil to stretch his six foot three inch frame and down another sip of water. After doing so he was finally ready to speak. He was beginning to feel more like Lawrence Olivia on the opening night of Hamlet in London.

"Gentlemen. My name is Dr. Phil Blair. I am the senior mission controller for onboard security assigned to monitor the Spacelab mission and the scientific and engineering projects evolving therein, both classified and unclassified. You may know our orbital lab as *Spacelab*; however, we also refer to it by its proper acronym. That would be…S.L.O.B."

Frank wanted to object to the word 'evolving' and the uncalled-for humor, but Phil stopped him cold by pointing to a small voice recorder that was recording Phil's mock presentation. Frank's critique would have to wait until Phil had completed his words.

"As you probably already know, Spacelab was designed to carry out scientific work deemed too dangerous to be conducted here on planet earth. This facility is especially useful for the viral research projects funded by the Advanced Research Projects Agency, which we know as ARPA. It is the singular success of ARPA's robotics studies that has made this all possible.

"Spacelab is the first orbital station that is capable of performing meaningful *in situ* scientific research on toxic biological systems without the presence of a human staff or crew. Here, by toxic, I mean systems that pose some defined or undefined danger to humans or our ecosystem in general. The laboratory and its experiments are operated by a team of sophisticated robots designed specifically for this station and these projects by ARPA and NASA scientists and engineers. We also have received considerable help from several university laboratories at Princeton and Stanford. Without reference to the biological work, I must say that our robotics studies have been an enormous and unqualified success. Mark my words. These robots will save countless human lives over time."

Phil paused to clear his throat and adjust his imaginary tie. So far, Frank seemed somewhat satisfied, even pleased.

"On certain well-defined occasions it is possible that humans will be required to attend the station, but under normal circumstances these human incursions must be kept to a minimum. Such visits are authorized only after the access volumes within Spacelab have been purged of possible hazards and security subsystems are one hundred percent operational. The nature of several of the viral entities currently onboard Spacelab present known and unknown hazards to human cells and transfer to earth by a human or any other mechanism is a situation to be avoided at all costs. Safety and security, which go hand in hand, are our first and main considerations. Neither has priority over the other. Both must be absolutely maintained without compromise."

Again, Phil paused for effect. Monitor 19 was still blank, a fact that he noticed out of the corner of his eye. It would have to wait.

"Believe me, the potential research and scientific advances make the risks we must take well worth our while. But, because we currently have an abnormal situation aboard our orbiting laboratory, let me focus on security immediately.

"To answer the obvious questions first, let me assure you that Spacelab's emergency systems are well designed and have been tested especially for a situation of the type we have encountered here. In case of a terminal event aboard the laboratory, the spacecraft is designed to leave orbit in a trajectory vertical to the plane of our solar system. Once it is well into space, an onboard sensor would be activated from earth and Spacelab and its contents would be systematically incinerated and then blown to smithereens! That's one of the reasons we don't want humans aboard especially when we are experiencing problems.

"Of course, the valuable data accumulated from experimentation would be transmitted to our labs here on earth prior to destruction. That data would have several levels of encryption so that only NASA could retrieve the data. The same is true should the craft be boarded by unauthorized personnel. Because of our international space agreements and treaties, this possibility is quite remote, yet it is a contingency we have planned for."

Phil could see Frank shaking his head, but the latter remained silent.

"I am certain that you are aware of the breakthrough work of Professor Victor Laurie of Princeton University. It was Professor Laurie's hard work and exceptional dedication that made Spacelab a possibility in the first place. Without belaboring the point, suffice it to say that several of the Spacelab projects are essential to his work and that of the ARPA defensive weapons projects.

"Because of the unusually successful nature of these experiments, it became advisable for Professor Laurie to visit the Spacelab facility with a small team of ARPA scientists. Unfortunately, during the visit an incident occurred which has required the quarantine of Professor Laurie and two other scientists onboard Spacelab. Our current data show that the possible release of the dangerous viral components is highly unlikely, actually, non-release is currently an established certainty, and that the subsequent danger of exposure to these men is essentially nil.

"However, safety considerations for the men and our planet require them to remain aboard Spacelab under strict observation and quarantine for a minimum of forty-eight hours. Certain non-invasive decontamination procedures are being implemented as required and exposure tests shall be conducted again before the men return to earth. This redundancy is necessary to assure their safe return to earth.

"Once again, I can assure you that we are prepared to handle this situation and that the danger to our space travelers is inconvenient but minimal. The robotic entities are also programmed to handle deviations like this, and we owe a debt of gratitude to those scientists and engineers whose hard work accomplished this. We shall learn a lot from this incident, but luckily it seems that our planning for this type of situation has been on the right track.

"After Professor Laurie's return to earth, I am sure that you will have a first hand opportunity to hear about the details of the incident straight from the horse's mouth, as it were. I know that he is a man involved in several controversial studies that have spawned a considerable number of nay-sayers in the scientific community, yet his candidacy for a Nobel Prize and considerable guidance rendered on these important defense research projects aboard Spacelab stand as proof of his ingenuity and the kind of single-mindedness required of great inventors and discoverers such as Columbus, Hawking and Einstein."

Phil reached over and clicked off the voice recorder and handed it to Frank with a smile and terse response.

"Q.E.D."

Frank stared at the voice disk for a moment after removing it from the recorder, then he placed the disc in an inside pocket of his suit coat as he posed a question to Phil.

"How much time do we have before they're actually breathing down our necks? And I sense that you are steering clear of the possibility of robotic malfunctions. That's a wise strategy for now. We don't need to add more fuel to the fire until we get more information."

Phil just shrugged his shoulders and nodded.

"The robots aren't involved as far as I can tell so why even open that door. We'll have our hands full shielding Laurie. But we do have the advantage of looking rather sane and organized compared to him. Let's keep it that way.

"Minimum of three…maybe four days before the little bastards get organized themselves. It depends on whether anything weird happens between now and then, between now and the landing. Keep your fingers crossed, and it might be a week or even more. But, if there was exposure up there, all bets are off, and we have a long term problem."

Despite Phil's last comment, Frank seemed to relax just a bit. He got up from his chair and started to pace up and back as was his habit when he was nervous. Phil took this as a positive sign because it meant that Frank was on to worrying about a different problem. Phil knew that he had passed the first test. But, at the same time, he finally realized that the Spacelab camera feeding monitor 19 was definitely malfunctioning. He decided to wait until their present discussion was concluded before pointing this out to Frank.

"Is Laurie the only one working on this space-folding stuff?" Frank asked in a serious tone of voice. "Isn't there someone he's always mentioning in the footnotes of his papers?"

"Yeah," Phil mumbled in response, his eyes still glued to monitor 19.

"Pence. Dallas Pence. He's a physical chemist at Stanford. Pence has done a lot of work at SLAC. You know, the old Stanford Linear Accelerator."

"I thought that facility was shut down long ago?" mumbled Frank.

"Not so. It still has plenty of uses even though it can't compete with facilities like the Large Hadron Collider in Switzerland. For example, you can't produce mini-black holes at SLAC, even on a good day.

"But Pence's interests are in high-speed computing. I really don't know much about it, but I believe he's using a benign form of the same class of virus Laurie is using on Spacelab. That's probably classified. I'll give the library a call and have them send over some of their work. I know there are pieces in the Journal of Chemical Physics and the Review of Scientific Instruments. A little light coffee-table reading to say the least. We need to be current on this stuff."

A sly grin crept across Phil's face. He could see that Frank was impressed with his reasoning and preparation.

"Just one more thing, Phil. You'd better define Laurie's project in some publicly acceptable way or the mob will ask some embarrassing questions we will have difficulty answering…if we let them pose the original questions. And here I refer to a general statement that doesn't violate security. You can bend the truth a little bit to make it palatable."

Phil thought for a second, then motioned for Frank to insert the disk and turn the voice recorder back on.

"As you already know, Professor Laurie's work aboard Spacelab involves the development of a class of viruses to combat the chemical warfare threats posed by Iran and North Korea. I am sure that all of us, including our allies in the Middle East, wish him good fortune in this crucial endeavor.

We like to think of this work as the development of a viral anti-missile system."

Both men already knew that this was the cover story they were required to use in situations like this. In reality, neither man knew anything about the specific goals of the viral research on Spacelab.

Satisfied with his rehearsal performance, Phil decided that it was a good time to re-fill his coffee cup. As he reached for the empty cup, his attention was drawn back to the blank screen of monitor 19.

"Now what the hell has gone wrong, Frank? Monitor 19 has gone dead. That's all we need now to top things off…an equipment malfunction aboard Spacelab! And I was looking forward to a quiet weekend of over-eating and heavy drinking."

3
Legislation

A thousand years have come and gone, time has passed me by. Stars stopped in the sky, waiting for the world to end, weary of the light, praying for night prison of lost Xanadu.

Xanadu
Olivia Newton-John

Washington, D.C.

He was nearing the end of the first month at his new job, and Ollie Blair had his uncle Jim back in Chicago and his cousin Phil in Houston to thank for it. He had lived most of his life in Columbus, Ohio and was a rabid Buckeye football fan. But, he wanted to get out of his hometown and see some of the rest of the world so he ruled out attending Ohio State University. Several of his close friends opted to stay in Columbus, but that meant living at home and missing out on the excitement of a completely new life.

Ollie had just completed his freshman year at James Madison and was anxious to spend the summer working inside the government to gain some firsthand experience. During his several intense interviews for his present job, he tried hard to hide his strong liberal political leanings because he had heard through the student grapevine that the congress and its administrative functionaries tended to be very conservative and unforgiving of liberal political views. Anything new and any sort of suggested change even for the better was always viewed with suspicion by the conservatives. Besides, because of his interest in world history and very interesting and well-read history teachers, Charlotte Cordoy, Karl Marx and Vladimir Ilyich Ulanov, also known as Lenin, were three of his favorite historical characters. That would be enough to make a conservative roll over in his grave. The political joke at James Madison was that a conservative was a person too stupid to get a liberal education.

But this hurdle was no problem for Ollie who had performed as an actor in six plays in high school including his favorite, *Death of a Salesman* where he played the lead. He practiced his art on his friends by telling off-the-cuff stories mostly about fictitious relatives and acquaintances. The more unlikely the factual situation, the more his audiences enjoyed the tales.

One of his favorite stories was about his non-existent cousin Phil, not to be confused with the real one in Houston, who was born in Mexico City on the same day as Phil was born in Columbus. His Uncle Jack who worked for the U.S. embassy in Mexico City and his father were brothers, but neither knew of the other's family plans back in those days. As it turned out in truth, Phil was named after his Uncle Phil who had passed away two years before Phil's birth. His death was caused by an accidental poisoning on an Ohio farm. Both fathers chose to name their child after their deceased brother so Phil and his non-existent cousin Phil have exactly the same name and birthday. When Phil would tell that story, his friends immediately realized all of the nefarious possibilities this coincidence allowed.

His next eleven months were to be spent working as a page on the floor of the United States Senate. His grades were good and his work schedule would have little impact on his studies although his social life was sure to take a hit. But it took all the string pulling his uncle could muster to land the position. Typical of almost any activity in the nation's capital, the political maze surrounding the appointment proved to be horrendous even for a gopher position like that of a page. But Ollie's interest and aptitude in science, particularly physical chemistry, and his strong mathematics background and mastery of matrix theory and partial differential equations at such a young age far ahead of his peers finally won the day.

Again, it was one of his high school teachers who set him on the mathematics path. She ran the mathematics club at the high school, and in no time at all, he and several of his friends breezed past algebra and geometry into the arena of math needed to easily understand subjects like chemical physics. Her letters of recommendation for his entry into college were wonderful.

This was only the third year that college level students were again utilized as pages in the senate. A series of embarrassing scandals after the turn of the century and the increased complexity of the activities in the legislative branch made the prior system using high school students completely obsolete. For some unknown reason the Republican leadership seemed to prefer the high school students over college students like Ollie. Ollie was sure he understood the reasons why this was the case, but he wanted the job so he kept his mouth shut as visions of Catholic priests and altar boys danced through his head.

Ollie would really rather have gone straight to the Air Force Academy in Colorado, but in spite of his academic record, he didn't quite make the cut. The recent blossoming of activity among international space stations and the recent successful manned landings on Mars had stirred the slumbering imaginations of the American public and those of the world as well. The predictable result was that there were well over seven times as many highly qualified applicants to the academy as there were available positions in the class of 2032. As a result, his second choice became reality.

Yet, Ollie wasn't completely disappointed with this situation. The university was excellent, and he enjoyed all of his classes. This experience in Washington, D.C. would enhance his chances for admission to the Academy next year, should he choose to try again, and the possibility of a career in politics was still a viable alternative for him despite the dark underside of politics in the nation's capitol.

He was tall, good-looking, athletic and relatively intelligent. Who knows what connections he would make in the seat of national government over the next months and where those connections might lead to down the road. Besides, it was Friday, and he had a date after work with Nancy Wilt, a really beautiful redhead with a great intellect who was a freshman at James Madison. Nancy was from Philadelphia and seemed to enjoy Ollie's company because she too was interested in politics. Life was good. But it was finally time to get back to work.

Ollie made his way toward the Senate mailroom as he always did right after lunch. One of his gopher jobs was the hand delivery of important mail items to senators who were working between sessions on the floor of the senate and for those who were just too lazy to pick up their mail by themselves. The good part about this task was that he got some much-needed exercise by running up and down the several staircases rather than taking the elevator. As he turned a corner, a familiar and very friendly face came into view.

"How's it going, Ollie? Despite your most dire predictions, you seem to be surviving remarkably well these days. All this running around will keep you in shape for sure. Washington is a far cry from Columbus, but if you stay busy, the time…your sentence will pass faster. And you never know; the Buckeyes might need a running back next year! And you might even enjoy the company here…just don't drop your bar of soap near any of the senators!"

The soft melodious but aggressive voice was that of a female intern from St. Louis who had been assigned to the mailroom. Angela was very friendly, but what Ollie liked most about her was her intelligence and sense of humor. She seemed to understand the undertow of politics much better than anyone should at her age. And she always had her ear to the ground, which allowed her to pick up the latest rumors from the institutional grapevine.

"Okay, I guess, Angela?" Ollie replied. "I haven't been fired or arrested or molested, and I haven't stooped to being a conservative yet. That's a good sign for sure! But, those sneaky government agents hiding in the shadows are still following me everywhere I go. It's to the point where I'm afraid to use the paper towels in the bathroom or talk on a pay phone, and leaving the Laundromat when my clothes are in the dryer is out of the question. I'm positive that Nixon's ghost is still hiding in this place somewhere waiting to strike. He wants me to break into Watergate again!"

Angela wore a bright smile as she handed a thin weather-beaten tan package to Ollie.

"This is for Senator Jensen. You've heard of him, haven't you? It looks like someone…not me…put this baby through the meat-grinder this morning! If you shake it, it sounds like there are stones or marbles on the inside. Actually, it's probably a new supply of drugs for the old boy. He's been acting really weird ever since that trip he took to Europe and Moscow. Maybe it was those sexy Russian women that got to him?" There was definite sarcasm in her voice.

Ollie noticed the unusually worn condition of the wrapping. It looked to him as if a cat had used the surface of the package to sharpen its claws. The return address label on the back was completely unreadable.

"You mean the guy trying to block the Spacelab project?" mumbled Ollie as he examined the package a second time. It was different from others he had handled on his job so far which all conformed to proper labeling and wrapping standards. The envelope or what was left of it was also covered in places with a sticky brown material which he couldn't identify.

"That's the one," Angela replied. "He's in high cotton right now with that problem occurring on Spacelab just when he needed it. These conservative republicans just love adversity and failure for anyone else. It's what they live for ever since they got the crap beat out of them for their position on global warming. Their only resource is fear and more fear and more fear. The people that elected them…the voters, are the last people they worry about. It's all me, me, me! And I must say that those voters are idiots for sure."

"What problem on Spacelab?" mumbled Ollie, not really interested in the political aspect of things at the moment. "No one ever tells me anything around here…except you, of course. Here I am working at what is theoretically the very center of our semi-powerful government, and what I never hear is news from the outside world. Nothing! My cousin works for NASA down in Houston and even he's hush-hush about everything that's going on. He's got more security clearances than the president!"

"Quarantine!" spouted Angela with enthusiasm. "You don't think those Green Sky people…you know, the college dropout types trying to shut down outer space research or maybe it's the religious right for that matter, did it somehow, do you? Or it could be aliens from the planet Oggle? I'm putting my bet on the aliens! I just wish they were a little better looking and smelled better.

"Apparently, the robots up there spilled some chemicals or something and NASA had to lock down the spacecraft so the germs wouldn't get down here. Something like that."

Ollie recalled a conversation he recently had with a classmate of his at the college who was majoring in biology. Pesumably, Spacelab was put into orbit because the research being done there was too dangerous to be conducted here on earth. That thought seemed to make sense. He'd also heard that the work onboard Spacelab was being done by robots instead of astronaut-scientists. His school friend Harold kept suggesting that maybe this was the kind of research we shouldn't be doing at all because it was inherently too dangerous to humans.

"By Green Sky, Angela, you must mean those latter-day hippies who want to bring the 1960s back again? From what I know about that epoch, I'm all for it for sure. Just think about it. Smoking grass all the time and free love everywhere…ah, and long hair to boot! And the music was the very best, not like the modern crap we are subjected to now. They got to enjoy Bob Dylan, The Grateful Dead, Eric Clapton, Steve Winwood, Little Feat, The Who, Pink Floyd…hey, they were the best ever."

Ollie paused to consider his own words. Once again he convinced himself that he was right. He had been born too late! Oh, to be twenty years old in 1965! He pictured himself protesting the Viet Nam War and then going to Woodstock to party for a week straight. Those were the days all right! But he had missed them.

"Actually, that's not such a bad idea, Angela. Great music and free…"

Ollie began to blush as Angela laughed and pointed at him.

"You don't look at all like Jerry Garcia or Meatloaf, Ollie. And I know you can't play a lick on the guitar or the drums or sing for that matter… except in the shower! But, maybe you could learn if you got another shot at it. That's all any of us really needs for happiness…a second time around to correct all of our mistakes."

Ollie tried to change the subject to bail himself out of the situation.

"Who hasn't heard of Jensen? I'm not an expert on these things…yet, but isn't he the republican't senator they call *Semi-conductor Jensen* because he believes God told him that CPUs should only reside on silicon? He believes that germanium is a Muslim plot…a Marxist plot to take over the world! Karl Marx is the real enemy here. Taking care of your fellow man is a sin! If you fail at capitalism, you should die without a whimper!"

"I don't know, Ollie, but I heard one of the democrats call him *Old Silicon Head*! He is from Kansas you know. Didn't *Brown v. The Board of Education* come out of Kansas? These fellows are not very kind to their own people, especially when they're not in Kansas any more. Makes one think twice about making politics a career, doesn't it? Once you choose a side, you're stuck with that decision…forever…unless you join the Lieberman flip-floppers. Who the hell was Lieberman anyway?"

"Angela, should you use your head and get smarter and after some deep thought and experience should you change your mind…admit you were wrong, then they will label you as a stupid flip-flopper! But Lieberman was just the opposite. He went from right to wrong trying to feather his senate seat. He was a flop-flipper!"

"But, Ollie, you haven't been here long enough to reach an opinion on that score, have you? You haven't seen enough of the real dirty underbelly of Washington yet. But mark my words, Ollie, you will! They get under your skin like the vicious little worms that they are, and they pervert the language and use it like a weapon to carve you up and enslave you. And they lie like dogs, to be sure. Kafka was absolutely right!"

Angela just closed her eyes and shook her head as she continued.

"You know, Ollie, that Kafka studied law and chemistry. He must have discovered the inherent flaws in lawyers for himself. Did you know that his three younger sisters were gassed by the Nazis after he died? How's that for going out on a sour note?

"Why are we even working here, Ollie? There must be a real life for us somewhere…anywhere else. Something honest and productive that we can be proud of."

Ollie smiled remembering his uncle's warning about the cesspool of politics he was immersing himself into.

"Angela, isn't there an old saying that goes something like this? *Sticks and stones may break my bones, but names can never hurt me.* Is it *names* or is it *words?*"

Angela just smiled and shrugged her shoulders as Ollie continued.

"I wouldn't care what they called me. I'd just come up with something better to call them. That goes for turkeys like Senator McDonald. He referred to his defense initiative as *Rolling Thunder.* I think he and his initiative deserve to be called the *Rolling Blunder.* But, of course, I'd expect that from a conservative. You've heard of a *Liberal Education* I'm sure. But, I've never heard of a conservative education. It means no education at all or at worst…home schooling."

Angela was quite familiar with McDonald and couldn't help but laugh at Ollie's remark.

"Help me out here, Ollie. Why is Jensen so hell-bent on opposing Spacelab funding? It's run completely by robots, which should be right up his alley. The scuttlebutt about the accident…actually, they're calling it *an incident*…last night is that it was the NASA people who caused the problem. It was human error if you can believe what little they are telling us. That's a ringing endorsement for Jensen's position that Spacelab should remain one hundred percent automated. No human tinkering allowed! It's hard to believe that he could actually be right about something?"

Ollie just shrugged his shoulders, too. He hadn't really given the subject of robots much thought although the concept appealed to him.

"I'm shooting from the hip here, Angela, because I really don't have a well thought out answer for you. But something deep inside my skull tells me that it's a mistake to program humans completely out of things like this. Pretty soon those robots will develop some sort of awareness and take over the world, which might not be all that bad. Remember the replicants in that sci-fi movie with Harrison Ford? The female replicants were pretty good looking for sure! It would make marriage and divorce obsolete, that's for sure. Each female robot would come with a guarantee…"

Ollie tried to suppress his laughter but was unsuccessful.

"You've been reading too much science fiction and watching old movies, Ollie, just like that professor from Princeton. What's his name again?"

"Victor Laurie, I believe," Ollie responded. "Is he involved in this… incident?"

"Apparently, he's in quarantine up there…at least for another day or so. They're worried about possible exposure to those viruses the robots were supposedly working on. Imagine being killed by your own experiment!"

Angela started nodding her head as she continued.

"It's a matter of safety and control. You've got to admit that we humans have acquired a very high standard of living because of our control over our silicon-based assistants. This Spacelab incident was probably a one-time thing caused by human intervention.

"But, you know what?" said Angela, "From everything they've said down in Houston, I can't honestly say that I'm convinced that the robots didn't malfunction in the first place. I sense a cover-up going down over there. I know that's not what Jensen wants to hear, but we shouldn't let the Congress jump to any conclusions yet…as if we have any control over that. Artificial intelligence combined with strict software control has given us the assurance we need to go ahead. Silicon-based systems don't evolve unless we tell them to evolve, unless we make them evolve. Darwin tells us that evolutionary processes are for living things…right? Professor Laurie says the same thing…I think? But, Jensen's from the religious right so you never know?"

"Now I remember!" shouted Ollie loud enough to be heard quite a distance away. "Laurie! He's the guy the Washington Post blasted last week. And I must agree with them. What a nut case! I've read several of the *Dune* series, and the sci-fi is great. But, come on! Folding space for real to travel from one place to another without moving? And they say he's working on creating a mini-universe in the laboratory. What's with that? It's probably a black hole that will eat all of us."

Ollie could see that Angela was deep in thought so he paused to give her a chance to organize her ideas.

"He never actually said that…not in the exact words," Angela responded. "At least I don't believe he has. And he hasn't to my knowledge mentioned *the spice* Herbert uses in his books, not to mention the need for the worms that produce the spice. But you should…scientists should theoretically be able to *fold* something two-dimensional that is already curved…shouldn't they? And we know that space is curved…don't we? So, the pieces are in place."

Angela rolled her eyes in response to her own words.

"Ollie, the next time I do a line or try some hash, I'll try folding space just for fun to see if it can be done! And I'll travel to where you are to prove my point."

Angela pulled a blank piece of paper out of a folder she held in her hand and drew two small stick figures on the sheet near diagonal corners. She drew an 'A' near one figure and a 'B' near the other.

"Suppose you are at point 'A' and you down some of the spice and fold this sheet which represents space so that 'A' and 'B' touch. Bingo! You've moved from point A to point B without moving…so to speak.

"But right now you'd better get going because I can't seem to fold this space we're standing in right now. That's probably because we're short the spice we require. The senator needs all the help he can get, and Jerry upstairs told me he's been looking for this package all day. And, remember, he probably doesn't want his pages doing his physics for him on company time."

Ollie took the small parcel from Angela's hands and gave her a smile and a wink with a thumbs-up. As he began to turn back toward the senate floor, Angela grabbed his arm.

"Don't give this to anyone but the senator himself…in person. No assistants, security people or the like. No exceptions whatsoever. I called a few minutes ago so he knows it's coming. If you can't gain access to him, bring this right back to me in the mailroom. Remember, no exceptions!"

Ollie set forth on his mission wondering what could be so important about this package.

It's probably one of his constituent's lobbyists delivering some off-the-record campaign money. This package is about the right size for something like that.

Just as Ollie cleared the vestibule and turned into the entryway leading to the main floor area where the senator usually held forth, a man in a dark suit wearing horned-rimmed glass with thick lenses stepped in front of him.

"Is that Senator Jensen's report? What took so long?"

Before Ollie could respond, the man tried to grab the package out of Ollie's hand.

"I'll give it to him!" he muttered.

Ollie almost let go, then he pulled the package out of the man's grasp.

"I can't do that," Ollie whispered firmly. "This is for the senator's hands only. I have strict orders!"

A look of anger and then frustration passed over the man's face as he started to make a second attempted to take the package from Ollie. Just then one of the senator's security personnel appeared around the corner.

"Page!" he shouted to Ollie, seemingly ignoring the other man's presence. "This way, before the senator leaves."

The man in the dark suit froze. Then after a second or two, he adjusted his glasses and turned away and without a word headed up the runway in the opposite direction. He seemed anxious to avoid a confrontation with the approaching guard.

Immediately, Ollie obeyed the security guard's commands as he followed him at a brisk pace down onto the senate floor. After some bumping and jostling with a group of people who were blocking their path, they finally reached the area the senator occupied.

"Crap!" shouted the security man as he scanned the senate floor. "We've missed him! He has a fund-raiser in Virginia and a briefing on the Spacelab. He won't be back until tomorrow morning. You should be here tomorrow morning at eight straight up, package in hand. Got that?"

Ollie nodded.

"What's your name…first name?" the man demanded.

"Ollie."

"Okay, take off, Ollie. Secure the package in the mailroom safe, and be here tomorrow at eight o'clock sharp!"

4

Tachyons

Looking through a hole in the sky seeing nowhere.
Through the eyes of a lie. Getting closer to the end
Of the line. Living easy where the sun doesn't shine.
I'm living in a room without any view.
I'm living freely because the rent's never due.

Hole in the Sky
Black Sabbath

Chemistry Department
Stanford University

The two scientists had been very good friends for several years ever since Dallas Pence arrived back at Stanford to take a faculty position in the chemistry department. Because their training and experience only overlapped a little, they loved to argue the latest scientific theories from different points of view which had the effect of broadening both of their ways of thinking about basic research. They were both avid sports fans so their bantering and discussions often lasted well through happy hour each working day.

Terry Swanson paced back and forth and waved his arms in the air as he talked just as if he were a standup comedian at a local comedy club.

"Tachyons? What will they think of next? This is pure science fiction, my friend. These are particles traveling faster than the speed of light which I grew up knowing as the fastest one can travel no matter what; particles that can never ever slow down. There is no Cherenkov Radiation here! And, it's said that they are particles with an imaginary rest mass? What does that mean in the real world? Or are those tardyons by any chance?

I always thought that tardyons were some of my students who are always late for class! That's what I call them. What do I know about it anyway? I'm a mere mortal on planet earth."

Terry bowed gracefully for his audience.

"Nonsense! It's nothing like that at all. Even the nefarious Richard Ogg might agree with me on this one for a change. There is something at work here that a simple virus easily and completely understands, something that we great complex humanoid scientists do not have a clue about. It is wound up in complexity theory, in the self-organizing capabilities of a complex system. It's chemical natural selection hard at work on the molecular level. These little guys know exactly what they're doing, and they're keeping us in the dark! These are nanorobots…nanobots with internal brains."

Pence was shaking his head and laughing, but he knew better than to interrupt Swanson when his friend was on a roll like this. The laboratory phone began buzzing as it was wont to do, but Pence let it ring and bade Swanson to continue. This presentation was too good to miss for anything.

"But let me clean the slate and go back to the very beginning, Dallas. What do we have to work with here? All we have in the first place are naked strands of nucleic acids. That's it! Take your choice. RNA or DNA? Or take them both for all I care. Then surround the little darlings with a cuddly sheath of protein. That's basically it. You have created a tiny little organic machine that is outsmarting us. But, before you proclaim yourself to be the creator God…well, at least a God…there are so many these days, consider some of the shortcomings of your little creation. Let's call him Barney. I like that name. It sort of fits, don't you think?"

Pence knew the name well. It was the name of Swanson's most loved pet golden retriever.

"Left alone, Barney cannot perform the required organic functions that define life. I'm sure that you're familiar with the most essential function because I've seen you eyeballing that new secretary in the chemistry department office. Reproduction is completely out of the question…for Barney, not for you. Thank God for small favors, or we'd be in bigger trouble than we are now!

"But give it…give Barney and his pals easy access to a proper host cell, let's say in your brain and…bango, who needs reproduction skills! Pirates off Africa should do so well. Barney commandeers the cell and rides it like a bicycle or maybe a motorcycle. Your cell becomes a willing slave doing just what the mean old virus wants it to do. And you just can't say 'no' because your cell won't listen to you. Well, most of the time at least. It reminds me of my ex-wife quite a bit. She couldn't do anything by herself, but with me in tow, the world was hers. Now that I think about it, it's a perfect analogy. I was the slave cell and she was the virus!

"Yet, this very power means that on its own, it is as dead as a rock… if a rock can be dead, that is. Viruses are incomplete organisms in the truest sense, and here I leave out any references to our old friend, Professor Ogg."

Dallas Pence listened to his longtime friend from the biophysics department, Professor Terry Swanson, but the smile forming on his face told Swanson that Dallas didn't necessarily agree, at least with the approach. But, at least Pence found the discussion entertaining as he always did. Despite their numerous friendly arguments, this was actually the first time in a long time that the two cronies were not on the same page. Swanson thought it was about time to let his pal express his opinion.

"It's the wrong paradigm, Terry," Dallas whispered under his breath while a smirk covered his face. "When I say this, I'm leaving out any reference to your ex-wife, Isadora."

Swanson paused and looked down at his right hand, which held a pair of dice. He seemed to be eyeing the plastic cubes with suspicion, as if they were alive in some sense and trying to mislead him.

"Pence, you are just lucky we can't do the experiment again right now. There's some trickery afoot here, that's for sure. I'll bet your pal Victor Laurie put you up to this when he was on drugs. Admit it! As he sits up there in the Spacelab decontamination area, he's probably smiling to himself because he's always got you to do his bidding for him here on earth. When things get too hot for him down here, he becomes an astronaut and splits the scene so he won't have to explain himself! You've got to tell me how you two got this little sideshow to come out this way. This play should be on Broadway or at least downtown Palo Alto."

Dallas thought about his mentor and occasional colleague who was now out in space and smiled to himself as he pondered the situation. Victor had always been a challenge to work for and work with, but this situation was even more complex even though they were working on different aspects of a general problem.

"Terry, right about now, old Victor is second-guessing himself about his little trip to Spacelab. But as long as his precious V-122, or whatever he calls it, is okay and his experiments are intact, he'll have that sarcastic grin on his face when he lands down here tomorrow…if he lands tomorrow?"

"If he lands tomorrow?" Swanson retorted without hesitation. "But that raises another pet peeve of mine. He never follows the correct naming conventions for his viral friends. And don't give me that security business. You're just encouraging bad science by labeling your media V-102 or V-122. If..."

Dallas finally felt compelled to interrupt his friend.

"To get this benign version of Victor's virus...the one we are using in these little experiments, I had to swear on a stack of Bibles six feet high that I would call this stuff what he wanted me to name it although I must say that Barney is now my favorite viral representation. He doesn't want his weapons research program compromised by mere mortals. The money flowing into his Princeton lab is going to fund his work in perpetuity... or longer and some of the crumbs might just land here on me...on us. That's worth a few nomenclature errors, isn't it? He's about as paranoid about classified research as it's possible for any human to be. He even told me about some of his weirder dreams...James Bond was after him in one of them!

"Look, he was stuck in that wheel chair, probably for life, but he worked his way out of it, at least a little. He can actually walk most of the time as long as the distance isn't too far. We shouldn't begrudge the fellow something as small as several tens of millions of dollars for his research. Besides, he now has superstar status in the press to be sure, and he might just drag us along with him into the spotlight one of these days. His ugly face has been on the front pages for three days running. And, I'll bet that you didn't know that the average American owns four Bibles!"

"Us...?" Swanson croaked in confusion.

Terry Swanson knew that it was fruitless to directly argue this subject with a former student of the infamous Victor Laurie. But he still wanted to nip away at the edges if for no other reason than the fact that his scientific ego demanded it.

"Who was it, Dallas? Not Einstein or Schroedinger or Heisenberg or Planck. No, it was a Frenchman as I remember. And you know how Americans dislike the French even though they saved our collective ass in our War of Independence. He was an anthropologist, not a physicist or a physical chemist such as you and your illustrious mentor. No! As far as I know, anthropologists never travel faster than the speed of light and do not have an imaginary rest mass! And all anthropologists that I know obey the tenets of general relativity, of that I am certain...I think? Still, there is that fellow on the Notre Dame faculty..."

The sarcasm in Swanson's voice was clear, but Dallas just shook it off. It was fairly hard not to laugh when Terry went off on one of his friendly tirades. His style was his way of communicating, badly. But, he was a good sounding board for new and off the wall ideas that most other scientists either couldn't get their arms around or who were too busy with their own agendas to spare the time for intellectual combat. If you could get your idea past Swanson, it had a chance in the scientific community at large.

"If my mind is still working," whispered Swanson, "I believe that it goes something like this. Stop me if I get it wrong, will you? I want to make sure that we're on the same page here."

Pence smirked as he nodded his acquiescence, so Swanson continued.

"A complex system, like the virus you have in your hot little hands, can attain various degrees of consciousness. Now I know that consciousness is not the right word, but humor me for a while. It's a word that feels comfortable to me in this context. The big difference between that chair you are sitting on and...say, you yourself, oh mighty scientist, is that you are aware of your own existence and the chair, presumably, is not aware of its existence. You know that the chair will probably be here long after you are gone to your just reward."

"That's a first for you and for me, Swanson," countered Pence as he leaped up and pointed to his chair. "I've never been compared to a chair before as far as I know. At least not so favorably!"

Swanson seemed to ignore the humor as he wrapped his arms behind his back and began pacing.

"There comes a degree of complexity, which when it is exceeded by the system, in this case by your virus, where the system achieves the ability to begin organizing itself. I believe that it was Aristotle who said something like 'by possessing life one implied that a thing can nourish itself and decay.'

"Now Dallas, I'm a mere biophysicist by trade, yet I do sort of subscribe to this complexity thing. I think that's because it's the way my fellow humans act. We do a piss poor job of it, but we do try to organize ourselves on occasion. And sometimes, like in war and in ice hockey, we try to play together as a team. This is a second level of organization. That is, between organized entities as opposed to inside an organized entity. Now that's a kind of organization that also comes after a threshold. The entities somehow become aware of each other."

Pence grabbed his head and leaped up from his chair again.

"My head's beginning to hurt," whispered Pence as a small joke. At the same time he reached for a cup of coffee that was resting on the table in front of him. Then he sat down and Swanson continued.

"But I have trouble with the communication thing, especially because the virus is relatively macroscopic. You're telling me that old VIC-122 here has organized and achieved instantaneous communications capabilities with substantially all of its member elements in this room. Am I right? Without central nervous systems as we know them, and without functional brains or equivalent, they communicate with each other. You're saying that these blobs of protein with their nucleic acid cores are firing and detecting tachyons right in front of us, and that the tachyons' contents are coded with a primitive language.

"Hey, these things can't even reproduce themselves for Heaven's sake! They need the cell structure of another organism to do that. Doesn't sound like a fun group to me. It's like going to a party where you have to listen to everyone else's jokes, and you can't tell any of your own.

"Well, but then again, Dallas, I know some computer geeks...silicon based types right here in Northern California, who when left alone naked with the opposite sex, probably could not reproduce either. Maybe there's something to this? Tell me again about that heat experiment at Cal Tech."

Pence lumbered over to the blackboard.

"We had two blobs of this virus in tubes across the room from each other. They were imbedded in an inert substrate. A hot glass rod was pushed into one of them to create a hole in the substrate. Presumably, the imbedded virus 'felt' the heat, too. In a short while even though eighteen feet away, the second substrate had a deformation in its surface similar to the first hole! Just to be complete, we did the experiment without the virus. No hole across the room. Makes me wonder about tachyons."

Terry laughed and then was reminded of something he'd seen on television earlier in the day.

"You forgot to mention Victor's old pal and associate, Richard Ogg. If there ever was someone after Victor's hide, he's the man. I don't see it, but he alleges that his experiments and calculations on ammonia prove that he had the idea first. The government should have sent Ogg up there with Victor, and they could have fought it out hand to hand in outer space for all the world to see. It would be 'Winner take all!'

"But, hey, not to digress too much because that was very interesting, but I saw that Iranian fellow you introduced me to at the Physical Society meeting last spring on TV this morning. I forget his name, but he's the NASA physician…"

"Mahadavan!" croaked Pence proudly. "His grandfather, or maybe it was his great grandfather, was one of the lucky…smart ones who got out of Iran when the Shah was deposed. Fortunately, he took Maha and his mother with him. That was a cloak and dagger operation for sure. Maha was born in Tehran but got U.S. citizenship as a boy and made it to medical school at Harvard. Maha even has a Bostonian accent to prove it. He's as good a scientist as you'll ever find on this planet.

"Most of the physicians I've encountered just process patients to harvest the medical insurance money. They're so-called capitalists living off of Medicare money. Doesn't that make them socialists? But this guy Maha actually treats his patients and tries to heal them. If you're ever sick, he's the fellow to see.

"A couple of years ago I got bit by a snake…I guess it was a snake, and I broke out in a rash all over my leg. I was on a cruise ship off Belize at the time. The ship's physician just sort of yawned at the whole thing. 'If you're not dead yet, everything should work itself out' were his final words.

"By chance I told one of my contacts at NASA in Houston about the incident during a phone conversation. Well, no sooner did I put down the phone than I had an incoming call. It was Maha. He wanted the complete scenario and then insisted that I fax him color photos of the bite and the rash. In three hours I had a tube of some steroid cream that I was supposed to apply to the rash three times a day. Well, in two days the rash was gone, and the bite was healing. End of story!

"Well, except for the unexpected personal apology I received from the ship's physician. Apparently, Maha called him and read him the riot act. The guy was whimpering like a beaten dog when he talked to me."

"Is Maha the guy with the good looking daughters…granddaughters?" asked Terry with an obvious element of hope in his voice.

"You bet! Three of the smartest and prettiest girls on the planet for sure, but a little too young…and too smart for you."

Just at that moment the phone on Dr. Pence's desk began buzzing again. Dallas picked up the receiver this time and after about thirty seconds began nodding his head vigorously. Obviously, it was good news. He hung up smiling.

"Terry, ARPA has approved funding for our experiment. Laurie will be doing cartwheels in his wheelchair."

"Good," Swanson replied. "Now, please start from the beginning and explain your approach. Keep it simple. Assume I'm on the faculty at Berkeley, and I have a very short attention span!" Terry couldn't resist getting in a dig at the University of California.

Dallas retrieved two glass beakers from a nearby shelf.

"This is the benign virus in acetic acid solution. As you know, acetic acid is a weak acid. The positive proton has a strong affinity for the negative acetate ion. In this other beaker is the same trace of virus in a strong acid solution. Notice the difference in color. The virus is colorless in a weak acid and violet in the strong acid."

Dallas placed the two beakers back on the lab bench. Both were now sitting on plates, which contained temperature-measuring devices.

"On the other side of the lab I have placed two similar beakers. Now, there's a heating coil under each of those samples. I can control the temperature of those beakers across the room with this power supply."

Sitting on the bench was a small rack containing two DC power supplies. Pence threw several switches as he talked.

"As you can see, Terry, both of these samples are at the same temperature within a tenth of a degree Centigrade. Similarly, the samples across the room are within a tenth of a degree of each other."

Terry checked the digital readings and nodded. Dallas could tell that his cohort was enjoying this demonstration to the fullest.

"Now for the baseline test. I'm going to raise the temperature of the weak acid solution across the room by five degrees. We'll do it slowly and see what happens."

After Dallas changed the power supply settings again, the two scientists watched as the temperature in the weak acid solution methodically climbed by the prescribed five degrees. When the temperature rise was complete, Dallas gestured toward the temperature readings in the beakers on their side of the lab. They were relatively unchanged.

"Not much excitement there?" said Pence with a laugh in his voice. "It's as if they don't know each other exists."

Swanson agreed as this friend returned the heated beaker to its former temperature. They each had a cup of coffee as they waited for the beakers to reach the same temperature within a tenth of a degree. It took about ten minutes but there was no reason to hurry.

"Now, I'll heat the strong acid solution in the same way I heated the weak acid solution. Watch this!"

Much to Terry's amazement, as the other remote beaker gained temperature, the strong acid solution of the virus on the bench before him rose in temperature also. In five minutes this beaker was four and a half degrees higher in temperature than its counterpart.

"Wow!" shouted Swanson. "They're…communicating with each other. They are actually communicating…if that's the right word. How in the world could they do something like that?"

Pence had that *I told you so* look on his face.

"Tachyons, Terry. It's the only explanation I can come up with. These beasts are utilizing energy or particles moving faster than the speed of light whether we like it or not. These virus molecules, under the right conditions, have primitive transmitters and receptors for tachyons that actually work. Now, for the Nobel Prize all I…all we have to do is prove it."

"I need a drink!" mumbled Swanson as he slumped back into his chair to ponder the situation. "I know that we're good friends, Dallas, but, what do you need me for? This experiment right here is worth the Nobel Prize just the way it is. Don't get me wrong. I appreciate your generosity, but…"

Pence shook his head. He had an answer for Terry.

"I need help with the biophysics. Remember, Laurie is running around in outer space with a much more dynamic form of this virus doing even crazier things. I can't even imagine what that thing might be capable of…other than killing all of us? And he really doesn't know what he's doing! He's not aware of the danger…only the opportunity. He's a physical chemist like me, for God's sake. This is biophysics. We need your help!"

Swanson liked the idea, and he agreed. Then he had a suggestion.

"Let's see if these fellows can communicate over a substantial distance more like a city block instead of a few feet," he suggested as he pointed out the laboratory window. "Your lab has this very convenient porch, and my lab is also on the second floor. We'll take one set of these guys over there and see if they can find each other like they found each other here. We can do it at noon and then at midnight to see if there's any difference. What about tomorrow? This could be fun!"

"You're on!" said Dallas Pence with a smile. "But right now it's happy hour as far as I'm concerned, and I don't care what's going on anywhere else! I need a drink, and you're buying."

5

The Press Conference

Very superstitious…writing on the wall.
Very superstitious…ladder's about to fall..
Thirteen-month old baby broke that looking glass.
Seven years of bad luck, good things in the past.
Very superstitious…

Stevie Ray Vaughn
Superstition

The Houston NASA Space Center

Forty-eight hours of quarantine in space were completed, apparently successfully, but Professor Victor Laurie realized that the greatest dangers to him and his reputation were yet to come. With the entire news media and most of the scientific community focused on him and his voyage into space, Victor felt more pressure than he recalled enduring on the day of the oral examination for his Ph.D. at Harvard University. His dissertation in the field of microwave spectroscopy had been approved by Professor E. Bright Wilson, the acknowledged leading researcher in the area of rotational spectra of molecules, yet there were those professors on his orals committee from organic chemistry and the physics department that worried him. Would he remember the structural formula of sucrose and the simple definition of pH with robots dancing in his head?

His research efforts as a graduate student were exemplary, yet personal interactions with the faculty and other students were often quite rocky. Part of the problem was his physical condition, which made it difficult for him to seriously pursue any member of the opposite sex. As a result, he focused his mind on his research and future projects it might lead to.

As he recalled, the night before the oral exam he could hardly sleep a wink. His roommate in the dormitory, an organic chemistry major, wasn't much help either. Ray Buchholtz was from the Bronx, and he snored something fierce. Ray had no trouble sleeping because his orals were over a year away. Victor wanted to silence him, but in the end he endured the racket as he contemplated his ultmate fate. Just one more hurdle to clear and he could rid himself of Ray forever.

The exam was scheduled for 10 AM so breakfast was no easy matter for Victor either. One of his friends took him to a restaurant for an omelet and oatmeal hoping to calm him down. Luckily, his friend came up with a good calming strategy to help the situation.

Who knows more about this stuff than you, Vic, he recalled Harold saying. *These guys no more want to challenge your research than the Man in the Moon! They all want to get back to solving their own problems and rest assured, they have plenty of them. Just make sure you define all your terms carefully and clearly, and they'll all go to sleep as if you hypnotized them. Physical chemistry is as boring and mystifying to an organic chemist as organic chemistry is boring and mystifying to us. Plus, remember, they don't want to make Professor Wilson look bad because he's the big man around here and you're his student. That's your ace in the hole!*

Victor recalled being asked that simple question about pH he had worried so much about and how he stumbled for a few moments trying to structure his answer properly until Professor Wilson stood up and told Victor to relax because he was among friends. The faculty was impressed with Victor's research and Professor Wilson told him as much in front of them. That was all Victor needed. He defined the concept of pH, discussed examples of strong and weak acids and bases, and was home free the rest of the way. That happy memory gave him some much-needed self-assurance for his tumultuous future.

Despite the predictable nervousness brought on by the looming prospects of a press conference where he would be the main attraction, Laurie felt amazingly well, at least physically. He wanted to ascribe the unusual, almost giddy feeling his body was now experiencing, to the extended period of weightlessness he just completed on Spacelab. There seemed to be no other reasonable explanation. He had never felt this free before, free of the inevitable force of gravity that was always weighing on him and slowing him down.

He had participated in several brief weightlessness simulations at NASA Langley, yet they were far from the real thing. Onboard Spacelab he found himself floating absolutely free of any restraint, and he developed a new respect for gravity. His relatively powerless legs seemed invigorated for the first time since childhood, and memories of playing ball in the schoolyard with his friends flooded his brain. He remembered his head spinning as he danced in the air above one of the robots while singing one of his favorite David Bowie songs.

"Ground Control to Major Tom…"

Yet, it was the chorus of voices that still rolled around in his head that both bothered him and inspired him most of all. These were voices he had not heard before his trip into space. He analyzed the situation and his feelings over and over.

It was like a dream, but it was real. Those robots actually spoke to me… or to something in my head! They called me by my name. And I was able to understand them when they told me what to do for them. Did they speak English or was it some binary language? I don't know. Somehow I can't remember. The words or the thoughts were just there…in my mind, clear and concise.

When did this all start? It happened on Spacelab for sure. I fell and lost my helmet and then everything went blank for a while.

But, why is this bothering me now? I can't be going crazy? My head is still in one piece as far as I can tell! But it almost feels like something else is in my mind with me. Something they…someone put there. Another entity is inside this head of mine…in here with me. Somehow, someway, I must control myself. Please let this just be a bad dream or spasm of my imagination! I could handle that. I know scientists are supposed to be a little wacky anyway, but this is carrying a good thing too far. I must relax and let the truth flow, and I'll be okay.

Laurie ran his right hand through his full head of jet-black hair several times. All this time his head was shaking negatively in response to his jumbled thoughts. It was almost as though his physical body was disagreeing with his mind. He knew he had to come to grips with this and soon…no, immediately! All he needed was a mental breakdown in front of all these people who could seal his professional fate forever. His space travel would make him a hero, but he'd be a dead hero for sure if he passed out on stage.

I can't let anyone know about these voices. They'll never believe me. And if they doubt my feelings, what's next? My research. All this work I've done will be in vain. They'll find out about my mini-universe experiment. They'll shut it down because they fear that I'll loose a black hole on them…on the earth. But the risk is worth it. Still, they'll never agree if I appear mentally unstable and out of control. I've got to calm down and act normal starting right now.

He took off his reading glasses and placed them on the table in front of him. He knew he looked less like a mad scientist with them off his face. After a deep breath, he seemed more encouraged and ready to press on.

I'll just tell them that the extended weightlessness aboard Spacelab disoriented me because it affected my balance. That's believable especially with my leg problems. I have too much riding on these experiments, and they know it. I risked my life by going up there to make sure all was well! Goddammit, I'm a modern day hero. Scientist...space traveler...who knows what else? We need more people like me and fewer second-guessers to propel our society forward.

I just have to remain calm, keep a smile on my face...and laugh at my obvious inexperience in space. I just can't do that quarantine stuff again. It's just like being locked up in a very small cell with another person who talks all the time. Or as Pence says, 'Locked up in a small room with Led Zeppelin!' I like Led Zeppelin! Go ahead, lock me up in that room any time you want as long as I can listen to Led Zeppelin all the time I'm in there!

For the past three hours the space-traveling academic had been examined from stem to stern by a team of NASA's best physicians who after much consultation thankfully gave him a clean bill of physical health. A complete MRI took over an hour and even now three specialists and two neurologists were peering at the results. About every fifteen minutes one of them would visit him and tell him that all seemed well. He wanted to believe them so he would smile and express his thanks.

Even his legs felt better although he was still stuck in his same old wheelchair most of the time. As a matter of fact, they felt so much better that he was seriously considering a return to the physical therapy regime his physicians had suggested but that he had ignored long ago. It was ironic that he was contemplating a new type of space travel in his research, yet he was sure he couldn't walk three steps unaided in any direction without falling down.

Suddenly, his smile faded quickly from his face as he reminded himself of the mysterious incident that had occurred aboard Spacelab during his extra-terrestrial visit.

Just my luck to be aboard Spacelab for my first time ever when something goes wrong up there and with the whole world watching my every move. And I was one of the ones insisting that the station be run only by robots! And all was going so very well. I should have followed my own advice and sent Elmer.

A robot Laurie had worked with at NASA was nicknamed *Elmer Fudd* by the lab technicians because his audio responses were often slurred.

Viral development was ahead of schedule, so promising as a matter of fact, that we wanted to advance the media development. Come to think of it, all these projects are classified. I've got to be careful not to spill the beans. If that's true that this whole thing is classified, how come every Tom, Dick and Harry in the press corps seems to know so much about them? The Russians even volunteered to come aboard Spacelab and help during the emergency. What kind of cold war is that?

Victor thought back to his meetings at Langley before the mission. It wasn't his idea…at first, anyway, to go up. Yet, at the moment he couldn't remember who suggested it first. It could have been Maxmovich or those guys from Houston, but he couldn't recall. Then it hit him like a bolt of lightning.

It was that wacky senator…Jensen who did it! And he did it all from behind the scenes so he could deny it if there were any problems. How could he get elected to the senate when he seems drunk all the time?

There were plenty of military and civilian technicians and robots completely qualified to install the new modules. Why didn't I point that out when I had the chance? My ego got in the way! That's it! I offered no resistance to the idea. I put my own head in the noose and jumped when they told me to!

I never should have let them talk me into going up there. And it was my idea to make it look like my idea! If only… Well, it's too late now. I've got to go along with the company story regardless of what happened or happens. I really wish Pence were here to cover for me. I need an ally real bad. He's good at taking fire and counter-attacking. After all, I taught him, didn't I? Why can't I do it myself? I can direct, but I can't act worth a lick. My life is like a Cohen Brothers movie.

Professor Laurie's thoughts were interrupted as his assistant entered the room and without a word began wheeling his chair toward the door to the main conference room. It was obvious that his medical exams were over. Victor pointed back at his reading glasses and a pile of papers sitting next to them. His assistant dutifully retrieved these items and asked it there was anything else the professor wanted. Satisfied that he had all the materials he needed, Victor waved him on. It was time to face the real music of the public news conference.

Soon Professor Laurie was seated at a table with several NASA bigwigs as the government spokesman opened the meeting. From his first glance, Victor could sense without looking that the room was packed with interested reporters eager to pounce on him at the first opportunity. They knew raw meat when they saw it, and Victor was determined not to disappoint them. For a second time he told himself that it was time to face the music but to relax while doing it!

However, then it happened! As his eyes scanned the audience he froze as if he had just seen a ghost…or rather the devil! There in the first row sat his archenemy Professor Richard Ogg. Here was the so-called scientist from the University of California who claimed that Victor had stolen his ideas about space travel. Ogg's eyes seemed to glow in the low light of the room. Flashing from red to green and back like an out of kilter traffic light, they mesmerized Victor…almost hypnotizing him until the house lights came back up again.

A man from NASA stepped to the podium. After some initial remarks about Spacelab, another NASA spokesman stepped forward to introduce the scientist. At the same time a microphone was placed on the table in front of Victor next to a bottle of drinking water.

"Ladies and gentlemen, Professor Victor Laurie of the Princeton University Chemistry Department has kindly agreed to try to answer your questions about the Spacelab incident. Please restrict your queries to a general nature as some of the details of the Spacelab experiments are still classified. Professor Laurie has agreed to make an opening statement, which should clarify much of what happened while he was onboard. Thank you."

Victor tried to smile at the two hundred or so newsmen assembled before him. Then, after clearing his throat, he decided to dive right into the subject at hand. He was convinced that if he could put the listeners into his position, if only momentarily, they would understand and be sympathetic to his cause. He didn't see too many friendly faces in the crowd, so he didn't expect any help from third parties.

"This was my one and only trip above the earth's atmosphere, and hopefully my last trip, too! Not that it didn't have its exciting moments and visual rewards and all those things you see in the movies, but over time I've developed a certain respect for gravity. Besides, it's just that the dangers associated with sending a novice like me into orbit become fairly obvious after you've been through what I've been through and doing it on a regular basis produces too many and too serious a range of problems for the average guy like me to face. Our highly-trained astronauts are truly a brave and resourceful team, and they deserve all of our admiration and support for taking on these tasks."

The assembled journalists gave Victor a polite round of applause.

"The spectacular view of the earth and the sensations induced by weightlessness were very distracting, even for a supposedly experienced scientist. I am sure you can appreciate my feelings on the matter and my reactions thereto. Fortunately, I've worked with prototypes of the robots aboard Spacelab extensively during their development so I had no trouble communicating…ah, interacting with the units up in the laboratory. At least that part went well.

"They carried out their protocols flawlessly and spoke clearly and distinctly… Their language capabilities make it much easier for us humans to work with them. We should be very proud of the scientists and engineers who developed these robots because they do tasks much too dangerous for human organisms."

Laurie knew he had made a big mistake, not with the word 'organisms' but with the implication of spoken language, and he moved to cover himself.

"The robots don't actually speak, of course," he said with a mischievous smile on his face, "unless you count bits and bytes. But after you've worked with them for a while, they communicate by their actions and digital code responses. I imagine that soon they will actually have full speech capabilities. After a while you start to consider them your friends. It takes some of the edge off space travel and the dangers inherent in the mission."

The looks on the attendees' faces told Laurie that he had succeeded in covering up his snafu. The fact that he himself actually heard voices was his secret and had to remain his secret.

"The NASA technicians and I encountered no difficulties installing the new equipment modules on Spacelab. The successful completion of this installation was the main reason for the mission, because the installation was not a task the NASA robots were designed to perform on their own. This was not unexpected because the complex design of these advanced experimentation modules requires expert hands-on installation and setup. We anticipated using new advanced robots to do the installation, but because of some fortunate results putting us about two years ahead of schedule with our experimental program, we decided not to wait for robot development to catch up. The time and money saved were worth the risk.

"I do not want to sound political with these statements, but I feel that it's essential to keep the congress and our taxpayers as up to date as possible on this project because of its national defense aspects. Security issues prevent me from laying out the details for you, but rest assured that minimizing the costs of this project while maintaining its scientific integrity are foremost in our minds at all times."

Laurie knew that he wasn't quite telling the real truth. In fact, both the main installation robot and its backup unit unexpectedly failed when the standard installation command was given from earth. Laurie realized that someone might notice the fact that the new units had been aboard Spacelab for six weeks prior to his mission and were not transported by the human crew. So, he had an answer ready just in case the question should come up.

"These current robotic units are highly developed and fully capable of successfully performing most activities a human technician could accomplish. Yet, these particular modules required a few tricky manipulations, and they are specially designed to perform some crucial experiments, which became necessary based on our scientific progress.

"Also, several significant modifications in their control circuitry required the human touch. So, we decided that it was worth the effort to attend to these installations ourselves now at the most efficient point in the program. After all, in the end these experiments are our responsibility, and the taxpayers deserve a maximum of efficiency and results from our labors. An error of omission at this point could have cost us significant funds and extended delays in our research."

Laurie smiled to himself as he pandered to the American taxpayer in a way that would make any politician proud.

"We were able to successfully connect and initialize the new modules, and as we were leaving the central laboratory, several warning sensors came on. The robots immediately conducted a system-wide check of the entire spacecraft as they are programmed to do automatically upon any warning of this type. Fortunately, no breaches were found either in the spacecraft or in the experimental systems and our experiments were set back only a day or two.

"It was during this period that I lost consciousness for several minutes. In accordance with emergency procedures, oxygen therapy was applied by our robotic systems, and I regained consciousness, apparently rather quickly. I was then isolated for forty-eight hours as required by our safety procedures, and here I am...alive to tell you the tale. Our electronic friends aboard Spacelab performed their tasks flawlessly, and you might say that I owe my life to them."

After another polite round of applause, the audience of reporters began to ask a series of questions about the future of Spacelab and the reliability of its robotic workers, which Laurie handled quite well. However, the question that he knew would eventually surface finally was voiced by a female reporter from Chicago. Her name was Cathy Benes.

"I'm not a scientist, Professor Laurie, but I have heard the rumors concerning the ultimate goal of your extensive research and I have, of course, picked up on the connection to Frank Herbert's novels...you know, the Dune series. I just read the first book in the series and even rented the movie, which is vintage 1988 or so. Do you really think there is a chance of...folding space and are these experiments headed in that direction?"

The room fell absolutely silent waiting for Laurie's response. He cleared his throat and focused his eyes firmly on the reporter who had posed the question. He couldn't count the number of times he had tried to compose a short but clear answer to this question but had failed. Yet, he pushed ahead trying to calm himself as he went. And, as the NASA people had advised him, he spoke very informally.

"Cathy, I'm just a physical chemist. I doubt I could write a novel...a fictional or should I narrow it to a science fictional novel. And, you realize that our Spacelab work has nothing to do with space travel, at least not as far as we know. Our research is for our national defense. The particulars are classified, but I am authorized to tell you that my interest in space travel is not part of this work.

"Frank Herbert has proven that he was quite capable of writing science fiction. But the point to emphasize here is the fact that what he wrote makes sense and remains science fiction then and now. No matter how brilliant his ideas and his presentation...and I have read all of his Dune novels several times, they are not to be taken as factual science. Maybe some day in the distant future we can address the concept of folding space, but not now.

"And please remember that this fictional travel was made possible in the book by using a powerful drug produced by giant worms resident on the planet Arakkis...ah, I think that was its name...maybe? We don't have a clue where Arakkis is, we don't have the spice, we haven't found the worms yet...none of these things are aboard Spacelab...I can vouch for that."

The audience finally began to see the humor in his remarks and a roar of laughter rolled through the crowd.

As Professor Laurie smiled, he began to experience some dizziness. He stopped and reached for a bottle of water, but only managed to knock it over. Suddenly, a look of panic spread across his face. He could hear the voices in his head once again as he toppled slowly to the floor. His problems were only beginning.

6

Contact

The Houston NASA Space Center

The image of the space traveler's face on the monitor screen conveyed a sense of weariness commensurate with his protracted ordeal, but the major managed a smile and a wave of the hand as he looked up from his makeshift bed at his two electronic visitors. The astronaut searched both faces visible on his flat-panel interface carefully, but at first he failed to recognize either man. That wasn't unusual in this business. However, he did make note of the prominent NASA label on each man's shirt. Under the circumstances he was very pleased to have human visitors no matter who they were.

His video visitors were well aware of the fact that this man had been secretly in quarantine in space aboard Spacelab for almost three days now and was facing at least two more weeks of close medical inspection upon his return to earth. They also realized that they had the distinction of being the space traveler's first non-medical visitors during that period, and that he was sure to be somewhat confused and disoriented after his recent experience.

But NASA couldn't risk sending the inexperienced Professor Victor Laurie into orbit alone, so Major Vostry was the logical choice to accompany him. Vostry had been into space on seven previous missions all of which he had completed successfully. He was certainly the most qualified astronaut available for this complex mission.

"Finally," he whispered in a hoarse tone that sounded more like a grunt, "human visitors not carrying hypos and pills! And those needles better have been clean. I don't want a case of Hepatitis C out of all of this. I like my liver just the way it is and so does my girlfriend. You'll have her to deal with if I don't make it back clean and in one piece!

"Still, whoever you are, you're a sight for these sore eyes. Thank God, you're not with the military! I don't feel like saluting anyone just now. Tell them for me that they can take the chain-of-command thing and shove it where the sun doesn't shine!"

Vostry paused briefly to clear his throat and rub his tired eyes, then he continued his rant.

"I believe we have met before, fellows, but as you might expect, my brain is mush right now, and I've never been particularly good at correlating names and faces, unless, of course, you were good-looking women. That dates back to grade school and high school. Everyone had a nickname and an ugly face back then. It was a lot easier to keep track of people. Still, you look like friendly types even though these screens are a bit fuzzy right now. Well, it's probably me that's fuzzy right now."

Seemingly somewhat stunned by Major Robert Vostry's friendly and informal response to their appearance, Frank and Phil both hesitated and responded with smiles and waves of their hands after casting quizzical looks at each other, opting to wait for the patient to continue. They both had occasion to speak with the major several months ago, but then only briefly during a conference call. So both men listened intently when the space traveler finally broke his silence again.

"What's with the total silence routine, boys? I thought that we were all friends up here, you know…on the same side of the earth? For some unexplained reason, I get more conversation out of these damn robots than out of their human counterparts. No one told me that these tin cans had English-speaking capabilities. Actually, if I'm not mistaken, I believe that one of them actually asked me out on a date! I couldn't tell the robot's gender, so to be safe I declined the offer, at least for now.

"Would you two fellows mind telling me exactly why I'm still here aboard Spacelab? Don't lie to me. I can take it even if it's real bad news.

But, I'd better be getting overtime for this! And if you don't start talking soon, I'm going back to *I Love Lucy*!"

His voice seemed calm and had a resigned and sarcastic quality to it. Frank was the first to respond to the major.

"I know that you know this already, but you've been through quite a harrowing experience lately to say the least, Major Vostry. We decided that you qualified for *in situ* quarantine. Because Professor Laurie was probably exposed, we wanted to delay your return so you wouldn't get any exposure from the professor. That's not saying we're one hundred percent sure he was actually exposed to a virus, but there was no need to take the chance with your safety.

"You may not recall, but we met a few months ago on a conference call between Langley and Houston. If you don't mind, we have a few questions for you. When you get back, they'll be all over you, so just look at this quiz as a practice session for future oral exams. If you don't mind, let me begin with do you recall entering Spacelab?"

For a moment the smile disappeared from Vostry's face. Then he began vigorously nodding his head and gritting his teeth.

"I certainly recall the launch from earth and ultimate docking with Spacelab like it was yesterday. It was the first time I've seen SLOB up that close. She's a big mother to say the least. Now I know why she was assembled in orbit. I was involved in the early stages of that mission, but I never thought the finished product would be this large. You can convert this flying laboratory into a retirement home for old astronauts when NASA's through with it.

"And Laurie, how could I forget him? Luckily, he's one of a kind. He's a lunatic…or is he a lunar tick? He was very quiet and reserved at first all the way up until the moment he entered this laboratory up here. Up to that point he was remarkably calm and professional…or just scared shitless, which is probably the correct description? I was actually starting to admire the guy.

"I don't know what happened in there after the craft stopped shaking… inside the laboratory itself, but once he came flying out, he was jabbering with those robots of his as if they were human and screaming at me to move this, carry that… I couldn't do most of what he wanted because I couldn't understand him. It was like he was speaking a foreign language, and believe me, I've heard quite a few crazy foreign tongues at some of my earlier duty stations. This was nothing even close to English or German or French. It was more like…Morris Code. Reminded me of my tour with the boy scouts. I was a Hamm radio guy as a kid, and Laurie was almost croaking C.Q., C.Q.

"But first, something else strange started things off. A few minutes before he came out, Spacelab began shaking as if we were docking with the Queen Elizabeth or something similar. That freaked me out...probably did the same to him, but I couldn't see him at the time. I was praying that the Spacelab's warranty hadn't run out! I checked around as best I could, but nothing physical had happened to the ship as far as I could tell from where I was.

"And another thing. When he came out, Laurie's eyes and his lips were wide open as if he'd just seen a ghost or two in that lab of his up there. And he was drooling out of the side of his mouth like a heroin junkie. Well, some kind of junkie for sure. And he was literally singing! Have you ever heard Lou Reed do *Heroin*? It sounded almost like that...slow at first, then fast, then slow...I'd like to have a tape of that to find out exactly what he said. I'm sure I heard *It's my wife, it's my life*...pretty sure.

"Without any explanation he dragged me back into the lab area and kept pointing at a cluster of sealed buckets that supposedly contained human tissues preserved in formalin...whatever that is? He kept pointing to his head and screaming unintelligible phrases. All I could do was shrug my shoulders and ask him to repeat himself. Finally, he gave up, so I got out of there as fast as I could.

"But in the process I did ask him what formalin was. He glared at me like I was a dummy and said it was formaldehyde dissolved in water... ah, aqueous solution is what he said. Then he screamed at me again... something about not letting it polymerize. He said that if it reached paraformaldehyde, we'd both be dead! That sure got my attention even though I had no idea of what was going on. What was I going to do? Talk the molecules out of polymerizing?"

"You and he were alone in the lab section?" asked Phil quietly.

"Yeah...except for the robots. There was no one else. Three of them followed him around up here like they were his pet collies. It was unbelievable. After a while he didn't seem to mind them trotting after him at all. It was weird science.

"These robots up here are almost human in their behavior. One of them was with me most of the time. He...I assumed it was male. Any way, he was very helpful, but it was hard to get rid of him. Sometimes I just like a little privacy. He seemed to anticipate what I was going to do even before I did, whatever it was I was doing. He wanted to wipe my ass whenever I even thought about hitting the lavatory. I used to think that my former mother-in-law was exceptionally bad, but this guy was psychotic to say the least!"

A smile broke out on Vostry's face. At least he seemed to be enjoying his monologue.

"If you really want to know, I even gave mine a name. Elvis! I never did find out if it could play the guitar or sing. Actually, he was labeled as 'Gamma' which isn't very artistic. My job up here was to install the new servo modules. Each of these robots is a little different so I had to pull each one's service sheet to be sure I replaced the correct module. It was a bit tricky under the circumstances. This was no time for a mistake, because I could envision Houston sending me back up here to fix it. No thanks! This place only gets one shot at me, and this is it. They'll have to fool someone else into thinking this is a great duty station.

"That's when another weird thing happened. I removed Elvis's...ah, Gamma's control module, and I could swear it had 'Minsk' printed on the side of the mother-board. I started to wonder whether we're subcontracting this project to the Russians? They don't have a satellite lab with these capabilities, and I can't believe they aren't interested in our viral research. Why would they knowingly contribute to our weapons research program and not get a share of it for themselves? This is weapons research! Don't deny it. It would definitely fly in the face of our new cold war spirit. When I get back, I'll quiz the boys about that board for sure. I know what I saw. I wasn't imagining it!

"And before I could ask any questions of Laurie, guess what? This Russian cosmonaut appeared. See, it's the Russians again. Honest, it was like the movie 2001 all over again except that I was in it. I knew I was losing it...my mind, that is, when I saw this guy. I mean...he even pointed to a nameplate on his space suit in an attempt to introduce himself. It said 'Leon Yengoyan' as best I can remember. I never remember names, but that one I'll never forget.

"Weirder yet, he was talking Russian, too, but I could actually understand him. And I don't know a word of Russian, reading or speaking! That's when I realized that I was hallucinating big time! Like I said, I usually have a terrible time remembering names, but for some reason I remember his as if it were burned into my brain. Leon! It reminds me of Frankenstein or the Wolfman or Count Dracula! It was that weird!

"Worse yet or maybe better yet, he took the replacement module and installed it for me...no questions asked! How in the world did he know...?

Don't even ask about that. He just nodded his head a few times, did the installation, and walked out. He even told me to be sure to check out the system. He did that in English! I guess I was just stunned to silence. This all came to me from what was probably a Russian robot and a Russian cosmonaut out in an American spacecraft in earth orbit? That's when I was sure I was nuts!

"Then, to my great surprise, I realized that the whole internal configuration inside Gamma was very different from the other robots. Very different! Elvis definitely doesn't have the standard ARPA configuration although externally it looks exactly the same as the others. I would have gotten the installation started but…it was finished! Leon did it for me in no time at all and correctly as far as I could tell. As I said, no questions were asked either. Ah, I know that I'm repeating myself…sorry."

Vostry paused to clear his mind and thoughts. He appreciated the fact that Phil and Frank let him purge his confused thoughts. He began to calm down and speak somewhat slower as he searched for answers to his questions.

"Then, I must have passed out…whenever that was? They, the robots that is, or Leon, must have moved me into the port and connected me to Spacelab's life-support on their own. I guess I'm the only one left up here now…human that is. You haven't seen a Russian cosmonaut wandering around with a bunch of robots, have you? Is it really hour 221 of the mission?"

Phil and Frank seemed equally stunned by the major's story. Slowly, Frank responded to some of his many questions.

"That's affirmative, Major Vostry. We were worried, but Professor Laurie said you were coming along fine. And he didn't mention any Russians as far as we know, at least not yet, or any unexplained vibrations aboard Spacelab as far as I can remember. Don't worry. We'll have you back to earth in a day or two, and we can start to figure all this out a piece at a time."

"He's not here…Laurie that is, so I imagine he split immediately," mumbled Vostry sarcastically. "Whatever happened to the 'no man left behind' thing? He must have seen the Russian, too. Well, he's a civilian so I guess it's to be expected. I'll have our motto changed to 'no civilian left behind'."

The major's sarcasm was a sign that he might have recovered from the effects of the Spacelab incident and his remarkable experiences. But first, his story about the robot and the Russian cosmonaut definitely needed some investigation. Phil made a mental note to grab Gamma for a hands-on inspection at the first opportunity. He wondered how a rogue robot made its way onto Spacelab if indeed that was the case.

"Major, this is Phil Blair. I'm Frank's assistant. Initial indications and safety procedures specified an extended decontamination stint for you because of your proximity to…to the event. Here I'm not talking about Leon or Gamma.

"According to flight control, Professor Laurie was apparently more distant and less likely to be affected, but now we have reason to question that scenario. Houston ordered his return on the first shuttle, but he should probably have been the one lying there instead of you. A shuttle will undoubtedly be dispatched to pick you up within the next few hours. I have already notified command that you have successfully completed the decontamination procedures."

Major Vostry nodded his appreciation as a broad smile of relief broke out on his face.

"Do you recall what happened in the other lab?" asked Frank. "If you don't feel like talking about it right now, it's perfectly okay. We understand completely."

"Son…," began the major who then hesitated. "Sorry, it's a silly habit I picked up from my dad back in Chicago. He called everybody 'son'… except the ladies, of course. Well, I got up off the floor. I was a little dizzy. I had my flight report in my hand, but I don't remember writing it. That's another strange thing…very efficient but a bit disconcerting. Who wrote that flight report and put it in my hands?

"Phil, I don't remember anything after I walked into this communications center to file that flight report. As I stepped in the door, I was hit by a bright flash of light, and I was in la-la land for God knows how long. There was no discomfort or pain. I was just gone…again. It was like someone knocked me out with a very soft pillow. No pain at all…just poof! It was like the very best hangover I've ever experienced. I got all of the alcoholic buzz and none of the headache.

"Next thing I knew, it was fifteen minutes ago, and a robot was dressing me in a clean suit like I was going to my senior prom. And then it put me back on this cot so I could rest. The back of my neck itches like hell, and I was a little dizzy at first, but that's about all the negatives. The intravenous chow must have been tasty because after who knows how many days of being out of it, I'm not hungry at all? Weird! Normally I'm always hungry?

"The only thing that seemed out of place at that point was one of those plastic buckets that are kept under refrigeration in the main lab. When I was coming out of my trance, I happened to spot one floating up near the ceiling exhaust vent. Later, when I went to look for the container, it was gone. The robots policing the area must have cleaned it up. It could have been shaken loose from its moorings by all that vibration. And, believe me, there was some serious vibrating going on for a brief time.

"I believe those containers are used to hold the test brain tissue samples, and like I said, are filled with formalin to preserve the tissue. But I guess I'm repeating myself. If you've ever smelled the stuff, you'll never forget it. But on Spacelab, of course, that's not a problem because the lab atmosphere is checked closely. You might want to take a look at the chromatographic data that monitors our air supply to see if anything spilled in the lab. But when I passed out, whatever caused it was too quick for an atmospheric system contamination alarm. The onboard electronics must have thought everything was normal."

At that moment Phil raised his hand while shaking his head dejectedly as he checked some electronic data.

"Unfortunately, Major, the chromatograph is down...well, went down simultaneously with the incident. So did a whole section of video equipment that was positioned right where we needed it most. Bad luck? Coincidence? Or was it just good planning by someone else?

"All systems are back up now...since this morning anyway, and nothing unusual has been reported. I'll have them recheck the video for that floating plastic bucket. But we have no data from the moment you said you saw the Russian or of the vibrational incident."

Major Vostry just seemed to shrug his shoulders.

Frank motioned to Phil that he wanted to ask Major Vostry another question or two. Phil nodded that he was finished.

"Major, did Professor Laurie ever mention what the brain tissue samples were for? I know you didn't get to speak with him much and that some of his work is classified. But, it could be important."

The military man hesitated for a moment, then he responded rather slowly in a hushed tone.

"Are we on the air, Frank? I must be sure that we are talking privately."

Frank nodded in the affirmative although he knew the risks involved.

"Well, I hesitate to even speculate because some of Laurie's work is currently very highly classified. If I happened to guess right, I'd probably be eating next Thanksgiving's turkey in Leavenworth, Kansas, or being shot out of a cannon at the circus."

"That's a good point," Frank replied as he unsuccessfully searched for another way to ask the same question. "We'd better get some clarification first. But, I would definitely mention the plastic container floating in the lab when you are debriefed again. We need to know why that particular container was loose. We can talk about this in private when you return."

Suddenly, Vostry raised his hand as if there were a new problem. He was scratching his head as he spoke.

"I wonder how Elvis got his module installed if I was imagining the Russian…if he was just an illusion or a figment of my imagination? I'd pulled the motherboard just before I saw him and slipped into lah-lah land. One of the other robots must have…nah. That's very unlikely. Professor Laurie must have cleaned up after me. No one else would know how to accomplish the reset. I saw Elvis running around here after I came to, but he…it just seemed to ignore me from that moment on. It reminded me of my ex-wife. I've got to remember to tell Oscar about that motherboard from Minsk and have it checked out."

Frank looked at Phil and decided that they had accomplished as much as possible under the circumstances. The major would soon be back in Houston where they could discuss these matters in greater detail in person. They could also see what new data could be retrieved from the damaged surveillance systems.

The major sat up straight in his bed and began pulling up the covers as if preparing for a nap.

"If you don't mind, fellows," Major Vostry whispered, "I'm going to take another snooze while the opportunity presents itself. See you later down below."

7

Pull the Plug

Staring blindly into space, getting
Up to splash my face, wanting just
To stay awake, wondering how much
I can take, should I try to do some more,
25 or 6 to 4.

Chicago
25 or 6 to 4

Cape Canaveral

The facial images of Phil Blair and Frank Hurbert appeared simultaneously on the teleconference screen. A single male viewer of some girth adjusted his chair and then flipped on the camera, which would return his image to Houston. He had been expecting the video-conferencing call for some hours now.

"How are you boys doing these days? When are you comin' over to visit us? Not that I care very much, but what are Houston's orders?" came the questions in rapid-fire succession from Milan Maxmovich, the current administrative chief of satellite operations for NASA. They were directed to Phil Blair who was sitting at a conference table in Houston, a pile of papers neatly stacked in front of him. Because they had worked together before, this kind of outburst was expected.

"I assume that you're secure on your end, Miles," Phil responded quietly. "The way things are going I wouldn't be surprised if the whole world was listening to our conversation and taking notes to use against us later if things go badly."

Maxmovich smiled immediately. He was also familiar with Phil's privacy paranoia as a result of prior situations. He started his response comically by moving his lips with enthusiasm but not actually speaking. It drew the laugh from Phil that he expected.

"You can tell me your deepest, darkest secrets, Phil. Only the Russians can hear us right now…that's a joke…I think? Well, don't quote me. I never said that."

Conversely, Phil was familiar with Milan's brand of humor. It was something that was necessary if you wanted to survive the stress that Milan's job brought with it so Phil didn't mind the jokes at all.

"Miles, our chances of reaching any city limits in Florida these days are truly absolutely zero, so put away your fishing gear and that silly hat with all those handmade lures stuck in it. First and foremost, we have to retrieve Major Robert Vostry from Spacelab with as little fanfare as possible, of course. From our recent video conversation with him, I'd say he's ready and eager to go. As I'm sure you've been able to see, he's in the recovery module doing well and ready for the return trip. He's a little agitated to say the least, but who wouldn't be under the circumstances? I've spoken directly with him, and the medical instrumentation seems to say that he's physically stable enough for the return trip. Mentally…well, that might be another thing altogether. He did mention that he's experienced some strange dreams and had some strange visions since he's been up there all alone…the only human anyway. But, that's probably normal under the current circumstances.

"As a starter, I do have one…very unofficial question for you, Miles. Take a deep breath before I ask it."

Maxmovich gave a positive thumb up sign to his friends so Blair continued despite some reservations.

"This is probably going to sound a bit crazy, but bear with me on this so we can figure it out. Have we been collaborating with Moscow on this number…on anything else aboard Spacelab? No one ever tells me anything over here. One day it's the cold war all over again, and the next day we're in Happy Valley together playing hockey. They keep me confused to say the least."

"Are you nuts?" laughed Milan who couldn't resist the choice of words. "Can I…should I ask you why you ask or will they send me to the funny farm or the slammer with you if I do? I do have some new jokes so the jail time wouldn't be totally boring."

Phil thought for a moment and decided against it. Telling Milan the whole story wouldn't help at this juncture. It was evident from Milan's response that he knew nothing about any possible Russian Spacelab joint-venture.

"It's a small thing better left for later. If anything develops, I'll keep you in the loop, Miles. I just don't want to be guilty of starting any rumors just now. It's the worst possible moment, and we've got enough problems ahead of us to keep us busy for months. If anyone asks, just tell them that my brain just short-circuited from over-work and under-pay. That will sufficiently explain everything and cover our butts!"

Milan sensed that it was time to change the subject. But he did make a mental note to corner Phil about this issue after the major was safely on the ground and they were very much alone.

"Are any of the robotic elements returning with him?" asked Milan. "I would hate to have our friend and passenger, Major Vostry, suffer a medical event en route with us having no means to aid him. As you inferred, we have enough public relations problems on our hands now as it is. If we lose an astronaut the caliber of Major Vostry in transit back to mother earth, you might as well shut down the whole project...forever. I'd bet every cent I have that that creep in the senate will blame it on a virus and then blame the virus on us instead of Victor Laurie. That's the way those retarded republicans work. I call them 'retardopubs!'"

"Affirmative," Phil replied. "Two elements have been assigned to accompany the major on his return to earth. One piloting type will be onboard, of course, to drive him home, and one with a medical protocol capability will continuously monitor the major's condition and transpond the data to us. The major has some valuable information and observations on the incident involving Professor Laurie from what you said in your report, at least as far as the powers that be are concerned, and we all want to assure his return in one piece, both mentally and physically.

"Next and separately, probably within twenty-four hours, the balance of the robots are to be downloaded to earth."

There was a pregnant pause before Milan replied. He hadn't considered this possibility prior to the call.

"All of them? Really? Without robots aboard, how are we...they going to operate Spacelab? Or are they..."

Phil cleared his throat.

"That's as far as the directives go, Miles. I didn't say this, but use your most vivid imagination and don't discuss this with anyone else even in your sleep. I'm serious. No jokes either!"

Again Maxmovich paused.

So they've decided to abort Spacelab, thought Maxmovich to himself. *Shoot it into space and blow it to smithereens! It's too dangerous to destroy in earth orbit. Who knows what kind of anaerobic bugs or germs are festering up there thanks to that bastard Laurie. And how will the administration explain this one hundred million dollar mistake to their constituents? Blame it on us, of course!*

I'd better dust my resume off and fast. I'm going to need it and probably plastic surgery and a name change, too!

"Okay, Phil. Thanks for the update. See you in the unemployment line! If you need an alibi, remember that we can always go fishing or at least say we went fishing off the coast."

Seconds after Milan's image disappeared from Phil's monitor, the phone buzzed and Frank took the call. With few words, Frank hung up the phone and was vigorously tapping Phil on the shoulder.

"We have to talk, Phil. In private, preferably outside under the sun where no one else can see us or hear us. Now!"

The two men retired to Frank's office without another word. Frank pulled up the chair behind his desk and put his feet up on the desk indicating that this was going to be an extended conversation. When he flipped on his CD player and turned up the volume, Phil also knew that Frank had some secrets to divulge. Led Zeppelin proved to be the perfect audio cover.

"It would be a total understatement to say that a lot's happened in the past hour or so, Phil. As you already have noticed, the FBI gave us a friendly visit this afternoon. Guess what? They have reason to believe that our Spacelab incident was espionage! How do they know about Leon?"

"How...how could that be?" mumbled Phil under his breath in complete denial and disbelief.

"Wait...there's more!" ranted Frank over the blaring music. "I know I've asked you this a hundred times, but you know who Senator Jensen is, don't you? The congressional turkey who's always trying to block our efforts especially as far as Spacelab is concerned."

Phil just waited for the punch line.

"Well, he's missing. Disappeared! Kidnapped or so they say! Terrorists? Foreign agents? Green people? Or maybe he just went bonkers on his own?

How lucky can we be that this should happen right now when we need help? We're so lucky we should be in Las Vegas playing craps!"

Now, Phil's face held an expression of complete confusion. Jensen was one of the space program's worst enemies. Frank often described him as a right-wing religious nutcase. Jensen was famous for his belief that outer space was solely his god's domain and that man should stick to living his time out here on earth where the Holy Ghost could keep an eye on him. Opponents were quick to point out that the senator never talked about his rumored cocaine and heroin use in the same sentence where he invoked the will of God. Nevertheless, Oklahomans kept sending him back to Washington if only for the entertainment value of his antics. Phil reminded his boss that Jensen was qualified to be the governor of Alaska.

Frank continued. "I remember the time he said, 'Who needs science when we have Intelligent Design!' I didn't stop laughing for a week... after I stopped crying! If he doesn't like the data or experimental results, he just makes things up to suit his purposes. Actual facts can be irrelevant to a conservative, you know. And finding the real truth can be time consuming, too. That might cost money better spent on booze and drugs and sleazy women."

Phil was scratching his head.

"Kidnapped? Who would kidnap that asshole and why? I could see you and I doing it just to save our jobs, but who else would waste the effort? From our point of view, Frank, that's the best news we've heard here in years," yelled Phil as he pounded his fist on Frank's desk with a flourish. "I want to give some sort of very large award to whoever did it...and you can quote me on that!"

But Frank had only begun. There was more.

"That's not all, Phil. A little bird tells me that our illustrious Professor Laurie is beginning to get weird. No, don't be confused. I mean weirder than his normal screwed-up state of mind. He's admitted to hearing voices...from his robots while he was up there. You know full well that he never takes our advice so he wasn't hearing our voices, if you get my meaning. He claims that he hears the robots talking to him...in his head and in binary, even when they're not around. Let's see you beat that!"

With these three quick punches, Phil found himself completely disoriented. Frank let him think for a few moments before continuing.

"Is this whole thing...Laurie, Jensen, Spacelab, Russians, viruses...is this just an elaborate test of my sanity? If they want me to retire or quit, why don't they just ask me. For a tidy severance package I'd be on my way with no questions asked…to the Bahamas. Why waste the time and effort to put me…to put us through this fiasco? A little cash and I'm history."

Phil had no answer and opted to let his boss complete his mental purge. What could he say to explain this?

"Phil, you're my strategy guy. I've always been able to count on you to come up with the unexpected. What do we do, if anything, in response to all this crap? You know they will blame us for everything if it looks like we're just sitting here and doing business as usual and according to the book.

"Now imagine our Major Vostry telling congress that a Russian cosmonaut was on Spacelab with him and that one of the robots was made in Minsk! They will beat us to a pulp. We're dead meat, Phil, unless…"

Phil's head was still down in his hands as he pondered the many unanswered questions. Then, to Frank's surprise, Phil leaped out of his chair, hands above his head.

"I have the answer! I…we both need a drink! Now!" shouted Phil. "We need to loosen our brains to deal with all of this stuff."

Frank immediately glanced at the clock, which read three-thirty.

"Absolutely goddamn right!" said Frank as he reached for his coat. "Friday's bar in thirty minutes. I have one little errand to run first. Bring a recorder and a notebook just in case we get some magnificent ideas. Oh, and a pencil, too. And you're buying the first round! If I don't show, just assume I committed suicide!"

With those words and a comment to Frank's secretary, Marian, about an important meeting across town, both men were on their way to their vehicles, smiling in the face of what surely was an imminent total disaster.

Just as planned, at precisely four o'clock, Frank found Phil sitting at the bar nursing his first frozen margarita. He ordered one of the same from Kevin, the bartender, and settled into his seat with an unusual smile on his face.

"Stop me if I'm wrong, Frank," were Phil's first words to his boss. "First, we have a spy somewhere in our midst. Second, we have a kidnapped opposition senator unable to attack us. Third, our project's lead scientist is wacko and hearing strange voices in his head. Fourth, one of our best astronauts is seeing things that may not be there! It's almost…it's more than a Gordie Howe hat trick."

Frank was clearly confused. Phil immediately moved to the rescue because he knew Frank wasn't an avid sports fan.

"In ice hockey a Gordie Howe hat trick is a goal, an assist and a fight in the same game. When Gordie played for the Detroit Red Wings way back when, he did it all…I mean he was a one-man team. He scored goals, dished out assists, and protected his teammates with unmatched authority. The only problem here is that we are the ones being scored against and beaten up! We are just not sure who's doing it to us, or who is going to do it to us in the near future."

Frank patted Phil on the back as he began to break down the problems that faced them. He knew that between them they could come up with a viable solution…maybe. All that depended on it were their jobs and reputations.

"Phil, Laurie's mental problems can wait for the moment. He's going to see a psychologist and a psychiatrist…I must admit that I don't know the difference. Hence, there isn't much we can do to him or for him right now. If that was our only problem, we'd be in the clear."

"Hence?" mumbled Phil in response.

"Okay," whispered Frank with a smile on his face. "Henceforth!"

Phil finally smiled and said exactly what Frank was thinking.

"The fourth horseman…or is it the fifth horseman…is…the destruction of Spacelab. Am I getting closer to the apocalypse?"

Frank tapped his fingers on the table as he spoke.

"At a moment like this we need…some chicken wings. Our brains need some greasy nourishment to find the spy, figure out what he knows, find out what's going on with Laurie, come up with Senator Jensen even though it would be nice if he stayed missing for a very long time, figure out who this Russian cosmonaut is, prevent the ultimate destruction of Spacelab, and…figure out what we're missing so we can keep our jobs. I'm thoroughly convinced that something we don't see that is right in front of us is causing all of this. No matter how hard I try, I can't see how any of this stuff is related. But that's what makes me think it is all related, all one big murky problem."

Phil was nodding his head as he waved for the bartender to bring more fuel. As usual, Kevin had anticipated their needs, and in a few seconds the welcome drinks appeared before them.

"This problem…these problems are too big for us two alone, Frank. But, we can't just roll over and die. That would be too easy. We've got to do what we can with what little we have left. The most interesting problem is the newest one. Who could be the spy, if there actually is one? And what are they after?

"These guys in Washington are so paranoid that anyone could look like a spy. You're not a spy, are you, Frank? Please tell me that you're not. But, then again, it would make things easier to solve if you were the real spy."

Frank gritted his teeth, stuck out his tongue and then went back to his drink without a word.

"Okay, we have to assume that you and I are on the same side in this fiasco. We have to protect each other's back. But, eventually, they'll dump the whole mess in our laps after the damage is done," Phil continued. "And we'll have no one to pass the buck to. Our legacy will be one of total failure…failure and incompetence and stupidity. I hate being able to see my own ultimate and shameful demise and not being able to do anything about it. And we're innocent on top of that! Our obituaries should certainly note that fact.

"I feel like Cassandra. I know the future, but I can't do anything about it no matter how hard I try."

"Cassandra?" asked Frank.

"Yes…Hector's sister. She and Apollo had something going on between them, so Apollo gave her the power to know the future. But then the bitch dumped him. Those Trojans are all the same. That was a really big mistake because Apollo cursed her foresight by causing no one to believe her. She predicted the fall of Troy, but the Trojans laughed at her. Like me, there was nothing she could do to avoid her future even though she knew about everything in advance. And I have always particularly liked Apollo; is this fair?"

Again, just like back in the office, Phil jumped up from his barstool and pounded his fist on the bar even more vigorously this time.

"I can't just sit in the control room and wait for my execution. I do not want to be a dead man walking! I want to inflict some damage on whoever or whomever is responsible for this."

Frank didn't know whether to laugh or cry. But he knew Phil was right. But he also knew that they would have to be careful or they could make things even worse. What they needed was not a noisy tank but a plan with a stealth bomber and a trap with irresistible bait.

"We won't be able to find Jensen from here, and we can't obstruct the Spacelab blow if it's ordered. So, we have little choice. We need to probe for a spy…whether we have one or not. We need to get security probing so that they don't have a choice except to keep Spacelab in business or at least in existence. Something inside Spacelab has to be the ultimate bait for any espionage. And no one even remotely attached to the project is above suspicion. Wouldn't it be neat if Laurie or Jensen were the spy? That would be killing two birds with one stone for sure."

"I'll drink to that," gasped Phil while gritting his teeth again.

"First, we make a list," Frank whispered. "Then we check every possibility as fast as we can. We can't rule out anything, and we can't trust anyone other than each other. Not even Maxmovich is above suspicion!"

"I need some more chicken wings for my last meal," whispered Phil under his breath. "This could turn out to be fun!"

After a trip to the men's room and some wings, Phil and Frank settled down in a booth near the rear of the restaurant to begin an attack on their problems. They started to compose a list of problems and sources.

"Frank, you start. I'll be recording secretary and write down our ideas...good and bad."

Frank nodded and closed his eyes as he began to speak.

"First and foremost is Professor Laurie. I liken him to 'The March Hare.' His classified experiments are being conducted in orbit by robots. This tells me that there is something contagious about whatever is going on up there. I've seen him talking to himself while waiting to testify before congress. His buddy Jensen has done the same thing. Hence, they are both infected by the same thing, by the thing being studied up in orbit... whatever it is? Whatever it is...is still onboard Spacelab. We send Laurie and Jensen back up and get Maxmovich to blow the thing up. Problem solved.

"I'm done, Phil. Your turn."

"This will never work, Frank, but let me write a few things down. They're probably minor, but under the circumstances...well, here goes.

"I want to inspect each and every robot down to the last microchip. Those semiconductors must somehow be involved in external communications. There's no other way. I'm still perplexed as to how anyone could have made a switch, but then again, we haven't been focused on the little buggers. We get distracted by Professor Laurie and phantom cosmonauts and the viral experiments while the robots have the run of the ship twenty-four seven.

"Next, I want to inventory and inspect every transmitter on Spacelab. The robots' maintenance reports and flight inventory just don't match up. There's an inconsistency here and an error there...and we don't even pay attention. I'll take the blame, Frank. Don't worry about that. But, something or someone has done some modifications to one or more of them, maybe even before they were launched.

"And finally, remember when the ship went into that unexplained vibration for 45 seconds or maybe more? It's the same as when we dock with Spacelab except this was a lot stronger, and we weren't docking at the time. Something external that we didn't see was messing with Spacelab right under our noses. How's that for starters, anyway? It has to be the Russians docking with Spacelab and stealing Laurie's experiments! Who else could pull off something like that and leave a cosmonaut behind?"

Frank smiled and went back to his drink. Both men leaned back with thoughts racing through their minds. Unfortunately, there were no absolutely sure answers, not yet at least. But the possibilities were interesting.

Suddenly, Phil sat up straight indicating that he had an idea.

"We've got to get Dr. Mahadavan to do a complete physical on Jensen, particularly full blood tests. That might be a little tough to sell the senator on, but we should be able to get him near Laurie and then tell him that Laurie had some communicable virus on his person, and we're just being safe. The more I think about it, the more I like your infection theory, Frank! We can use it for cover."

Frank was suddenly silent for half a minute or so.

"What if Jensen wasn't kidnapped? What if he just went over to the other side? As chairman of that space committee, he has access to all that classified information on the experiments. He could be the Russian spy we need to find! Nah...that would be good news for both of us and reality is never kind to us!"

8

The Decision

It is one thing to make an erroneous
Hypothesis; it is quite another to make
An unscientific hypothesis, which is entirely
Or partially incapable of verification.

T. Gomperz
Lawyers in Love

Command and Control Center
Cape Canaveral, Florida

The nearby fax machine was busy belching out a lengthy transmission from Washington, D.C. as Richard Lundgren and his fellow astronaut, Richard Goldsmith, studied technical drawings of Spacelab for at least the tenth time. Neither had ever been aboard the orbiting laboratory after its construction in orbit; however, that situation was about to change very soon. It was obvious that they would be sent up to investigate the situation onboard the orbiting laboratory.

They were particularly interested in the main laboratory area where the classified viral research was presumably being conducted. If there was contamination onboard Spacelab, as far as they were concerned, this location was undoubtedly where the problem started and where the danger was currently the greatest.

"What does a virus actually look like?" asked Goldsmith of his partner, half seriously and half in humor. "You hear all the time about people catching viruses and contracting viruses and getting vaccine shots to fight viruses…are those airborne things where you catch them by breathing or do you have to ingest them in food or water? What about touching someone who's infected? I'm really confused here to say the least. All I'm sure of is that they're bad! Is there such a thing as a good virus?"

Lundgren tried to ignore his fellow astronaut, but after a while he finally forced out a retort even though he didn't want to.

"Do I look like your doctor...your physician or your biology teacher or your garbage collector? I don't have the slightest idea what a virus looks like. I've never seen one face to face...excluding you, of course. You should ask that famous Professor Victor Laurie for a complete explanation when we see him...if we see him, that is."

Goldsmith made a mental note to do just that even though he knew that his partner wasn't the least bit serious.

"I still don't understand how these robots communicate with and track each other because they're so limited in what they can do," mumbled Goldsmith under his breath. "As far as I can tell, each of these lab areas is a Faraday Cage, and they...the robots aren't connected by any wires. Any low frequency radiation like radio waves and microwave radiation they generate should be trapped inside each the room where it's generated. And I don't see them accessing the antenna system either. So, how do they do it defying the laws of physics?"

Goldsmith never trusted the electronic beasts even during training. The robotic elements he'd trained with were anything but error-free, and his faith in their performance under stress was absolutely zero. The thought of being physically isolated with a number of them in orbit while trying to combat a biological contamination added to his many fears about the upcoming mission. It wasn't the kind of duty he had envisioned when he volunteered for the space program.

"Notice the signature on this print, Goldie?" said Lundgren with a laugh as he pointed to a signature. "It's hard to read at first, but when you really focus your attention on it..."

"You know goddamn well who it is!" Goldsmith shouted a little too loudly for his own good.

"It's Colonel Milner," whispered Lundgren quietly. "Isn't he the guy who tried to get you scrubbed from the corps a while back? Colonel Richard Milner to be exact? And this makes three Richards on one space project doesn't it? If I were you, I'd think about changing my first name to Jose or Jesus or Tabby. Then they'll never find you. Just to be safe, I'm changing my name to Lorenzo...or maybe Hannibal! I want to give my brain a little time to find just the right alias. I need something the girls will like, too. Humphrey Bogart...how about Humphery Lundgren? Nah!

Too bumpy and old time for me. Sounds like the name of an elephant. But, bogarting this whole scene wouldn't be a bad idea. We'll just deprive everyone of it…huh?"

Goldsmith didn't respond to the attempted humor immediately even though he had the perfect retort. Deep inside there was no love lost for his former commander. They had had some accidental, yet serious misunderstandings during prior assignments, and Milner was rather unforgiving of mistakes, even during training exercises.

"Come on! You're almost a civilian now, Goldie. Think about that for a moment. And you're over forty, too. You'll be able to retire soon with full benefits and just goof off all the time…which isn't much of a change for you, of course. You can call the colonel any name you want whether or not you can spell it. You're not planning on another stint in the military after this one, are you? Don't be such a wimp! It's much too late and far away for him to get you on this one. This will make your name a household favorite, which is a great form of revenge! He'll have to sit at home and watch you on the talk show circuit for years."

Goldsmith somehow managed to hold his tongue in check as he sipped from his coffee cup and contemplated his available options. Finally, as Lundgren was about to harass him further, Goldsmith grabbed his partner firmly by the arm and looked him right in the eyes.

"Look, pal, I want a good final mission, but robot retrieval is not quite what I had in mind no matter what fame awaits me. The fact that Milner was involved in the design of this germ factory is not my fault in any way. My question to you is what in the hell you're doing here with me if you're so damn smart? This is a kamikaze mission if there ever was one, and I'm not even Japanese!

"Last week they told me that Jordan was to be my partner on the Spacelab trip. Okay, he's way overweight and a little bit rusty on technique and a little slow on the uptake, but at least he doesn't spend his time constantly picking on me and harassing me to death. I have enough problems of my own without you always trying to trip me up one more time. I shouldn't say this, but you remind me of my mother! She was always kicking the crap out of me every time I made a mistake."

With a silly grin on his face Lundgren just shrugged his shoulders and turned up the palms of his hands in innocence.

"For your information, I confess that I didn't think I'd be here either. I was looking forward to spending some time with my favorite white supremacist friends in West Virginia on a float trip on one of those rivers of theirs. I was going to call it 'Deliverance II'. We even thought about inviting Bert Reynolds, but I couldn't find his phone number.

"Then, yesterday, the phone rang, and it was that bureaucrat Maxmovich who's in charge of satellite operations from the NASA side. He knows that I have some training in chemistry...so here I am. I still don't see what chemistry has to do with Spacelab or the mission.

"Besides, yes, you were totally correct. He said that your pal Jordan was overweight for this type of mission. Too much beer and too many pretzels for your drinking buddy, and he got himself scrubbed! There's no way we could squeeze him in the door of the launch module and then get him out again. Which makes me think that he's a lot smarter than we give him credit for. At least he won't spend the rest of his life fighting some strange virus."

Lundgren glanced nervously at his watch.

"Maybe we'd better head for the conference room about now," he suggested to Goldsmith. "We're supposed to meet with that Princeton Professor Laurie in almost half an hour. I'd rather be a little early for this one if you don't mind. As dumb as the military is, these civilians scare me even more...much more. This fellow has quite a reputation on the grapevine, and I want to see him and hear him up close and personal. Besides, he's been aboard Spacelab and survived, and he might give us a heads up or two if we're nice to him. So, watch what you say!"

Goldsmith nodded reluctantly and in a short while both men were headed across the NASA campus toward the main conference room. A light rain had begun to fall as they walked causing them to speed up their journey. As they approached the headquarters building at a jog, Lundgren thought he'd better prepare for the mission ahead by giving his partner a little last minute advice.

"Look, Goldie, I know these people a lot better than you'll ever know yourself. They will want to have it both ways and totally at our expense. Right now, they need to appease public opinion and follow what appears to their superiors to be the correct strategy...politically. That means the destruction of Spacelab and all the dangerous germs running around inside of it...after we retrieve astronaut Vostry from the craft, that is.

"But, while we're there, they'll want to save some of those samples of their precious research to stockpile for another orbiting laboratory. And they won't have to wait long because Spacelab II is already in the works over at Boeing. I really don't want to be hauling around jars full of germs all day and night!

"If so, this retrieval sort of defeats the purpose of blowing up Spacelab. I hope you realize that if I'm right and we make one small mistake, we could be responsible for wiping out all, or at least most, life on our beloved planet earth. But, at least there's some consolation. We'd be famous...for a very short period of time amongst the few remaining humans! They might even put up statutes of us in Central Park?

"But I still have that one very serious and obvious question running around in my head, and it won't go away. If those robots are so good at their job, why are they sending us up to retrieve the major? The robots are perfectly capable of putting him in a module with two of their kind and launching. That's one of their main capabilities. The remaining robots could then launch Spacelab into space where they could activate the destruction sequence, which would permanently solve the problem without endangering...us! Sounds like a plan to me. We could watch the thing blow up on television just like everyone else is going to."

Lundgren paused as he scratched his chin and thought about another complicating factor.

"Unless they think our friends the Russians will steal the whole thing from right under their noses...? I can't imagine how they would do it, but I guess there must be a way it could be accomplished."

Goldsmith didn't respond immediately because his thoughts were somewhere else. He just shook his head as he opened the main door to the conference area. Inside, three men with serious expressions on their faces sat at a small rectangular table in the far corner of the room having a rather animated discussion.

"I need to take a leak," whispered Goldsmith. "Come with me. There's something you should know before we do this encounter. Trust me on this one."

After Lundgren saw the faces of their interrogators he realized that his partner was right and a little more planning was advisable.

"Go ahead, Goldie. I'll tell these guys we'll be along in three or four minutes."

Soon the two astronauts found themselves alone in the men's room.

"Look, Lundgren, I know that I'm an alarmist, but the rumor mill has it that there's a Russian spy or two embedded in this project. With my current tax problems with the damn IRS, the last thing I need is some kind of security background check that goes through my investments and checkbooks. I like my job! I don't do shit, and I get paid well for it. So, please, don't give those assholes a reason to break us down. My personal life is…personal…very personal. They'll figure out that I've been banging that secretary in security, and they'll think it's a spy thing. That would be worse than knocking her up…well, second worst!"

"Got it," Lundgren responded. "Let me take care of business, and let's get this over with fast. But I wouldn't worry about Lena. I know three other guys who have…had relations with her. I'd be more worried about the crabs or V.D. or Hepatitis C if I were you. She gets around, you know."

"How do you…?" Goldsmith decided to save this interrogation for later.

The two astronauts quickly found themselves seated across from three government bureaucrats dressed in conservative suits. Lundgren immediately noticed that each wore a red tie. The two astronauts wisely waited for their hosts to begin the conversation. The fat one on the left spoke first. No introductions were made.

"Gentlemen, the current mission has some very sensitive aspects over and above the obvious safety considerations. There are several very important national security interests involved. There are several major countries actively trying to penetrate our security. These include some of our closest allies. You cannot let your guard down even for a moment!"

The man paused for a few seconds, but neither astronaut responded. He was pleased to see that they were giving him their full attention.

"The two of you have been chosen for this mission not only because of your astronautics capabilities, but because of your high security ratings. This mission is both scientific and political and those two aspects cannot be separated for even a moment.

"I won't lie to you. This mission is extraordinarily dangerous and will require all of the courage you can muster. Your loyalty to your country shall be sorely tested."

Lundgren nodded but kept the serious expression on his face. He didn't want to communicate his misgivings about the mission to these people just yet.

"Sir, we understand completely. I wouldn't want the American press looking over my shoulder and second-guessing every move I made. You can count on us keeping our mouths shut during and after the mission. We are definitely on your side. We will follow whatever protocol you set."

The interrogator seemed satisfied with the astronaut's reply and attitude. He was ready to move forward.

"Then, Gentlemen, let's get on with the mission's details. In short, this is what it will entail. Reduced to its simplest terms, you're to dock with

Spacelab, secure Major Vostry and check his overall status, launch his reentry capsule to earth with two of the robotic elements aboard, secure the remaining data from the viral experiments, and then return to earth with all of the data and the remaining robots."

There was silence as the astronauts absorbed the information which was not full of any surprises.

"Do you want us to put Spacelab in termination mode?" asked Lundgren immediately before he could stop himself.

The three men sitting across from the astronauts squirmed in their seats and were silent for an uncomfortable moment. It was obvious that the interrogator was displeased with the question.

"Gentlemen, no one has said anything about termination. We've stated the elements of the mission. Let's stay focused on these elements and resist the temptation to speculate needlessly. Spacelab has been cleared for human re-entry just as Major Vostry has been cleared for return to earth. At this time there is no reason to become unduly alarmed. No mention of termination has been made. I hope you can forget the question you just asked?"

"Yes, Sir," Lundgren replied anxiously. At the same time Goldsmith looked around the room for a moment and then posed another interesting question to try to change the subject.

"Sir, I was told that Professor Laurie would be attending..."

Quickly, Goldsmith's words were interrupted by the small man with thick glasses who sat in the center of the three men briefing the astronauts.

"Professor Laurie was unavoidably detained in Houston. We were informed that he would talk with you before your launch the day after tomorrow. The bound documents before you on the table are to be reviewed before you leave this briefing."

"Is there any chance of moving the launch up in time?" asked Lundgren. "I know that if I were in Major Vostry's shoes, I'd want to come home as soon as possible. Goldsmith and I are ready to go tonight if necessary."

The man on the right side of the group finally spoke.

"It's a matter of allowing the robots to complete their cleanup aboard Spacelab. We are also waiting for certain data to be downloaded to Houston. This thing is expensive enough so we need to get all the information we can right now. Congress is looking for a report or two, and as you are well aware, they hold the purse-strings that affect all of us.

"Besides, Major Vostry gave us his thumbs up for this schedule. We've assigned him some minor tasks to keep him from getting totally bored up there. So, I wouldn't worry too much about his welfare until you get up there. By that time he'll be really glad to see you."

With that said, the three men quietly left the conference room single file, and the astronauts began perusing the mission statements.

"I guess we don't get to ask questions about any of the details," mumbled Goldsmith sarcastically.

"If you did that," laughed Lundgren, "they'd think you were the spy and so would I for that matter! Questions are out of the question...pretty good, eh? We'll have to play it by ear once we're up there. That's probably an advantage for us anyway. Better than letting those turkeys call the shots."

Goldsmith pushed himself away from the table and then propped his feet up on a nearby chair.

"Spies? In this day and age? Come on. You and I are in the midst of this crap and we don't know diddley-squat about it! Spy on what? Even these assholes know that Laurie is the only one who knows anything about the...payload on Spacelab. If he was the spy, then why wouldn't he just go to Peking or Moscow and do the experiments there instead of wasting his time here?"

"I'll bite," whispered Lundgren. "They'd think he was spying...for us!"

Goldsmith pounded his fist on the table.

"Exactly! The only question is who pays for the experiment? Do the Russians have a Spacelab equivalent? I don't think so, at least not in orbit. But I'll bet they're doing the same things we are down here on the surface of the planet. If you read about a bunch of Russians keeling over dead, then you'll know where their lab is!"

9

The Russian Connection

Our soul being air,
holds us together.

Anaximenes, the Ionian
Master of the Gods

Siberian Listening Post
near Vladivostok, Russia

Vladimir Koslov was a civilian technician from Minsk with a reputation among his peers for being a hard and dedicated worker with top-notch scientific and technical skills. He was twenty-eight years old, loved to play ice hockey, and had very recently been assigned to the Russian satellite communications facility near Vladivostok, the largest Russian seaport on the Pacific and home of the Russian Pacific Fleet. The site was near a small town some seventy kilometers northeast of the Russian seaport and was noted for its advanced space communications capabilities. Despite its remoteness, its proximity to China and Korea and Japan deemed it to be a high security post by the Russian government.

Among his skill sets, Koslov was an efficient software programmer. He was also an up and coming robotics specialist to boot. It was this specialization in robotics, which caused him to be assigned to this remote outpost on a very sensitive high profile mission, surveillance of the U.S. Spacelab vehicle, which was known to utilize extensive robotics in its operations. His secondary task that served more as cover and which had so far required very little of his time or efforts, was aiding the station in communications with orbiting Russian spacecraft. At his past duty stations he was fortunate enough to have met most of the active Russian cosmonauts including Tomas and Leon Yengoyan. At the present time he was not yet aware of the disappearance of either of these men.

Things had been pretty quiet lately between Russian space missions. This lull in activity permitted most of Vlady's attention to be focused on the U.S. Spacelab, particularly on direct transmissions between robots onboard the spacecraft. The Russian security services were very interested in the actions aboard Spacelab, particularly those who were well aware of what was going on at the Russian Institute for Biological Sciences in Saint Petersburg. The majority opinion held that the Americans were pursuing a similar line of viral research in earth orbit. Both sides knew full well that the winner in this contest could well hold a distinct advantage over the entire population of the earth. Koslov suspected that the political future of the inhabitants of earth was hanging precariously in the balance, and deep down inside he wasn't sure which side he should root for.

Koslov didn't particularly want to be working as a spy, but there was little he could do to avoid the espionage inherent in his job and still pursue his technical interests. Under the circumstances he decided to make the best of the situation and concentrate on the technology. At the moment he was studying a blueprint purportedly showing the design of the Spacelab's control panels. He didn't even want to ask how his partner at the site came into possession of this information.

"I'd really like to know how he did it, Zeg. This is unbelievably brilliant. The little machine…our little machine planted a concealed transmitter onboard Spacelab during its assembly in orbit that the Americans didn't detect and can't see or hear? How is that even possible? I've got to see this first hand some day to believe it. And I know the Americans take security very seriously. They have visual surveillance of every cubic inch of Spacelab and yet…. They are really going to be pissed if they find our little bug. Outsmarted by a Russian robotics chip in disguise as one of their very own chips. Now, that's worthy of a novel and a Hollywood movie!"

Zeg just shook his head as he adjusted the monitor sitting in front of him. He wanted to get a sledgehammer from the tool chest and crush the monitor into tiny bits, but he didn't have a reliable replacement. Zeg had been working at this site for over a year and a half now, mostly alone except for two security guards. He was very pleased to have a new partner as open and friendly as Koslov appeared to be. He particularly wanted to practice his recently improved English, and when he learned that Koslov had attended Oxford University in England, he was very happy indeed because he was a big fan of the old program called Mystery Theatre that appeared on BBC television.

"No big deal at all. It's right up your alley, Vlady! And, remember, we're not only clever, but we're tough and ready to pounce! You've noticed our municipal coat of arms, haven't you? It's right up there on the wall near the door. The Siberian Tiger! And, if you're worried about Command showing up to look over your shoulder…relax. We're 6500 kilometers from Moscow, and they hate it over here. The Chinese are much too close for comfort, and it's too far from Paris, which is where they'd rather be."

Koslov obviously disagreed with something.

"Then tell me how that three and a half tons of body parts with bullet holes in all the skulls got here…Stalin era stuff you'll say. But, if they want you bad enough, it doesn't matter how far away you are from Moscow. I'm not relaxing a muscle on that front. For all we know, they're probably listening to this conversation right now. If we make a misstep, Spacelab be damned!"

Zeg paused for a moment to study the expression on Koslov's face and decided to change the subject. He had swept the office several times for bugs, but Koslov's remark shook his confidence in their privacy for just a moment. No sense in tempting fate, he thought to himself.

"I want you to notice that I've picked up most of your western colloquialisms…as best I could. Russian or not, anyone who goes to Oxford is a westerner by trade! Believe it or not, I can do metaphors, too. But, just in case, if I do screw up, let me know right away. I want to perform on Broadway or in London one of these days. What do you think? Standup comedy or should I do Shakespeare? Hamlet is my favorite, and I haven't even been to Denmark!"

Koslov just shrugged his shoulders and fought off a big smile as he studied an image of the Siberian Tiger on the wall. He waited for Zeg to continue because he was sure that his new partner knew a lot more than Command gave him credit for. And that was a very good thing considering the level of security their communications were constantly subjected to.

"The…our robot does all the work for us. You should be proud of the little guy. He…well, it placed the transmitter right where it should be during tests the Americans were running. With theirs, of course! Once planted, that little beast I call 'Son of Robot' then jams the external transmissions from Spacelab with bursts of noise that seem solar in origin and directs the info straight to us for our perusal. It also screwed up their security system for twenty seconds while our robot was placing it in its new home. The whole operation was just like falling off a log…pretty good, huh?"

Zeg seemed particularly proud of his use of the word 'perusal', but he resisted the temptation to brag about it and went on.

"It's just a tiny unnoticeable sideband on white noise bursts…relatively microscopic when you hide it amongst the other data they are pushing around up there in orbit. That's my specialty, as you already know, since I've been bragging about it for weeks before you got here. Well, you weren't here to hear me bragging but Command might have if they have this place bugged. I have to warn you that I talk to myself a lot when I'm alone. It beats the hell out of getting lonely.

"Well, it took me eighteen months to perfect the little bugger so it wouldn't be detectable unless you know exactly where to look and how to look. White noise is perfect cover and literally undetectable because it's there in space all the time. Nobel Prize anyone?"

Koslov slapped Zeg on the back and bade him continue. Vlady was certainly happy to have a friendly and relaxed partner out here on the isolated Russian frontier. He couldn't imagine what life would be like trapped out here alone with an anally retentive government type.

"Then those geniuses at command in Saint Petersburg kept me here in Siberia for another term. They said I'd like it here after a while. That figures. Why reward me for hard work and loyalty with a promotion? They've gotten what they wanted from me without any complaints. Mark my words! One of these days, Vlady, there will be hell to pay for all of this crap unless I get assigned to some place with an ocean beach complete with a fine waterfront cabin and eighty-degree temperatures, not to mention the good-looking women in little bikinis! That's all I ask. Is it too much for all the things I've done for them so far?"

Koslov laughed aloud and patted his new partner on the back a second time for effect. He realized that his new friend liked to blow off steam using his recently acquired foreign language capabilities. He wanted to ask Zeg how he picked up his English skills but thought better of it for the time being. As they got to know each other better, Zeg would certainly tell him every gory detail. Actually, Kozlov was amazed at Zeg's command of his English vocabulary for someone who hadn't spent any considerable time in the west.

"So, I've confessed my very life to you and opened up my soul. Now it's your turn to tell me something creepy about yourself. What's bothering you the most other than me?" asked Zeg. "Don't worry about the situation.

You'll get used to the system soon enough. And for that matter, my lips are sealed forever. You don't squeal on me, and I don't squeal on you. That's how things work around here. The tiger up there on the wall enforces the rules…in our favor every time!"

Koslov just shrugged his shoulders this time, grinned and nodded to Zeg. He had a few things to say that Zeg might find interesting.

"Ever since I arrived here in the east, I've been…well, having some strange dreams. I'm not sure that's the best way to describe it? But, that's definitely not your problem, Zeg. I should really stick with the work at hand and not clutter up your mind with this stuff."

Zeg jumped up to make his point.

"No, Vlady, I'm your goddamn partner, and what bothers you, bothers me, too. Tarot Cards, crystal balls, magic wands, psycho-dreams…they're all within bounds out here. This area is a melting pot of Chinese, Russians, Koreans, Japanese, and plenty others, so nothing is off limits. Even if you were just kidding about this in order to get a rise out of me, which I'm sure you're not, at least it would be entertaining for me to say the least. If you want to wait until later to spill your guts, that's okay with me, too. But, for you, my friend and partner, I'm all ears all the time!"

Koslov was happy to hear those words but decided to stick with the subject of Spacelab for the present.

"From what I'm hearing, I get the impression that the robots on Spacelab are worried that this recent incident might result in termination of their mission…and I mean permanent termination! Maybe 'worried' is the wrong word for a robot? I guess that's my most pressing concern right now based on the data I have so far. I can't bring myself to express that kind of thought to Command in a report. They'd think I was crazy and bust my ass for sure!

"I'd hate to come all the way over here and have the Americans shut down or ground Spacelab or, worse yet, blow the thing up in orbit before I can figure out just what they're doing out there. I'm certain that complete destruction is one of their options if things go badly."

Koslov paused for a moment to consider where he was going with this line of discussion, particularly if Command could hear this conversation.

"Can robots be 'worried' about things like that, you ask?" Zeg responded in spite of Vlady's comment. He had already seized the role of resident comedian. "Are they entitled to some sort of unemployment compensation, minimum wage and hospitalization if things go badly for them? How about a retirement plan when they get phased out? Do we…

do they give them personality profiles back in Minsk…or Houston, too? Do they or should they have a labor union to represent them? Hmmm… so many difficult and unanswered questions."

Vlady realized that he was the butt of Zeg's jokes, yet he persisted because it was having a relaxing effect on him. At least with Zeg around he knew that this assignment would be a lot of fun. He didn't mind Zeg testing his language skills on him either. But now it was Vlady's turn to up the ante.

"I know these systems are advanced even beyond what I saw in Minsk, and those were very advanced units to be sure. And your white noise bursts show we could probably hide anything in the little bastards and get away with it. The more complex the robotic system, the easier it is to hide little simple devices inside them.

"But the external robotic queries we are intercepting are sounding more and more like questions between humans would sound rather than questions between machines. That wasn't at all the way they were designed or programmed. The controlled and concise response precision is disappearing, slowly but surely. If I wasn't an amateur scientist, I'd say the robots, particularly ours, are learning colloquial English in their spare time, among other things! They seem to be…dare I say it? They seem to be evolving with their language skills just like you have, Zeg! Meeting and talking with you has made me realize this. You should be able to appreciate that situation and the irony of it all. Call me a dummy, but…"

"You're a dummy!" Zeg responded loudly with a big laugh. "Okay, all kidding aside, we'll take a look at it as soon as I decode this crap incoming from the Saint Petersburg lab. Now, Vlady, I really do like those boys in Saint Petersburg, and I know that they're friends of yours. They've always tried to treat me right. But, they're in a complete goddamn panic about something right now!

"This thing is classified 'Top Secret' as the Americans would say, so why don't you take a break for lunch a little early so that I can get this done without violating my oath of office. When they send me your clearance, I'm going to let you deal with this stuff yourself. I've had enough of spy games for one lifetime! Besides, I've already seen the movie…*Spy Game*… the one with Robert Redford and Brad Pitt. They leave us alone in that one. It's directed at the Chinese for a change. It's not as good as *Apocalypse Now*, but it's in my list of top ten old movies."

Vlady nodded his agreement and pointed to the modest porch outside their work area, which was where they took their occasional work breaks. The porch even came with a small swing, which both men liked.

"I'll be out there under the stars pondering the universe and lesser things. But, I'd much rather be playing hockey right now. Are there any amateur hockey clubs nearby? Anyway, come and get me when the coast is clear and your conscience permits it. I'll probably just be taking a nap."

Zeg crumpled over in laughter.

"Don't worry, Vlady, we'll get your clearance soon so I can go play golf while you do this crap for me! But I want to keep my front teeth intact…I've grown attached to them. Hockey just isn't my game. I like to watch once in a while, but you'll never get me out there on the ice. I'm probably the only Russian who can't skate and isn't a hockey fanatic."

Koslov left the laboratory smiling under his breath as Zeg settled in to decode the most recent group of messages from headquarters. The new security system was quite sophisticated requiring three separate transmissions and a physical decoding key. Zeg pulled the key from the safe and began his task with his usual enthusiasm. He was very curious about command's new problem.

Vlady sat down with a glass of iced tea in his hand. It was a brisk evening, yet he felt good. He scanned the cloudless sky just enjoying the myriad stars that were twinkling back at him with a full moon low on the horizon. They were a beautiful and relaxing sight especially for someone who loved the outdoors. He decided to lay his head back on the small padded pillow that was attached to his chair and take in all of nature's wonderful show.

As he looked up, he sighted his favorite constellation, Cassiopeia. Every time he saw the constellation his thoughts went back to his time at Oxford. In an astronomy class he wrote paper about Ptolemy, the famous second century Greek astronomer who identified forty-eight constellations in the night sky. He also remembered that ancient Chinese astronomers had divided the constellation into three parts with interesting names…The White Tiger of the West, The Purple Forbidden Enclosure, and The Black Tortoise of the North. He made a mental note to get his friends in Saint Petersburg to send him his astronomy books.

For a moment he began to drift into complete relaxation. But, as his muscles relaxed, he started to feel an itching on his left arm right where he had received several shots from the medical personnel in Minsk. He softly rubbed his arm and much to his satisfaction, the irritation slowly began subsiding. They were influenza shots to protect him from a minor outbreak recently reported in Vladivostok.

Why can't life always be this way? he thought to himself as he moved back and forth on the swing. *Why must we always be fighting each other, mistrusting each other, and spying on each other? It would be like hockey without high-sticking and cross-checking! Just fair competition in the marketplace.*

Slowly, he let his mind drift off again. He was sure that he soon would be fast asleep. Unfortunately, that was not to be.

Suddenly, Koslov snapped up straight in his seat! There, he heard it again. It wasn't a sound emanating from his surroundings, and he could see that Zeg was still working quietly on his messages. No, it was a small… very tiny voice…inside his head.

"Help me!" was all Vlady could make out. The voice repeated its message five times and then it was gone.

Koslov shook his head and again began rubbing his arm where the itching had returned. It was just like the dreams he'd been experiencing yet this time he was still awake. In his dreams there was a single voice crying out in the dark for help. The only other thing he could remember was some sort of offhand reference to the moon! As he glanced toward the moon, he noted that its shape had been covered by layers of some intervening cumulus clouds.

At the same time Vlady was hearing the voice in his head, inside their office, Zeg was busy shaking his own head. His disbelief was caused by the decoded message he held in his hands. This was something completely and totally unexpected. Apparently, a Russian cosmonaut had disappeared, and Command was very disturbed about the situation. What was even stranger and harder to swallow was the reason why this message was directed to Zeg and Vlady. Command thought there was a reasonable chance that the cosmonaut was onboard the American spacecraft…aboard Spacelab! Zeg decoded and re-read the message three times just to be sure he hadn't made a mistake.

"That's crazy," mumbled Zeg aloud to himself. "The spacecraft is run by robots. Most of the time there are no astronauts aboard, at least not normally and certainly not right now! And if there were any humans on that ship, Americans or not, the robots would have reported their presence to Houston immediately, and we would know about it, too. Command knows this just as well as I do. Has Moscow lost its marbles or have the robots gone rogue on us? Something just isn't right here! Maybe this is a test?"

Just to be sure, Zeg reached over to a nearby console and carefully scanned the recent transmissions from Spacelab, but there was no indication that a Russian cosmonaut was aboard any time in the last day or ever for that matter.

"Vlady is going to love this!" shouted Zeg to himself. "I'd better get him back in here so he can enjoy this, too. Screw the clearance! When the brass goes wacko, all bets are off! I won't tell him right away. It's definitely a test of our response. It's a dumb one, but it's a test!"

No sooner had Zeg made his pronouncement when the door to the porch snapped open, and a confused Vlady Koslov stumbled inside. There was a strange disoriented look on his face. Zeg waited for Vlady to speak.

"Have you heard any voices lately? I mean strange voices in your head. I must be losing my mind, Zeg! Please tell me you're hearing voices, too."

Zeg smiled and nodded, but he wasn't sure what Koslov was talking about.

"Yours! But that's about it, Vlady. I can hear your voice…loud and clear. Please don't start singing for me."

"No! I mean someone else calling out for help. Someone calling out the words *Help Me!* over and over and over."

The question confused Zeg to say the least. He looked at the data from the American spacecraft and decided that Koslov was just setting him up for a joke. Or maybe he was part of Command's test? But then he realized that his partner had no way of knowing that a Russian cosmonaut was missing. Were these two…things related or was it a mere coincidence? Zeg decided to remain quiet and let his partner expand on the subject.

"It's a…a tiny voice right here in my head," offered Koslov. "I know it's beyond crazy, but I heard it. Five times! I counted them. And I definitely wasn't dreaming. I was wide awake the whole time. Honest, Zeg, I'm very serious about this."

Zeg pushed himself back from his desk as he studied Koslov's face, and then he lifted both hands into the air with a flourish.

"This job…this business will drive anyone completely crazy. And now on top of everything else, Command is missing one of their prized cosmonauts. They say he could…no, they say he is probably aboard the American Space Laboratory. Now, that's crazier than hearing…tiny voices in your head…isn't it?

"Don't get mad, but I have to ask. Is Command telling you to do this? If they are, we should…"

"I need a drink!" whispered Koslov in a serious tone. "And…no, Command isn't involved. Let's go into the village and drop a few vodkas so I can relax and clear my mind. Then, if I hear the voice again, I'll know it's for real and not some hallucination caused by…who knows what!"

The next noises were the closing and locking of the security doors. Soon, the two Russians were on their way to some happier moments. As they got into Zeg's car, Koslov had something more to say.

"Zeg, I know that I'm going to sound crazy once again, but just humor me for a moment. Are you telling me that it's possible that there is a Russian cosmonaut aboard the American Spacelab…right now as we sit here? If so, how did he get there in the first place? I've been watching Spacelab like a hawk for several days and after the American shuttle left, there were no more dockings. Did the Americans put him up there without telling us? Maybe it's a Halloween joke on us? They found our transmitter, and they are horsing around with us."

Zeg just threw his hands into the air in complete confusion.

"If I were you, Vlady, I'd keep a close eye on Spacelab because they will certainly question you about it the first chance they get! But that can wait until we get back. We deserve a break."

"Well, I'm not sure exactly what it means, but I've seen some very strange things on the Spacelab photos, Zeg. Every once in a while the stellar background next to Spacelab…inverts! I know that sounds crazy, too, and I'm sure…or I hope that there's a rational scientific explanation for the data. There must be something wrong with our equipment on the satellite or over here. What about a loose camera lens or something similar? It's another problem we have to solve.

"What could be even creepier is the fact that the inversions might actually correspond to those reports you have of a cosmonaut on board the American laboratory. Now, a correlation like that would be really scary! A Russian cosmonaut flying an invisible ship up in orbit and docking with the American satellite right before our eyes, and we missed it."

Zeg didn't respond immediately, but Koslov could see him mumbling something like *I need a drink, too!* under his breath.

10
The Rescue

I'm living in a room without any view.
I'm living freely because the rent's never due.
The synonyms of all the things that I've said
are just the riddles that are built in my head.

Hole in the Sky
Black Sabbath

At Spacelab

It was time to retrieve Major Robert Vostry from his orbital prison on Spacelab. It wasn't much of a surprise that astronauts Richard Lundgren and Richard Goldsmith had been chosen by NASA to man the recovery vehicle. There was some discussion of sending an unmanned recovery vehicle and allowing the major and two robots to return on their own, but because of the publicity and attendant political ramifications, this was no time for a mistake. Besides, the political bureaucrats quietly concluded that it was better to have someone human in the rescue effort to blame for any mistakes or disasters that might occur.

Despite their personal misgivings, both astronauts were actually anxious for the rescue mission to proceed because it had been some time since either had walked in space. The final checks on the major's condition were positive, and he seemed ready and raring to go to say the least. The final plan was for Lundgren and Goldsmith to launch the major with two robots aboard, and then have the astronauts return to earth separately after securing the latest data and samples. What wasn't announced publicly was the option of destroying Spacelab; however, the two astronauts were fully briefed at the last minute on the destruction procedures and they both were informed that preparation for the elimination of the flying space laboratory was to be their main mission, just the opposite of what they and the public were told a day earlier.

Initially, there was a slight delay in the mission due to the weather, but that amounted to only thirty-six hours. This gave NASA additional time to electronically retrieve important data accumulated from Professor Laurie's experiments.

The launch was absolutely perfect and soon both Goldsmith and Lundgren were on their way to Spacelab, for better or for worse. NASA's new launch guidance system worked to perfection and soon their vehicle was in Spacelab's orbit only two hundred yards behind the mother ship. As they awaited permission to commence the docking maneuver, Lundgren began quietly reviewing what he called the basic floor plan for Spacelab. Goldsmith casually asked him why he so interested in the details at such a late date.

"It's a little late for homework, isn't it? Afraid you're going to get lost in there with all those germs and robots running around on the loose? I'm more concerned that they'll decide they don't need us any more after the major is secure and end up blowing the thing up with us onboard! I'm going to be a little extra nervous between the major's launch from Spacelab and ours. I hope you realize that the powers that be consider us expendable.

"Well, anyway, from the docking station, the control center is to your right and the laboratories are to the left. The recovery room holding the major is straight ahead then on your right. From there, the potty is on the left. Sounds easy, doesn't it? Just like when we were kids and in the cub scouts, and we went to the annual dinner where they passed out the awards."

Lundgren shook his head negatively without looking up.

"I'm not too worried about Major Vostry or us in the least. He's got so many sensors on him, even the robots know how to find him and treat him medically. All we have to do is ask the little bastards where he is and then follow them to the source! And the whole world will be watching so I think we're okay.

"I'm trying to figure out where this supposed Russian cosmonaut would hide if he's actually in there with Vostry and the robots. You notice that in our briefings the subject never really officially came up.

"I'm sure he's not sitting around drinking coffee in the lounge or watching TV or just shooting the bull with Vostry. But, of course, you never know about these things! Those Russians are getting quite sophisticated these days. Gone are the days of Lenin and the czars when most of them couldn't read or write. They all speak two or three languages well and, of course, they give the Canadians a run...a skate for their money in hockey every year.

"So, if he actually exists, and that's a big 'if', this guy is clever...if nothing else. He got into our Spacelab without us noticing, and I know NASA's been watching the place like a hawk. That's quite a feat! Imagine trying to sneak up on this monster satellite with all those eyes on earth glued on this place. You would need a stealth rocket ship for sure."

Lundgren paused for a moment to consider what he had just said.

"I'll believe it when I see it...when I see him for myself on the hoof," Goldsmith responded. Lundgren just shrugged his shoulders. Neither believed all the rumors about a cosmonaut. It was a bureaucratic figment of NASA's imagination. The 'incident' had pushed Major Vostry through a lot so it's easy to understand that he might be seeing things now.

The rescue module containing the two astronauts was finally secured to Spacelab and the air pressure on either side of the entry manifold was being equilibrated. It was a procedure they'd practiced and experienced many times. Richard Goldsmith and Richard Lundgren waited patiently for the pressure devices to indicate that all was stable and secure. In a little over a minute all was ready to go. A green light flashed on over the transition port and an electronic voice told the astronauts that all was secure.

Goldsmith was the first to enter Spacelab using standard entry procedures. Solar panels on the side of the space laboratory generated enough power to illuminate the entry portal leading to the central command console. As expected, a lone robotic element sat passively near the console. Only the utility section, which monitored power consumption, heating and cooling, and other passenger comfort processes showed any current data activity. That was the way it was supposed to be, and Goldsmith expelled a sigh of relief upon seeing the system work so well.

"So far, so good!" Goldsmith mumbled loud enough for Lundgren and Houston to hear him. "I've sighted one standard robotic unit, and the spacecraft appears to be in a normal status with no unusual vibration after lock-on. I'll query the unit just to check things out before we locate the major and prepare him for disembarkation."

Goldsmith approached and activated the report function on the nearby robot. Then he punched in a report code requesting spaceship status, a standard robotic reporting function. Soon Goldsmith was holding a printed tally sheet showing the status of each of Spacelab's subsystems. A nearby monitor indicated that it was safe for the astronaut to remove his helmet and breathe the atmosphere inside the laboratory, yet Goldsmith was hesitant to do so based on the accounts that he heard about Professor Laurie's incident. He wondered to himself whether Spacelab's systems were actually capable of detecting and then removing the possible viral components that might be in the air inside the craft's structure. He didn't want to be the testing mechanism for viral contamination, that was for sure.

Goldsmith then requested a summary report on Major Vostry's condition and his exact location aboard ship. After a few moments he had that report in hand and was nodding his head. It seemed to be good news. The major appeared to be ready to go according to the medical system report.

"All systems are go," were his next words to Lundgren back in the module. "According to Spacelab monitors, the major has apparently cleared the decontamination sequence without a hitch, and he's mobile and alert. He appears to be in excellent physical shape, too, as far as this report is concerned. Secure the pod and get onboard. Apparently, he's taking a little nap, but it's time to wake him up if he isn't up already. He's definitely in recovery room 2 as we thought. After we check him out and he's good to go, we'll round up his two special robot friends for their trip back to Houston. I'd rather not stay here any longer than we have to. The sooner we launch him, the sooner our taxi for the trip home will arrive.

"Besides, these robots give me the creeps. It's like they're watching every move I make and recording it for posterity. It's like they are the humans, and I'm the robot! Like I said, it's sure creepy!"

Lundgren acknowledged the communication and in a few minutes the two astronauts were making their way side by side back to Major Vostry's recovery chamber. As Lundgren made his way around a corner, he noticed that something was out of place. A laboratory container vessel seemed to be stuck to the ceiling. He pointed it out to Goldmith who just shrugged his shoulders and continued on but not before expressing his opinion.

"That's probably one of Professor Laurie's experiments…I think. We'll tell Houston and see what they want us to do about it. I'd rather not grab anything when I don't know what it is. That Laurie's a genius but also a nut case as far as I'm concerned. Still, the robots don't seem too worried about it, but, then, they don't have viral problems, do they? None of the malfunction indicators are lit and the chromatographs are absolutely quiet. Always a good sign!"

Then, suddenly, out of the corner of his eye, Lundgren saw movement. It appeared to be one of the robots disappearing around the corner.

"Goldie, I thought all the robots were shut down except this one? I think I just saw one of those machines headed down the hall toward A-3. How many robots are supposed to be left onboard anyway? We only have room for two at most on the trip back with Vostry."

Again, Goldsmith wasn't much help.

"It...I must have made a mistake. I was looking for the major and didn't really focus on those mechanical beasts. One of them must be doing the check routine again. They automatically scan the ship every hour or so. But you already know all that. The two Major Vostry needs for his return trip to earth are in passive mode up front. We need to check them out, but they're ready to go or at least they should be according to these printouts. We'll track this other one down later after we've seen our patient on the hoof. He's our main concern."

Soon, the astronauts were inside the recovery room and decontamination chamber where Major Vostry lay fast asleep. He seemed to be incredibly peaceful considering the circumstances. After a few gentle taps on his helmet, the major came around. His glassy eyes blinked several times in rapid succession and after a few moments a smile crossed his face as he realized that his rescuers had arrived.

"Ah ha! I hope I'm not dreaming, gentlemen, but it appears that my ride home has hit the driveway and none too soon. No sense wasting any more time up here just hanging out with robots. When's our launch window? I want to get the hell out of here as fast as possible. This place and these robots will drive you crazy!"

"An hour and five minutes," Lundgren replied. "How do you feel? Do you think you can stand up? If not, we can have the robots secure a gurney for your comfort. We've got plenty of time to secure you in the launch pod."

Again Vostry smiled as he started to sit up on his own.

"I'm feeling so much better now that you've arrived. I know that I'm repeating myself, but this is no way to spend a vacation paid for by the government. Am I actually clear to depart this palace?"

"A hundred percent," Goldsmith mumbled. "A few checks that are just formalities and we'll help you into your cab. Two of these robots are going with you. One of them will serve as pilot and one will monitor your vitals and provide you with medical aid on the way back, if necessary. They'll be packed and all set to go shortly."

"You're staying here?" Vostry asked in disbelief. "I can't believe that anyone in his right mind would stay…but then all three of us qualify as idiots for coming up here in the first place. How did they talk us into this kind of duty? We must have been drunk as skunks!"

"Those are our orders," Lundgren replied. "I'm not too excited about staying here even for just a few hours either, but orders is orders."

Vostry stopped and scanned his surroundings for a moment.

"What about the Russian?" countered the major, matter-of-factly. "That bastard has been bugging the crap out of me, but I can't understand him. He keeps ranting and raving in Russian…I suppose it's Russian? Well, somehow I can understand him, but it isn't because I understand his language, that's for sure. And, how did he get here in the first place? The auxiliary port is open. We had a little unexplained vibration when Laurie's experiment went bonkers, but other than that…nothing.

"He kept pointing out into outer space away from earth and mumbling something weird. It was probably a name, but like I said, I couldn't tell exactly what he was saying. My Russian, if that's what he's speaking, is a little rusty to say the least. I'm glad he's staying here with you! He is, isn't he? Don't put him on that ship with me no matter what. I couldn't take it!"

Lundgren froze in his tracks. It took him a few seconds to calm down as the subject of a Russian cosmonaut resurfaced. Finally, he responded to the major.

"Major, hopefully, there's no one here but us American chickens. Sir, that's Captain Goldsmith and I'm Captain Lundgren. And you are apparently you, Major Vostry. No Russians! My grandfather was a Swede, and Rich is from Brooklyn if you can believe it. Do you really think that there's a Russian up here with us or is it a joke you're working on for management?"

Vostry nodded as he carefully looked around the room.

"It sure does look that way right now," mumbled Vostry. "There have been some strange things going on in my skull lately. I'm hearing conversations! Maybe I just can't be trusted any more. I think I know what I think I saw and then…"

But the major kept shaking his head, and finally he got real excited and insistent.

"We need to contact Blair and Hurbert right now before I leave for earth. The Russian was in here a few hours ago. His name...his name is Leon. He is really messed up. He kept grabbing his head and asking me to help him! His English is much better than my Russian, but I still couldn't make much sense of some of it. I think he said he was hearing voices... in his head just like me, but that's only a wild guess. He was stumbling around like he was drugged...a drunken sailor on a binge for sure and pointing to his head.

"Now, don't get me wrong. He was friendly. He didn't try to hurt me. It was like he was seeking my help more than anything else. In my condition, imagine someone coming to me for help?"

Lundgren looked at Goldsmith with a deep stare and then a big smile broke out on his face causing Goldsmith to lurch backwards.

"That's what they said about Professor Laurie. Apparently, he was hearing voices, too! I thought it was all a big joke someone was pulling on me, but now it seems to be happening to everyone...except us...so far anyway."

"Well," added Vostry, "they...Blair and Hurbert that is, had me convinced that I was just seeing things because of all the stress I was under. That was fine until this cosmonaut strolls in here again and gives me some pills for my blood pressure. How he knew that I could use them is a mystery to me? I looked at them and sure enough, they were just aspirin tablets, nothing more I don't think. There were just two pills in the container. I took one and kept one here to prove what I'm talking about. The one I took tasted a little bitter for aspirin, but that's probably because it's been sitting around here for quite a while. Here it is for your evidence folder. The container and the would-be aspirin tablet."

Vostry pointed toward a small plastic case on the table next to the bed.

"I'll bet you'll find that that's not standard issue at NASA. Then, how did it get here on Spacelab? And don't tell me that one of the robots had a headache and Walgreens sent it by courier pigeon! Leon must have brought it with him."

"Do you want us to take the pill with us when we return to earth or are you taking it with you?" asked Goldsmith just to be sure.

"Definitely. I want you to take it and be my witnesses. If I take it, they'll say I found it in Houston and made the whole thing up just to become a celebrity. If you produce it, hey, they might even believe me and my story about Leon. That will be a first for those turkeys!"

Lundgren was standing by the bed staring at the pill container and shaking his head.

"If he was here...if Leon was here, he's still here. Let's search the ship very thoroughly and find him before the major leaves." There was sarcasm in the astronaut's voice, but nevertheless, it sounded like a good idea.

Goldsmith shrugged his shoulders and waved for Lundgren to follow him out of the recovery room.

"I know where he is...maybe. At least we can say we didn't ignore the major's request, and we are absolutely sure that there was no cosmonaut aboard Spacelab at least when we were here. I don't want to get sent back up here to look for him."

As soon as the two astronauts turned toward the exit of the recovery room, they froze in their tracks. A lone figure was stepping through the recovery-room door, staggering as he tried to move forward toward them.

"It's Leon!" shouted Major Vostry as the visitor slowly crumpled to the floor in front of the Americans. Goldsmith lunged forward a split second too late to catch the falling Russian who was mumbling something in his native tongue. Quickly, the astronauts rolled the unconscious cosmonaut over on his back and placed a spare pillow under his head. Then they checked his pulse and breathing.

"He's okay...for now," said Goldsmith. "Let's put him in the recovery room next door while we contact Houston. We need to determine whether we should send him back first or later or what? I wonder just how long this guy has been here and...how did he get here without being detected?"

"Major," whispered Lundgren. "Did you hear what he said? My Russian sucks big time!"

The Major nodded his head.

"I think he said...I'm sure he said that we shouldn't return to earth just yet! But I don't know why? He passed out before he could finish his thought. Who would want to stay here and why? I'm completely confused!"

At that moment the Spacelab began vibrating, slowly at first then more rapidly. The lighting in the recovery room dimmed, and, as if on queue, each of the American astronauts except Major Vostry fell unconscious.

Vostry tried to shrink under his covers as he watched in disbelief as a robot rolled in through the door and began dragging the body of the Russian cosmonaut out into the darkness. From his vantage point on the bed, Lundgren and Goldsmith were either dead or out cold. It was impossible to tell.

After several minutes the Spacelab began vibrating again. The shaking of the floor was enough to awaken Goldsmith from his trance much to Vostry's pleasure. The major remained quiet and waited for Goldsmith to speak.

"Where is he?" were Goldsmith's first words. "The Russian…Leon… where did he go?"

Vostry told Goldsmith what he saw as the latter worked to revive his partner, Lundgren.

"Rich, you saw him, too, didn't you? We passed out, and now he's gone. I'm going to search the ship just to be sure."

Somehow, Vostry knew that it wouldn't do any good. While sitting on the floor, Lundgren agreed.

"The vibration…something…not one of ours, took him off."

Just then Goldsmith returned.

"We'd better get on the horn and fast. Someone's stolen the return module. We're all going to need a ride back home and soon!"

11

Schizophrenia

On his shoulder he carries the silver bow,
in the quiver the unfailing arrows,
his countenance darkens as the night;
he descends far from the swift ships
of the Acheans and shoots the first
arrow amid the terrible sound of the silver bow.
First the mules and swift-footed hounds fall. But
soon Apollo aims his sharp missiles at the men.
For nine days the people die, and unceasingly the
funeral pyres burn…deathly to the miserable mortals.

Georg Sticker
Scaling Mount Olympus

Hospital Emergency Room
Washington, D.C.

Splashing through the unusually heavy rain, a large ambulance rolled up to the rear entrance of Saint Catherine's Hospital after completing a nonstop trip from a hospital in Norfolk, Virginia. Having been alerted to its imminent arrival, members of the hospital's emergency staff were ready to transfer their cargo to a special treatment area of the facility reserved for government officials. The hospital grapevine was afire with speculation about their newest patient whose name was well recognized in these parts yet there was little information on his condition.

The older man lying on the gurney seemed stable and appeared to be either unconscious or asleep. Careful observation revealed that his eyelids fluttered roughly every thirty seconds and that his lips moved every minute or so as if he were talking to someone nearby. Every few minutes his legs or arms would twitch, sometimes mildly, sometimes more vigorously.

Several yards away Doctor Mahadavan of NASA could be seen conferring with an emergency room physician about the situation. The two physicians were comparing notes on several written medical reports when a young FBI agent entered the room and approached the pair with some questions.

"Pardon the interruption, but is the subject still alive?" asked agent Eric Lundgren. Mahadavan nodded. "I don't want to interrupt your work, but the boys on the hill are bugging me for an immediate status report. After all, he is a member of the United States Senate for whatever that's worth. He reminds me of that republican senator from Kentucky that my father used to refer to as *Mitch the Bitch!* Well, that was probably more than you needed to know."

Mahadavan was used to situations like this because he understood Washington's complex bureaucracy and all the scuttlebutt politics that went with it. He had learned long ago that the best way to fend off probes like this was to be very polite and proceed slowly and appear cooperative even if you're not.

"That's quite all right," whispered Mahadavan to the agent. "You fellows have all my sympathy because I have to deal with those same people myself on occasion, and it's not always lots of fun. I'll do my best to provide you with everything you need for your report.

"Here's what we have so far. It's a very unusual situation for a man of his status and responsibilities to say the least. Pulse, blood pressure and temperature are fairly normal, at least for a male his age. He's a little over-weight and does have a minor alcohol problem according to an unnamed member of his staff. We've found traces of several drugs in his system, but he also has some prescriptions working, again according to a member of his staff. We're checking on those now to see if we can eliminate the possibility of recreational drugs. His family physician is sending us his medical records forthwith. We'll know a lot more in a day or two after more tests and observation. Right now we've got to keep him isolated for obvious reasons."

Mahadavan took a second look at the agent's I.D. It seemed to ring a bell with the doctor.

"By any chance, are you the astronaut's son? You know...Richard Lundgren, who went up to Spacelab recently."

Lundgren nodded and broke the grim look on his face with a smile.

"I try to keep that fact a secret. I don't want to advance on dad's coattails, and he doesn't want people to realize just how old he's getting while he's running around out in space. He's got this hang-up with his age, and he'd kill me if he knew I was admitting he was my father. I normally tell people that he's my cousin…once removed."

Maha nodded his understanding of the situation.

"My lips are sealed," Mahadavan whispered with a smile. "But I would like to talk with you later about something. Believe it or not, I know your father pretty well, and it is possible that he might be able to help us with this problem we currently have. But first let me bring you up to date just a bit."

As Agent Lundgren stepped back while nodding his head, Doctor Fred Zahn retrieved several sheets of paper from a nearby table and handed them to Mahadavan. The NASA physician leafed through the papers, stopping several times to study some of the information more closely, and then turned toward Lundgren.

"When the senator was finally recovered after what we're referring to as his 'binge' for lack of a better word, he was semi-conscious and muttering under his breath. They found him in downtown Norfolk of all places in an alley next to a dumpster with an empty bottle of Jack Daniels in his coat.

"It's a funny thing about the liquor. There was almost no alcohol in his blood, but his clothes were still soaked in it. It was almost like he had been taking a bath in the stuff instead of drinking it! Now that's something I would definitely call an alcohol problem. But the lack of alcohol in his system is interesting under the circumstances.

"According to the officers on the scene, he seemed to have a major problem focusing his attention and showed a complete lack of emotion, especially considering the circumstances of his recovery, but when they questioned him, he was completely disoriented.

"He thought he was still in D.C. When asked about any associations he might have in Norfolk, he asked the officers where Norfolk was? They initially attributed this to the alcohol although alcohol usually produces the opposite effect. Alcoholics are usually very sure where they are and like to talk about it even when they're wrong.

"He seemed to be suffering from what they termed hallucinations. He was hearing voices! At least he seemed to believe that some invisible people were talking to him. Those are the words in the report, not our conclusions. They mentioned disordered thinking and speech and bizarre and disorganized behavior. Senator Jensen still seems to have a major problem differentiating fantasy from reality.

"There was one particularly interesting thing in the report. They say he kept asking something about a package. 'Where's the package!' was all they could decipher for certain. Well, that and 'Give me the package!' He kept reaching out with his hands at the same time. It appeared that he was trying to grasp something he thought was there. We ought to check with his assistant to see if he was expecting anything.

"The rest is much the same. Delusions, self-neglect, inappropriate emotions, paranoia, catatonic, you name it. They found him standing on one foot. I mean still as a post and on his left foot like Captain Morgan in one of those TV commercials. There was nothing physically wrong with either leg. Still, this guy's got every symptom in the book."

"Symptoms of what?" asked Agent Lundgren who was getting really curious by now.

"Everything and nothing," was Mahadavan's gingerly reply. "That's supposedly our job. Determine the objective and subjective symptoms first. Trace those back to the causality and rectify the situation. Sounds easy, doesn't it?"

The agent seemed stunned. Actually, it was one of Maha's favorite joke lines. He apologized for the humor and went on.

"We need to nail this down and soon before he completely changes character on us. Several specialists are on the way. Stick around, and I'll introduce you to them. They will explain this much better than I ever could. You could probably write your dissertation for a Ph.D. in psychology if you can unravel this guy."

"Thanks," said Lundgren who shook hands with the two physicians. "I'll be right back." Then he made his exit as Mahadavan scratched his head and turned to Zahn with a comment.

"I wonder how the boys at NASA are taking this news? I doubt Senator Jensen will get any sympathy cards from Houston. Everyone assumed a kidnapping, but now it looks like a case of some loose screws and bats in the belfry. We've got to be careful here because with Jensen we have a lot of political quagmire and public second-guessing we need to avoid. His friends will allege that we're his enemies, and his enemies will accuse us of being his friends. It's the best of American politics! Everything wrong all the time. Reminds me of the Tea Party.

"On the other hand, I wonder what that reference to a package means? Either he was waiting to have something delivered to him or someone took something from him. I'm not sure which is the case."

Mahadavan walked over to the telephone and dialed information. Soon he was in touch with the senate mailroom. After some conversation, he was given the cell phone number of Oliver Blair, a senate page who last dealt with the senator. Mahadavan smiled when the woman on the other end of the phone told him that everyone called this particular page 'Ollie'. After asking some questions and getting some answers, Maha hung up the phone.

Mahadavan then dialed the page's cell phone number and had a short conversation with him. Then he turned back to Dr. Zahn.

"Well, seems as though this senate page may be the missing link because he might have or maybe had the missing package in his possession. He told me that he's tried to deliver several packages to Jensen in the last month. The most recent one arrived after the senator disappeared, so no foul play here if that's the package in question. But I am curious about just what's inside that's so important to Jensen that he remembers it even when he's completely out of it and didn't actually receive it. The page…Ollie said he would bring the undelivered package over in an hour or so if he can locate it. If possible, we'd better open it in the presence of our patient. Who knows, maybe he'll snap out of it when he sees the contents?"

Doctor Zahn agreed wholeheartedly.

A little over an hour later, Ollie appeared at Mahadavan's office package in hand. After introductions Ollie handed the package to NASA's head physician.

"I was really surprised at the ease with which they let me out of the building with this thing," said Ollie. "Usually, they don't trust me with anything, not even my lunch bag."

"We have to confess that the FBI helped us with that," Mahadavan replied. "We wanted to talk to you so we thought it best that you deliver the goods in person. The senator is pretty much out to lunch mentally, but he's got a package on his mind."

"So, what's new?" said Ollie before he could stop himself. "Sorry. I'm used to talking with the other pages. Some of these elected officials are complete nut cases for sure."

"No problem," Zahn responded. "If he was a little wacky to begin with, it could help us with our diagnosis. Don't hold anything back. We'll cover your butt. This is just between us, and its only purpose is medical diagnosis."

With those words Ollie seemed to relax bit.

"Well, he seemed much more normal during the first three months of my working tenure. He was nasty, but that's normal for most of them. About a month ago while I was nearby delivering some mail and packages, he started talking to me in spurts. And his head would…well, it would twitch every minute or so. His assistants must have noticed it if I did. You couldn't miss it, but it wasn't my position to intervene."

"Well, I guess it's time to solve the mystery of the senator's package," said Mahadavan in a serious voice. "I'm sure the senator won't mind… he's out cold. We have to assume that it's the people's business and not a present from one of his girlfriends…if he has any. So let's do it for God and country!"

With those words he broke the seal on the package and pulled out an inner envelope. Carefully, he opened the envelope and dumped the contents on the table in from of him and his fellow witnesses, Ollie and Dr. Zahn. The instant look of surprise on Mahadavan's face was reflected by the others as they stared at the table.

"Nothing?" he whispered under his breath. "It's empty! Who sends an empty package to a U. S. Senator…especially this U. S. Senator?"

Ollie grabbed the envelope and pointed to creases on both sides.

"There definitely was something in here! I had it a few days ago, and I returned it to the mailroom that afternoon when I couldn't find him. I saw them…the mailroom people put it in the safe! This thing never left my sight after they gave it to me again this afternoon. I thought it was a little light, but what do I know about packages?"

Mahadavan picked up the pieces that once constituted the package, placed them in a plastic bag and stashed the bag in a nearby storage cabinet.

"If the senator pulls out of this sooner or later, he may want to see what we've seen. Maybe he'll have an explanation for all of this? We can only hope so. Luckily, all three of us were present when the package was opened. They can't shoot all three of us for this, can they? I hope not."

Just as the group was about to break up, in the door strolled Agent Lundgren with some paperwork in his hands. He politely asked the three men to sit down for a few minutes so they complied.

"It appears as if our friend, the senator, was a lot busier than we gave him credit for. And this is just in Norfolk a few hours before he was found in the alley drenched in alcohol.

"First of all, he stopped for breakfast at Denny's and skipped out on the bill of all things. Normally, they let things like that go, but apparently Senator Jensen carved up the fabric in the booth he was occupying with a knife. He must have had a knife on him because what he did required a sharp blade. The manager said that it looked as if he was searching for something buried in the material of the seat he was sitting on.

"He…the manager also said that they found piles of beach sand in the booth. It matched the sand found in the senator's pockets so he must have been near the beach before he ate. Don't even ask me what I think that was all about?

"Next, there's the matter of his transportation. His car was found eight blocks from the alley. The only reason it was noticed was the fact that it was parked on a street in a residential neighborhood and was blocking a driveway. They checked the cab companies, but no pickups from near that site. However, a car was stolen that was parked a half-block away. They recovered that car near the alley with Jensen's prints all over it! And they went back to his car and found no other prints except Jensen's in it.

"Thus…Jensen went to the beach and then to breakfast and sometime in the morning stole a car even though his was running fine. Or…he was kidnapped and the perpetrators just made things look kooky?

"So…any questions?"

Before anyone could speak, Eric held up his hand.

"Wait…there's more! Down the block from the alley in question, there's a hobby shop. Apparently, the clerk caught Jensen trying to walk out with a portable telescope under his arm. The clerk said he was alone at the time. Jensen explained that he just wanted to test it so he pulled three hundred dollars out and left it as a deposit. He told the clerk that he wanted to test the unit at night. Well, since the telescope listed for two hundred and fifty bucks, the clerk naturally agreed. Jensen said he would return by ten the next morning and if he didn't to just consider it a sale. We found the telescope in the stolen car."

The room was very quiet with a lot of thinking going on among the listeners. Lundgren folded up the papers and reminded the men that it was still possible that more of Jensen's activities could be discovered as several agents were even now out canvassing the neighborhood near the alley where Jensen was found. There were also numerous surveillance tapes from nearby banks and businesses, which had to be checked out just in case he made any other stops in the area.

Before Agent Lundgren could escape out the door, Ollie did have an interesting question.

"How was the senator dressed during his jaunt through Norfolk?"

Lundgren hesitated before answering but then complied.

"He was found in the alley wearing a business suit, but...that's where it gets a little strange. The hobby store clerk and the waitress at Dennys both confirm that he was wearing a loud Hawaiian short-sleeved shirt and Bermuda shorts with sandals when they saw him. Ah, when and why he changed into the suit is still a big mystery unless someone did it for him. We haven't found any spare suitcases or gym bags yet."

Then, without another word and a wave of his hand, the agent shrugged his shoulders and went out the door.

12

The Debriefing

*And if you go chasing rabbits,
and you know you're going to fall,
tell them a hookah smoking caterpillar
has given you the call.*

Go Ask Alice
Jefferson Airplane

The Houston NASA Space Center

It was with mixed emotions that Phil Blair made his way down the hallway toward his boss's office. He had plenty of other things to do, yet he wanted to hear the story or stories first hand…straight from the horses' mouths, as it were, yet, he didn't like the idea of confronting eyewitnesses with comments that made their testimony seem implausible, especially when they were high profile figures like American astronauts. Worse still, because of morning traffic and phone calls, he was a little late for the meeting, which was scheduled to begin over five minutes ago. He knew that Frank was a stickler on timeliness so he searched for an excuse that would get him off the hook without too much damage to his reputation.

He remembered promising himself that he would call his cousin Ollie to find out what was going on inside the bowels of the government, and now with the astronauts just around the corner he realized that he could have used Ollie's perspective to some advantage in this meeting.

Testimony was a good word for this encounter because it was going to be more like a courtroom scene than a friendly chat among lifelong friends. The astronauts were on the spot to say the least, and they were well aware of that fact. But, there were three of them versus two interrogators. Phil would rather have interviewed them one at a time so that he could focus on each viewpoint, but Frank gave in to their request to hear each other's statements as they were made. He could hardly turn them down without losing their full cooperation.

Robert Vostry, Richard Lundgren, and Richard Goldsmith were their names, a major and two captains as Phil kept repeating to himself. A major and two captains were formidable foes for any mere civilian. Even though the mission was classified, the whole world seemed to be watching and waiting for some sort of explanation of the strange presence rumored to have been encountered aboard Spacelab.

Phil thought back over some of the missions these astronauts were involved in, and he began to relax a bit. They were always calm in their NASA and public interviews in the past so there was no reason to believe that they would be combative now. Phil realized that they had no apparent reason to make up the story about the cosmonaut, and that they needed NASA's help as much as NASA needed them.

As Phil entered the office, he was surprised to find only Frank seated at the conference table. Frank was engrossed in a fairly large pile of papers and didn't even acknowledge Phil's presence. Phil began to almost hope that the meeting had been cancelled for good or at least delayed.

"Sorry I'm late, Frank. I had to sign a bunch of press permits, and that damn phone wouldn't stop ringing. Where are the boys? If anything, military types can be counted on for timeliness."

"Hell if I know or care," mumbled Frank while shrugging his shoulders. "I just got a voicemail saying they'd be a few minutes late getting here. Being in earth orbit must slow one's sense of time. Or maybe they sensed that you were late so what the hell!"

Phil took the opportunity to sit down and pour himself a hard-earned cup of coffee. Then he took a deep breath and tried to let his mind relax again. His eyes flowed across the wall behind Frank where at least a dozen framed photos of early NASA craft like the Gemini capsule and the Saturn V booster were hung in honor of early American space science and engineering.

How things have changed, Phil thought to himself. *Now, everything's political and nothing's rational. Exploration and the betterment of mankind are totally secondary or nonexistent compared to political gain and contracts. Money talks and everything else walks, that's for sure!*

Phil's reverie was interrupted by the sound of shuffling feet as, one by one, the three space travelers entered the room, nodded greetings to Frank and Phil, and took their seats at the conference table. It almost looked as if they'd rehearsed their entry. The men were silent, politely waiting for Frank to speak first. That was probably a good idea.

"Gentlemen, it's good to see you safe and sound to say the least," said Frank with a forced smile. "We hope that your day has gone well. This is Dr. Phil Blair whom, I'm sure, you've met before one place or another."

After handshakes and the pouring of coffee, the official meeting settled down and came to order.

"As you know," Frank continued, "we are trying to get a handle on this…intruder thing aboard the Spacelab. "If this project weren't so highly classified, we could quietly write the whole thing off and forget about it. Probably, that's what we should do anyway; however, I thought it might be best to analyze the situation before Washington sticks its big nose in here."

Major Vostry raised his hand in a request to go first. He smiled and began to stand up, but Frank was quick to tell him to relax.

"Let me set one thing straight from the very beginning. There definitely was another…another being on Spacelab with me, and he tried to communicate with me. However, his speech was garbled or at least seemed that way to me. At first I thought it was Russian that he was speaking, but now I'm not so sure about that.

"He came up to me on two separate occasions before the two Rich's here arrived on Spacelab to rescue my ass. He wasn't hostile toward me in any way. After thinking about the encounters more carefully, I'm very sure that he was looking for something aboard ship. What could that have been? He didn't tell me, and I don't know! That's the question I have been asking myself ever since the incident occurred. What was the payload he sought from us?

"What is even crazier is the fact that somehow, I know his name. It's Leon! The name literally popped into my head. I know that I might have been exposed to one or more of those weird viral…whoops, chemical experiments being run on Spacelab by the Nutty Professor…ah, you know who I mean. But that excuse doesn't fly. I saw what I saw. And he didn't tell me he was Leon; it just popped into my head!

"What's more, all three of us observed him at the same time in the same place, and these two boys actually touched him when he fell to the floor. They laid their hands on his body…well, his spacesuit.

"He passed out right in front of us. What made him pass out or lose his balance…who knows? He wasn't shot or pushed or shoved, nor did he trip over anything. They…the robots, that is, dragged him over to the recovery room next to mine, but the HQ boys tell me the visual conked out so they didn't get a picture of it. Sure makes me feel warm and fuzzy about our technical capabilities. But since he was running around the spacecraft for hours, something must have observed him. What about the other robots? They possess visual recording capabilities…right? They were looking… well, pointed right toward him for quite a while."

Frank shook his head and pointed to Phil. It was just what Phil feared might happen. The finger of blame would start pointing at him. But he knew he had to remain calm and answer as clearly as possible.

"Major, I'm at a complete loss to answer your questions, mainly because I have the very same questions. Take the extraction data. We can fully follow your arrival and your extraction…the three of you and the robots. But no one else came or went after you were alone up there. Now a bunch of our subsystems zonked out right when we needed them, but we didn't cause that to happen from here. Something…someone intervened and shut them down.

"So, either he's still aboard or he exited Spacelab in the module or he does not exist or…! After hearing the words directly from you, I myself don't know what to believe except what you've told us. It's as if our surveillance turned a blind eye to…Leon. He's got to be aboard ship unless he left with the module, which is most likely. Then, we have to ask where he went?"

"Okay, let's send a search team up there again," Goldsmith interjected, "and resolve this once and or all. Give me a day or two, and I'll be ready to go. I know what I saw, and I know what I touched, and I know what to look for! This was not a figment of our joint imaginations. This was not mass hypnotism or hysteria. We just have to admit that we had a technical breakdown and that he's hiding or he escaped."

Phil reached into his coat pocket and pulled out a letter-sized piece of paper. Without reading it, he handed it directly to Frank.

"Frank, I received this just before I left the office for this meeting. I don't know if this simplifies or complicates things? Several of our robots have had their programming altered…the ROM code not the RAM. The boys at the lab are trying to figure out just what those changes are meant to accomplish. This could explain quite a few of our malfunctions."

"You mean they were altered *in situ*…aboard Spacelab?"

"Yep!" whispered a nodding Phil Blair. "Apparently, someone aboard Spacelab reprogrammed them right on site and didn't tell us, or more likely, didn't want us to know."

"Not me…not us!" shouted Lundgren. "And the Major was in no condition to do so. It must have been our mystery guest…Mister Leon!"

The room fell silent as each man pondered this new information.

"Look," said Blair in a quiet tone, "it appears as if we have a robot-cosmonaut conspiracy on our hands. I had the C.I.A. give me what they have on Russian cosmonauts in general and specifically on any of them named Leon.

"First, during the history of the Russian space program they were able to pinpoint two cosmonauts in training whose first names were Leon. One is Leon Spachek and the other is Leon Yengoyan. The second Leon has a twin brother who is also a cosmonaut. Luckily, we have photographs of each man; however, they are rather low quality shots and are almost ten years old. As we speak, the agency is attempting to enhance these photos, but you might as well look at the originals and see if you recognize either of these men."

Blair passed the shots to the astronauts and gave them some time to study them. None of the three men spoke immediately, but they all began nodding their heads as they eyeballed one of the images. Lundgren spoke first.

"This is definitely our visitor. No enhancement necessary. I could pick old Leon out of a crowd of people dressed up as cosmonauts for Halloween. He looked right at me up there in Spacelab. Those eyes of his will give him away every time. And I remember seeing him and his brother being interviewed on television several times. That's why his face seemed so familiar."

Goldsmith agreed just by nodding his head again, and Major Vostry also did the same.

Frank grabbed a second small stack of papers that were sitting in front of him and passed out several sheets to each of the other four men.

"I did a search on the possible cosmonauts who might be involved here, and this is a summary for Leon Yengoyan. Actually, without any of your information we might have chosen him because he has some interesting voids in his record. We even learned through Langley Field that he was reported missing recently by the Russians themselves. Now, this could just be his cover story in case he got caught, but at least we're pretty sure that we have the right man.

"So, I'd say that rules out the figment-of-imagination possibility. Next, we should probably discuss the vibration you both experienced. It's the other big unexplained mystery we have in our data.

"Something docked with...or undocked with Spacelab. There is no other explanation for this!"

Frank and Phil exchanged glances. Frank pointed towards the door.

"Boys," said Phil with a smile on his face, "I believe that NASA is about to buy you lunch and maybe a few beers? We can discuss the rest of this in a more relaxed atmosphere. I hope you don't mind the informality of this. I believe that we're making good progress."

The astronauts were pleased by the suggestion, but just then there was a familiar tapping on the door to Frank's office. Frank asked the men to wait until he could see what his administrative assistant wanted. Frank opened the door and a female hand passed some documents to him and the two exchanged a few words.

"Anything I can help with?" asked Phil as Frank read a few lines from the main sheet.

"Unbelievable!" ranted Frank as he threw his arms over his head. 'I guess that there's a crackpot for every cause."

Phil rushed over and grabbed the papers, which Frank had thrown on the floor.

'It's a telegram! Who sends telegrams these days?" asked Phil.

"What is it, Phil?" asked Major Vostry quietly.

Phil held up his hand as he reread the message. He was slowly shaking his head negatively the whole time. Then he turned toward the officers and began to read the text.

"Gentlemen. You must immediately abandon Spacelab and not reenter it under any circumstances. Failure to follow these instructions shall result in Spacelab being crashed into Washington, DC! Do not attempt to destroy Spacelab. Heed this warning or die!"

Everyone froze for a moment.

"Who would send such a thing?" asked the Major. "And how is Jensen involved. He is the country's worst enemy when it comes to the exploration of space. I still remember that photo in the New York Times. There he was standing with his arms around two Russian cosmonauts telling the world how brave they were and how important space travel was for the whole world. What a hypocrite!"

"There is no signature, Major. But this was sent to NASA from Norfolk, Virginia yesterday. Somehow Norfolk sounds familiar."

"Norfolk?" muttered Frank. "Isn't that where they found Senator Jensen? Was he on a binge or was he kidnapped? Phil, we've got to contact the FBI immediately. This could be a threat on Jensen's life or…he could be threatening us. We've got to find out and pronto."

The astronauts seemed surprised by this new information about Jensen. Phil grabbed the telegram and headed for the door where he stopped.

"Frank, I'll meet the four of you over at Ernie's Bar and Grille after I take care of this. We still need those drinks and something to eat!"

Frank agreed and soon everyone was on his way out of Frank's office until Vostry stopped in his tracks.

"There's one more thing that we haven't mentioned, Frank. As we were leaving Spacelab, we received a message from Houston telling us to leave several of the robots behind. I know it seems unimportant, but we were given no explanation."

Frank just shrugged his shoulders and continued out the door.

13

Frankenstein

Tonight there's gonna be a jailbreak
Somewhere in this stupid town.
See, me and the boys don't like it,
So we're getting up and going down.

Jailbreak
Thin Lizzy

Russian Institute for Biological Sciences
Saint Petersburg, Russia

The flashing green sensor suddenly lit up the darkened underground laboratory causing several inquisitive mice to head for their usual hiding places among the stacks of electronic equipment. The sensor itself was connected by a sheath of wires to a sealed plastic vat, which contained a fowl-smelling chemical solution and a wide variety of electrodes. Another sheath of wires ran from the vat to a nearby glass case that contained the apparently lifeless body of an unidentified man whose nametag read the equivalent of 'John Doe' in Russian.

Except for other equipment, the main laboratory room was otherwise unoccupied. Several equipment manuals and boxes of electronic parts were haphazardly spread across the wooden desk at the far end of the room. A small desk lamp on the desk's surface was doing its best to illuminate its surroundings. Parts from a D.C. power supply also cluttered the desktop standing next to a half-empty bottle of Russian vodka, several empty glasses and a half-full box of chocolate candy.

An obviously unhappy Dr. Alexi Karpov was the first on the scene in response to the sensor's labored activity. He had been napping in a nearby room. His near exhaustion evidenced by the heavy bags under his eyes was caused by his back-to-back fifteen hour work days. The long trek to his living quarters through the bowels of the old building had forced him to jerry-rig a hammock in his small office out of sight of the surveillance cameras. This permitted him to get some very much needed rest while he waited for his experiments to run their course. He hadn't seen the sun or the sky in almost a week, and he grunted some obscenities under his breath as he walked.

He went straight to a printer, which had belched out several pages of information during his absence. After glancing at the equipment and briefly at his patient, he sat down at his desk and began leafing through the report. Soon, he began shaking his head and talking to himself, which was normal behavior for him, especially lately. This had been happening to him a lot lately, and he was beginning to fear for his sanity.

Pavel will never believe this! Neither do I for that matter. The read virus thinks it's in a space ship and that it's re-entering the earth's atmosphere? I didn't think this fellow was anywhere near our...any space program. He's supposed to be a spy of some sort, not a cosmonaut.

What the hell is it reading? I thought he was supposed to be exposed to some speeches by Josef Stalin before they capped him! Instead, it looks like he's dreaming the plot of the movie 2001 according to the virus. But his response is almost the same as that of that poor cosmonaut fellow...Yengoyan we had a while back.

Now that I think of it, I'm sure that's what it was! Yengoyan watched a movie based on Hamlet before he was injected. And his response was almost the same as this, totally unrelated to the memory stimulus they gave him. As far as I remember, they never engaged in space travel back in Shakespeare's time, at least not when they were sober. But then, those Danes were a sneaky lot.

At that moment Pavel Malkin entered the lab in a rush. His heavy breathing told Alexi that he must have sprinted all the way from the surface. He had a very concerned look on his face.

"What's up, Alexi? Are we getting any data from this fellow? Well, are we getting any useful data at all?"

Alexi nodded in the affirmative and smiled at his friend despite his current confusion.

"It's very weird, Pavel. According to the improved read virus, our patient here thinks...thought he was in a spacecraft re-entering the earth's atmosphere just before our friends in Command injected him. Then he just fades away, at least according to the read virus. Of course, I'm assuming that it's the earth's atmosphere he's reentering in his vision."

Alexi grabbed his partner and friend by his shoulders and sat him down. He had some serious questions to ask of Pavel.

"When the boys wheeled this fellow into our laboratory, did you take a good look at his face?"

Pavel thought back in time for a moment, but then he was forced to answer the question negatively.

"His face was completely covered. The less I know about these poor bastards, the better I can sleep at night. My conscience just bothers me too much when things get personal…like seeing their faces. Their thoughts are something else again. As long as they stay away from family…especially children and friends, I'm in the clear. They are just patriots doing their best to help Mother Russia.

"But, more to the point, why do you ask?"

"I haven't seen his face either, but you surely remember our recent guest, the cosmonaut Yengoyan. Leon Yengoyan. The read virus is suggesting that this is him. Or rather, it's suggesting that he's a cosmonaut. Does that send a chill up or down your spine?"

"Can we take a look?" yelped Pavel as he started to get up from his chair but was restrained by Alexi.

"Not for another thirty minutes. But you should look at this read virus response first anyway. And then we should compare it word for word with the results from Yengoyan. I'm willing to bet that we won't be able to tell the difference between the two brains, at least from the read virus's perspective."

Now Alexi had really caught Pavel's interest.

"Can we reproduce it?" asked Pavel anxiously. "If it's in his head…his brain, we should be able to read it again. Somehow the read might have slipped by some neurons on us. But, you know, I checked everything twice before we started this run. And the equipment was spot on. I just can't see how Yengoyan's data could have leaked over to…"

"You're right!" shouted Karpov, covering his mouth as he jumped up from his chair. "Let's reset and try again. We've got the original output from both safely recorded. Let's clear the read virus and crank Leon…I mean this nameless fellow up again. I checked the input, too. There was no operator error during the first run. And the system checks out one hundred percent. Your methods for correcting the read virus seem to be working. At least that's good news. Now let's put everything to the test and see where the error...if any, lies."

The scientists set about rechecking and configuring their experiment and once completed they retreated to their makeshift lounge for coffee and conversation. It would be a little over an hour before the read virus would be ready to run again. They went to great lengths to appear relaxed and in control for their friends on the other end of the surveillance cameras.

Malkin breathed a deep sigh of relief as he sipped his coffee. His stress was contained but obvious to his partner, yet he began to relax and slumped back in his chair. He thought about his last vacation trip to the Black Sea and the beautiful woman he had encountered in a local bar. They were still corresponding, so he decided this might just be the perfect time to re-read her last letter and gaze at her photograph. As he reached for his briefcase to retrieve the letter and photo, Alexi grabbed his hand. His words were whispered in a low voice.

"I don't want to ruin your day, Pavel, but I snuck a glance at our patient's face. That subject lying in there in our lab is not the illustrious Leon Yengoyan we have grown to know and love. He's not the same fellow who visited us a while back despite the official papers. Well, either that or this is Leon and the other fellow wasn't the same Leon.

"But, strangely, he looks almost like Leon. Remember, Leon has a twin brother somewhere who was also a cosmonaut."

Malkin's face became a picture of disbelief. He tried to hide his expression by turning away from the security cameras. Then, he began laughing as if Alexi had just told him a great joke.

"They...someone switched bodies...subjects on us when we weren't looking. The fellow out there in the lab is about the same height and weight, but even with the helmet covering his head, it's the color of his eyes that give him away. I didn't mention it to you, but I did see them. This fellow has blue eyes. Leon's eyes were green! I double-checked my lab notes. Even in the dark and through the lab visor, I know green from blue!

"I didn't want to bring this up in the lab where they could hear us so easily. Can you think of any reason why this...tampering with our experiment is occurring? Nothing we do here will make any sense if the subject keeps changing and the results stay the same. But it does say a lot for our read virus, doesn't it!"

Malkin cleared his throat, turned and leaned over toward his partner. He postured himself as if he were telling a joke back to Alexi.

"If this guy isn't the original Leon, then who the hell is he if he isn't Leon's twin?" whispered Pavel in disbelief. "If our illustrious bosses went to all the trouble to come up with an almost exact replica of the first Leon, how could they screw up something as obvious as the eye color? That would have been easy to fix.

"And why the switch…now? And where is the original Leon? So many questions and not an answer in sight! Is this some sort of intelligence plot aimed at us…at you and me? Or is it just a perverted test of our powers of observation being conducted by our keepers? Obviously, they must seriously doubt our work product!

"What have I…what have we done to deserve this kind of treatment? We dedicate our lives, our special training, to this project, we work in the most miserable of conditions as if we were prisoners, and they treat us like the enemy! I'm going to call them on this right now!"

"Wait!" whispered Alexi as he restrained his scientific partner. "Let's let this play out just a little bit more before we act and get ourselves shot. We've got to be really very careful…very, very careful. I grant you that. Maybe they surgically altered his eye color? He isn't wearing contacts. I checked that when you weren't looking. Neither was our first Leon as I remember.

"But the eyes aren't the most interesting aspect of this experiment. Did you look closely at the optical result from the read virus? That was an American spacecraft he thought he was in! He visualized a NASA logo of all things. He saw data streams in English, and he interacted with several robots. There is something very strange going on here, my friend. The only American spacecraft big enough to match those optics and have robots is…you guessed it, the unit doing viral experiments up in earth orbit. Presumably, the same viral experiments we're into here in St. Petersburg are being run up there. The original Leon used to be a spy. So, if this is the same fellow or his twin brother, whichever, then he's still at it!

"If all of this is true, we need to put a date on this fellow's visit. We need ingress and egress data for that Spacelab visit. That should be easy enough. Siberia is supposedly watching the Spacelab twenty-four hours a day. We need to contact our friend Koslov without the committee knowing it. He might be able to give us the information we need for this analysis."

"I understand what you're saying, but why is all this so important?" asked Pavel. "Is it worth risking our very lives? Think about that for a moment. Basically, I'm chicken!"

Alexi hesitated for a moment. He was trying to simplify his explanation of the risks involved.

"I need more time on that risk analysis. But consider this. The real Leon had contact with several American robots not too long ago. I mean before his last jaunt into space. Don't ask me how I know, but he did. This fellow, whoever he is, did the same thing almost exactly. As we know, his optical data pictures several American robotic entities in very close proximity. And guess what? Both of these fellows end up in our lab or one ends up here twice! Something very strange is going on here, Pavel.

"Someone wants something we have. Maybe it's right here in front of our noses? What if someone wanted to steal our read virus? It's the only thing that's changed between Leon visits. What if our friend Leon is a spy…an American spy? That would make things really interesting, wouldn't it!"

The scientists finally decided that it was time to return to the lab and re-introduce the read virus into their patient and take a better look at his face and eyes. As they reentered the laboratory, Alexi froze in his tracks.

"He's gone!" Alexi shouted as he pointed toward the empty glass container that held their subject only minutes ago. "Those bastards from the medical facility must have taken him when they saw we were absent from the lab. Either that or he got up and walked out on his own, but somehow I doubt that was possible!

"How can we conduct our research when the government keeps removing our subjects without consultation before their treatment and analysis is complete? General Bedoyovich is going to get his ears pinned back by me…personally! I hope he hears this! I never agreed to get embroiled in their little spy games!"

Right at that moment the lab phone buzzed. Pavel, who was the calmer of the two scientists at that moment, picked up the receiver. He listened but before he could respond, the caller hung up on him.

"It was Command. They said that their surveillance of our lab was down for thirty minutes. They announced that we could proceed with the subject. Then, of course they hung up…immediately!"

Alexi didn't know whether to laugh or cry.

"They swipe Leon or Leon II or whoever, and then they cover their asses claiming that they were electronically blind? How clever of the little bastards. Now they can blame this whole thing on us…whatever *the whole thing* is?"

At that moment the ground began vibrating, slowly at first. Both men immediately hit the floor. As the ground shook, Alexi heard his partner mumbling under his breath.

"It seems like we've been here before, Alexi. Leon's taxi cab must have just pulled up!"

14

Voices in my Head

*Don't know where I'm going, but trying for
the kingdom if I can, because I'm a man.
When I put a spike into my vein, heroin be the death of me.
It's my wife, it's my life, I'm better off than dead.*

Heroin
Lou Reed

Princeton University Chemistry Department
Princeton, New Jersey

It had been a long and perilous journey, one he had never entertained in his thoughts and dreams until it was forced upon him by fate. Being shot up into earth orbit and thrown back in a pod smaller than his Mercedes was not what he had bargained for when he agreed to go. But it was the current reality of Professor Victor Laurie, and something he could never have predicted.

For a man confined to a wheelchair most of his adult life, it was difficult for him to explain even to himself the strange feelings and thoughts that were running through his body and mind both day and night ever since that fateful trip. He'd dabbled in the use of recreational drugs in his younger days, but this was so much more surreal. His life now seemed to encompass the harsh irrational reality of a dream driven by an overwhelming fear of falling from the sky, not just at night when he slept, but also during every waking hour of the day. But he wasn't falling back to earth. Somehow, in his mind he was falling down to the moon of all places?

When his mental exhaustion finally exceeded his physical energy and he actually slept, his slumber was fitful at best, and he remembered little of his real dreams except for the strangest images of spacecraft and robots fighting over him like raccoons after a church mouse. These were dreams within dreams within dreams, always with the soothing sound of an Allman Brothers song in the background. Pursued by bureaucrats in the daytime and alien demons at night, his nerves were worn to the point where he knew that quite soon he might just snap…permanently.

And the same visions haunted him time after time. The voices in his head were relentlessly calling to him for help. A swarm of robotic machines were incessantly staring at him and pursuing him wherever he would go. One Russian cosmonaut with eyes aglow chasing another Russian cosmonaut trying to kill him. Tiny viral molecules of his own creation were running up and back and into and out of his body like miniature worms. The earth he stood on…the ground beneath him…the floor of any building he was in would shake beneath him without reason or determinable cause.

Finally, after what seemed like weeks of continuous debriefing by a legion of NASA personnel, he was actually left alone with his own thoughts in a safe and secure place, his office at the Princeton University Chemistry Department. No other place in the universe felt as much like home to him as this cubical plot completely stuffed with science books, computers and boxes full of data. The familiar items that surrounded him seemed to form a shield against the bristling outside world because they were created during a much happier and peaceful time in his life. Even the voices in his head were relatively silent in this place. It was such a wonderful and welcome change for Victor that he finally managed a rare smile.

There were a few non-professional personal effects present inside this den of his but not very many. Photographs of his friends from Harvard and Stanford covered a small section of the wall next to a large window that gave him a soothing view of a beautiful garden. It was lush foliage that separated this building from a physics laboratory across the way. That always seemed appropriate to him because, as a physical chemist, he was really half chemist and half physicist. The lingering joke amongst his friends was that a physical chemist could be defined either as a chemist who knew little physics and thought steroids were a cereal preferred by baseball and football players or a physicist who knew absolutely no chemistry but could spell the words 'physics' and 'chemistry' without resorting to a dictionary.

These things didn't matter to Victor at all. He deemed himself a scientist comfortable in any of the sub-spheres of scientific discipline. He was as at home with a virus as with a quantum mechanical wave function. He just wanted to make his mark on the scientific community at large and realize his life-long dream of being awarded a Nobel Prize. Was that too much to ask for his hard work and dedication?

His heroes were Charles Townes and Arthur Schalow, inventors of the ammonia maser, which was really a giant step to the first laser. He remembered being told that they got the idea for amplification by stimulated emission of radiation during a casual discussion while sitting on a park bench near Columbia University in New York during lunchtime. He regretted not having a nearby partner with similar objectives off of whom he could bounce his numerous ideas. His best idea man, Dallas Pence, was thousands of miles away at Stanford University.

Two of the projects he had interest in definitely presented the possibility of realizing his goal of a Nobel Prize. He just had to work tirelessly and think hard and never give up, but he also knew that he also had to be very lucky. Many things had to break just right for him to succeed.

Probability theory was one of his favorite subjects and the story about Albert Einstein believing that God didn't play dice couldn't be beat. He knew that Einstein was wrong which meant that he had a chance of being right. He would never let religion or supernatural beliefs or fairy tales get in the way of his development of a valid scientific theory. He remembered all of those politicians who were now licking their wounds, politicians who debunked global warming in their attempts to preserve ill-gotten profits for large corporations, which were polluting the environment. When the polar icecaps began melting several years ago, these critics of science ran for cover.

Still, even with these positive thoughts and attitudes working for him, it felt like someone else was in the room with him watching and waiting. He turned on the lights and shut the door. He had been gone for quite a while so he slowly scanned the room, checking its contents and assuring himself that he was alone and that his possessions were undisturbed. It was past nine o'clock in the evening so the building was sparsely populated, if at all. His friendly desk chair beckoned to him and soon he drew a deep breath and laid his frame back into its comforting structure. Slowly, his eyes closed as his mind began to review the events of the recent past.

"How and why did I get into this area of research?" he spoke aloud to himself. "What freak occurrence of nature placed me on this track and sent me into a world I cannot escape from? If for some reason my plight was meant to be, where will this all lead me and why?"

Actually, he knew the answers to the questions he posed to himself. He had always been interested in time travel and often wished he could shrink himself down to the size and mass of an electron, which would make such an improbable action more feasible. And he loved the idea of traveling great distances by folding space, a possibility which most of the scientific community debunked.

Those concepts were all just dreams more appropriate to children than adult scientists or so said most of his friends and associates. Still, deep down inside, he held out a child-like hope that science had overlooked something very fundamental and that it was his job to discover just what that theory or concept was.

But then came that winter from hell when he got sick...very sick. His head hurt; his chest hurt; his stomach hurt! The discomfort and pain were almost too much for any normal person to stand, and he actually toyed with the idea of doing himself in. He was ready to try anything that might kill this 'flu' as his doctor was wont to call the cause of his discomfort.

Then it happened just by chance. For once he was in the right place at the right time. The university was working on a new post-infection serum that was supposed to convert an attacking virus to a benign form that wouldn't affect the nervous system of the patient. When he learned of the tests being offered, he was definitely ready to take the chance. What did he have to lose? Even just a small change for the better would be worth any of the possible risk.

He submitted to the test shots and placed himself in the university hospital for observation. As he remembered, there were seven other similar cases being tested at the same time. Still, to this day, he was unable to recall the exact scientific name of the substance placed in his body to fight the disease. He remembered that a week later, the scientific team conducting the tests issued its first public statement. There was some good news and some bad news.

The bad news was that of the group of eight patients involved in the experiment, only one seemed to make any measurable progress as a result of the serum. This was a kiss of death for the research project at least in the short term.

But, the good news was that he was that one success story! Soon, he was well and figuratively back on his feet and working with little or no noticeable side effects, at least at first. All he could remember was that certain ideas began popping into his head, ideas that his training as a physical chemist could not have easily spawned. But, there they were, so his experimental program began to shift in the direction of viral research and away from quantum theory. Maybe what had worked for him could be made to work for many others suffering as he had. It was certainly worth a try, and he was certainly interested in trying.

One thing led to another and over ten years the path led to reading the data stored in brain tissue of human beings. Government funding was almost immediate, and he was able to attract some of the best graduate students to his research program. There was only one problem, and for a scientist it was one that was most difficult to deal with. Most of his work would be classified because of the implications of the research. The government would be looking over his shoulder all the time. It would be constantly monitoring his methods and results with constant second-guessing.

But, Laurie was no fool. He knew that he couldn't fight city hall directly so he had to improvise. His tactics led him in two major directions. He convinced the head of the chemistry department to let him have two unused rooms in the basement of the chemistry building supposedly to use for storage of unused equipment. But these areas were not used for storage at all. Laurie used them as hidden laboratories where he could clandestinely carry on his research without being discovered by any collaborating government scientists and others interested in the security status of his work. Secondly, he privately funded his former student, Dallas Pence, at Stanford. The work there seemed independent to the outside world, but was essential to Laurie's research goals. Pence's main interests involved direct communications between the microorganisms.

There was one other matter that he kept in the spy versus spy category. It was his constant companion…his wheelchair. Over the past year or so he had discovered that under the right conditions he could walk on his own with the help of a cane. At first he could only manage a step or two. But improvement came with each attempt and as he worked his new walking skills, it was only a short time until the cane was no longer absolutely necessary. He wanted to tell everyone of his miraculous recovery, but a voice in his mind kept telling him that he might one day utilize that secret to his benefit. So, he kept his wheelchair for public appearances at least for now. It gave him some leverage and provided an excuse for escape on those occasions where he felt like he was being pushed into a corner by the press or the government. The wheelchair became an even handier tool than he had ever imagined.

So with his mind dancing with thoughts of the past, he pulled out a small pillow, which he kept in his nearby filing cabinet, and he settled in for a sit-down nap at his desk. It felt so good just to be able to relax for once in a place where he felt safe and secure. But no sooner than he began to drift off into a well-earned sleep, the phone on his desk harshly buzzed him back to reality. It was his private line so he reached over and picked up the receiver. With a tired voice he grunted into the receiver only to hear a friendly voice in response.

"Victor! You're sleeping at your desk again, aren't you? How many times do I have to tell you not to do that? Get a couch! You've got room for one in there…in your office. Just move that small file into the closet and vacuum the floor. I can sleep there when I come to visit!"

There was only one person in the known universe who would dare begin a conversation like that with Professor Laurie. It was Dallas Pence!

"Dallas, you pick the worst times to call me. I was just beginning to forget all of my numerous worries and problems…for a short time. In case you missed all the fun, I'm back on earth and on the loose again! This better be good news, or I'll kick your ass even from my wheelchair!"

Laurie could hear laughter on the other end of the phone line. Even though Pence had been his student, the two men felt more like distant cousins who rarely saw each other in person.

"You're damn right that it's good news! Stanford beat Cal again in the Big Game by thirty-five points. Oh, I forgot. Princeton doesn't really play football with the big dogs, does it? But, anyway, you'll have to call me back. I'm at the bowling alley with my honey, and it's my turn. Give me a couple of minutes so I can finish this game, and I'll tell you some new jokes."

The unspoken message was clear. It was time to complete this call from a public phone. The mention of the bowling alley was their own private code reference to a pay phone. Victor hung up the receiver without another word knowing exactly what he had to do. He reached into another drawer in his desk and pulled out a cloth bag holding a considerable amount of change, mostly quarters. The bag had the name of a Las Vegas casino imprinted on it. Next, he went through several files and collected several sheets of encrypted data. He had devised the code himself so he could read the information directly from the sheet with little difficulty. He didn't expect particularly good news so he had devised the next string of experiments he wanted Pence to perform in his laboratory at Stanford.

Then he pulled his wheelchair over, sat down, and headed for the elevator at a slow grinding pace. Five minutes later he found himself sitting in front of a pay telephone in the lobby of the next-door physics building. He pulled a small piece of crumpled paper out of the bag and studied the number scrawled on the sheet. Then he carefully began flexing his fingers. Soon, coins were being dropped into the phone, and the number was being dialed.

Two rings were followed by Dallas' cheery voice answering on the other end of the line.

"I love this spy stuff," said Pence to his former mentor in a hushed tone. "James Bond didn't do this well! After we're done, I want to make a movie about this whole thing. But you have to get a couch for your office first. I'll even volunteer to give you the spare one I have in my garage because it's very comfortable."

Laurie skipped the small talk and went straight to the subject at hand. He was anxious to make some progress and then get back to his nap. But first he needed some information.

"Give me the news!"

"Okay, Victor, here it is. V-122 is communicating with its twin brother at 100 feet using millimeter wavelengths. Instantaneous temperature tracking and some color tracking were positive. It was a beautiful thing!"

"Some? What do you mean by *some*?"

Dallas hesitated for a moment searching for the right words. He knew that they were assuming that this line was secure in the sense that no one was listening, yet he just couldn't blurt out what he had to say.

"You could say that dark blue came out purple."

"Instantaneously?" asked Victor. The frequency of Laurie's voice had gone up an octave.

"Just as good as the temperature shift. I took plenty of films and checked the clocks. It's reproducible. And no contamination whatsoever! I know you're sensitive about that. When can we expect to see you in person for an onsite rerun? It's worth the price of a ticket, believe me."

Victor thought for a while. He wanted to go to California this very instant, but the little voices in his head were against it for some unknown reason.

"I've got to get the feds off my back first, Dallas. Say a week…maybe ten days. There is no real reason to hurry, is there? Just keep a low profile until I can get out of here. But, don't tell anyone that I'm coming. This is very important. Okay, I'll give you a shout when the time is right so you can pick me up."

"That's not all," whispered Pence before Victor could hang up. "They see each other between buildings...a hundred yards!"

"That's all I need to know right now. Say hello to Swanson for me."

With those words Victor hung up the phone. Beads of perspiration began to run down his forehead as an indication of his excitement. He even went to the trouble of carefully wiping his fingerprints off of the receiver and faceplate of the phone just in case he was followed. He stopped for a moment to consider whether his considerable paranoia was justified or not. No clear answer came to him.

After looking around again to assure himself that no one was monitoring his words, he sat back into his chair and wheeled himself out of the physics building back toward the safety of his office. He wanted to celebrate by jumping out of his wheelchair, yet he knew that he had to maintain a low profile just in case anyone was watching. He concluded that a little paranoia was a good thing. He always pondered the possibility that he was being watched, and the voices in his head seemed to agree.

On his way to the pay phone, he thought he had seen several unexplained shadows zipping through nearby bushes. Was it the U.S. or the Russians or...was he just actually paranoid as he had always suspected of himself? He'd always been a bit extra cautious even before this research had commenced so he couldn't answer the question one way or the other.

As a compromise to his desire to celebrate the success of the experiments, he began humming one of his favorite songs. It was 'Almost Cut My Hair' by David Crosby. The lyrics were so appropriate. As he wheeled his chair and sang under his breath, he hesitated for a moment to run his hands through his own long flowing black hair. When he got to the part that mentioned looking in his rear view mirror and seeing a police car, he shook his head and moved on at a much faster pace.

I can't let this get to me. We're on the verge of success! Instantaneous communication by the virus samples over great distances! But, there's much more work to do...much more work for me to do to reach my final goal! Those assholes in Houston were laughing at some of my suggestions last week. But soon, they'll be eating those words.

Back on the Stanford campus, Dallas Pence was walking back to his lab from a nearby pay phone at the student union. He actually enjoyed the cloak and dagger methods employed by his former mentor even though they did seem a little silly at times. It was getting dark and the scientist wanted to finish a few things and go to a movie with his girlfriend, Melissa. Because of the demands of the experimentation, it had been a few weeks since he'd taken some time off to relax, and he missed her presence and company very much. Her soft voice and pretty smile had a way of calming him down and making him forget his problems for a while.

He wanted to call Terry Swanson and update him, but he realized that his call could wait until tomorrow. Besides, his cell phone was far from secure. It was a typically beautiful evening in Northern California, and he wanted to see Melissa's face as soon as possible.

One thing he failed to notice as he approached the main chemistry building was a black limousine cruising slowly westward on Palm Drive and nearing the point where the drive split and the northern arm ran directly in front of the old chemistry building. As Pence began to enter the walkway leading to his office thinking about his conversation with Laurie, the limo stopped and the window came down presumably to permit the man in the front passenger seat to ask directions. This was not an uncommon occurrence since the old chemistry building was one of the first structures visitors would encounter when they were coming onto the campus from Palo Alto.

Being a friendly guy, Pence approached the vehicle, listened to the question, which had to do with directions and began to point west toward the physics department. Before he could complete his answer, there was a popping noise and the professor began to slump to the ground. Before he could collapse completely, two men jumped out of the vehicle, grabbed Pence and carefully moved his limp body into the back seat. Slowly, the vehicle turned around and headed back east towards the city of Palo Alto.

15

Alice in Wonderland

We have to toe the line, it's so hard to take the pace.
You're a better man than I in the perfect human race.
See the writing on the wall in the city's caves of steel.
Hear the echoes of the night, will the anger ever heal?

Under the Gun
Asia

Saint Catherine's Hospital
Washington, D.C.

The hospital room was dark. The lone patient struggled unsuccessfully with the restraints that held him down flat on his back to his treatment bed. The official record sheet that was attached to the foot of the bed identified him as Emil Francis Jensen. His home address was simply stated as Washington, D.C. Lines on the sheet intended for age, height, weight, blood type and physician data were blank. A religious indicator near the bottom of the form identified the patient's religion as Mormon. His eyes fluttered but remained closed, and he was grinding his worn false teeth ferociously. Thoughts flashed subconsciously through his head at a mile-a-minute pace.

Where am I? Cut me loose. Cut me loose now! I'll make you pay for this... whoever you are no matter how long it takes. Don't you know who I am for god's sake? I'll break these bindings with my mind if I have to. The FBI and the CIA will hear about this and come for you; you can count on that! My friends in Moscow and my friends in the sky will crush you and leave your putrid body to rot on the moon...in the dark and you will be frozen solid! They are more powerful than you can ever imagine in your small, useless mind. They will rescue me soon and make you pay big time for this indignity!

Senator Jensen took a deep breath, flexed his weak upper body muscles as best he could…and then with one more gasp for air, he passed out.

But his mind was still the center of furious activity during the tenure of his unconscious state. Before long he slipped slowly into a lavish dream state. But unlike the normal dreams experienced by most humans, his dreamscape was displayed in full Technicolor like a first run movie produced in a Hollywood studio. And he could hear voices talking to him from an unknown location that seemed very far away. In a way the voices were familiar, yet he couldn't identify them with any certainty.

I'm…I'm inside a spacecraft, and for some reason I know it's not on the ground! We're moving but there's no sound. It's like I'm…I'm orbiting the earth. At least that object down there…it looks like the earth from here. Is this Spacelab? Am I aboard Spacelab? I can see Washington…the Capitol Building…the White House… from here so clearly even though they are so far away.!

Sarah Palin said she could see Russia from her window in central Alaska, but I can see the whole earth from here…from wherever it is I am now. How did I get this far up in the sky without any effort? I don't remember being launched in one of those absurd spacecraft like that clown Professor Laurie was. Those bastards over at NASA must have kidnapped me and launched me just to serve their demented purposes? They will all pay for their sins! There is no gravity holding me down, but I can't get up off the floor. How can this be?

After some moments of silence a gentle voice told him that he was among friends, and that he should relax and enjoy the ride. It told him not to worry about where he was. He couldn't tell who was whispering to him, but soon that would change. He was the center of attention of the voices.

And now, I'm surrounded by a bunch of little machines…little robots. They're talking to me as if they know me! They're asking something about a package? That one just asked me where the package is. What package? How can he speak to me…a machine knows my name and who I am!

Now I see two men in space suits! They're taking off their helmets now just so I can see them. Their faces are so similar and so familiar. I know that we have met before…in Moscow. Yes, it was in Moscow! It was at the space treaty meeting several months ago or was it years ago? We had some drinks… some vodka together and talked about space travel. They are smiling at me and telling me to obey the little machine. They are saying that it is my friend, too.

The two men look almost the same…like twins. Yes, they are twins or must be twins, the same in every way except for their eyes.

Now he, the machine…it tells me that when I get back to earth, the first thing I must do is to retrieve the package and its contents. It tells me that the package contains some magic pills. Magic? What will this magic do to me or for me?

Retrieve the package from where? When will I get back to earth? 'Soon' he said with a friendly smile in his voice. Can robots smile?

The patient didn't realize it from his dream state, but the lights in the hospital room slowly came on and someone released the restraints on his hands and feet. As the patient turned over onto his side, his dream continued without interruption.

Now they're taking me down a hallway and into a room. It's so bright in here! My eyes are in pain, but I can't close them no matter how hard I try. Everything's white…I can hardly see! It's not a big room, but it has machines… electrical boxes…equipment all along each wall and even on the ceiling. How do I know that when I can't see anything with my eyes?

Why am I here? No one is answering my questions any more! The two spacemen are gone, but there are more little machines all around me. I'm too weak to go on. I can't feel my arms and legs any more! Even if I could move or run, I wouldn't know where to go from here.

Now they want me to sit down. I agree with them. I must to sit down before I fall down. I'm so tired…I'm going to sit down in the chair I see in front of me. It looks like the chair in my dentist's office. There is a mask like they used to use for laughing gas…and electrodes for my arms. I don't want them putting any of those on…

Suddenly, the space ship began shaking, slowly at first, then more and more violently. Fear coursed through the space traveler's veins once again as he felt the overpowering vibrations.

They've changed their minds! They're going to kill me instead, or we're going to crash! Something has gone all wrong with the spaceship! What did I do wrong to make this happen? How did I get here in the first place? Let me go! I must try to run…run far, far away!

Before long, Jensen's eyes popped wide open as he burst out of his dream state! His anxiety was painted all over his wrinkled face. Someone was talking to…yelling at him again in a human-like voice, but it wasn't a robot this time. It was someone standing over him!

"Senator Jensen, wake up, please. Don't be afraid. We are your friends. We are here to help you recover from your fears. Can you hear me? How do you feel? You were dreaming something…"

As Jensen passed slowly into normal consciousness, he noticed that his arms were flailing about as if he was punching an imaginary foe and his legs were thrashing about in a running motion, both involuntarily. His body ached all over from the unusual physical exertion he was experiencing. What made things worse was that he was not a man known to exercise at all. Somehow he knew that it was Dr. Mahadavan who was now restraining and shaking him, but he had never talked to or seen this man ever before in his life as far as he could remember.

How do I know him? And how does he know me! Is he with the robots? Are we still in space? Why doesn't someone answer me? Where is that little voice in my head that tells me everything I need to know? Where is it when I need it? When I need help and some answers, it's gone!

Before the patient could control his grunting and moaning and voice his complaints and questions out loud so they could be understood, the doctor spoke again in a soft friendly voice.

"Ah, you are finally with us again, Senator Jensen. You had us worried for quite a while there. You've been unconscious for an unusually long time. We feared for your life several times! Your pulse and blood pressure were behaving erratically to say the least. At times, it looked to us that you were in what we call a physical dream state with all of that thrashing about going on. For your own protection we had to bind your hands and feet to keep you safe from injuring yourself."

Jensen caught himself and decided to try and calm down both physically and mentally. Slowly, his legs ceased their violent motion and his arms lapsed to his sides. It was with great relief that he finally took a deep breath.

"Where am I?" Jensen asked in a soft rather meek voice that he rarely used as his eyes scanned the room with blurred vision for signs of the robots and spaceships being present.

"You are in Saint Catherine's Hospital, Senator. You had a personal mishap in Virginia…it's quite complicated, and we still do not have all of the facts. We'll explain all of that later when you feel better, and you can tell us what you remember about your experiences. Right now you need to reorient yourself physically and mentally before you get up out of bed. If you feel funny…dizzy just now, it's because you have been sedated somewhat heavily for several days. But, your vitals are beginning to look better except for your pulse and blood pressure surges. Actually, once we normalize those factors and after some much needed, peaceful sleep, you will probably want to get up and start moving around once again."

Jensen flashed back to his dream. It seemed so real even now. He remembered what he was told to do by the voices in his head.

"Do you have the package…my package? I must have the package!" Jensen voice stuttered quietly but firmly as his eyes opened wide.

A surprised look crossed the doctor's face as he listened to his patient's quite unexpected request.

"You know about the package?" whispered Mahadavan with surprise in his voice. This was a question the doctor hadn't expected and a response the senator hadn't expected. "How in the world…?"

"So, you do have the package…my package," Jensen replied calmly. "They will be glad to hear that fact. They are so worried about it and kept asking me about it over and over. It is my job to recover that package for them and return it."

"They?" whispered the doctor to his companions as he shrugged his shoulders, but as Jensen's eyes closed once again, Maha decided not to pursue the issue further at this time.

"You get some rest, Senator. We'll have an aide in the room should you need anything. If and when you feel better, you can expect some visitors with some questions for you. Your family and friends were very anxious about you to say the very least. You were unaccounted for…missing for several days, and they were quite concerned to say the least."

Soon, except for the aide seated near the door, Jensen found himself alone. It felt so good to him to be able to roll over onto his side, and soon he was sound asleep. Once again a soft voice stirred from inside his head. His mind was a complete blank, but the words were clear.

When I awaken, I must rise up and seek possession of the package. Inside I will find three cubes slightly bigger than sugar cubes like the ones my mother would place in her tea. I am to swallow the cubes, and I will be returned safely to the spacecraft. But I must find the cubes first to complete the transit.

With that, Jensen fell into a deep sleep. The next morning he awakened to the strains of some pleasant music. Dr. Mahadavan was sitting next to his bed reading the local newspaper as Jensen came to. Jensen then stole some thoughts from one of his favorite science-fiction books.

"The sleeper has awakened, Doctor Mahadavan," he whispered. "Please get my cubes…ah, my package for me. I need my spice immediately! I must return to the spacecraft and my friends."

Mahadavan was surprised by Jensen's comment, but he had anticipated this moment so next to him on a table sat the remains of Jensen's package. He began to explain why the package had been opened.

"Senator Jensen, considering your condition at the time, we took it upon ourselves to open your package under the assumption that it contained a prescription from your personal physician. Your medical records indicated several persistent medical conditions, which your physician in Oklahoma was treating. He faxed the medical information to us while you were sleeping. We also needed to be sure that our sedation didn't interfere with any prescription medications in your system. The wrong combination of chemicals could have proven disastrous for you."

Mahadavan handed what was left of the package to Jensen who was now sitting on the side of the bed. The senator carefully leafed through the wrappings stopping only to notice a misspelling of his name on the top address line. The return address label was absent, yet the senator could somehow see what had been there.

"Emile Jensen, huh? Whoever sent this sure doesn't know how to spell. That's very careless when addressing a United States Senator of my standing! I'll have to look into this personally."

Mahadavan reacted to the remark with a look of surprise and took it as an attempt at humor. He had wondered all along who the sender was, but that label had been torn off the package some time ago. Jensen's physician in Oklahoma had indicated that no package of this type had been forwarded from his office to Jensen.

"Don't you know who sent this to you?" asked Mahadavan just to be sure that his patient had considered the question carefully.

The senator didn't respond immediately, but only shook his head and didn't make eye contact with the doctor. His hands fumbled through the package wrappings several times unsuccessfully searching for its contents.

"You took them…the cubes…you took them! They were supposed to be for me alone! Find them and return them to me…now!"

"There was nothing in the package when we opened it, Senator," Maha replied calmly. "Three of us were present at the time when it was opened. It was empty when it arrived here at the hospital. No one here took its contents."

"You'll pay," mumbled the senator. "All of you will pay for this, believe me. They will make you pay when they return and that will be very soon! If I were you, I'd run away as quickly as…"

With those fading words Jensen slumped back prone on his bed and seemed to lose consciousness. Mahadavan retrieved the torn envelope from his hands and placed it in a nearby drawer. He then hastily scribbled some notes describing the senator's condition and his comments about the package and a spaceship and placed them in Jensen's medical folder for future reference.

As he opened the folder, he noticed a set of records he hadn't seen before. They were dated several months back and dealt with Jensen's strange behavior after he returned from a trip to Moscow. As Mahadavan read the file, his eyes opened wider and wider in disbelief. Apparently, the current episode was not the first time that the senator thought he was kidnapped by robots aboard a spaceship. This was much too interesting to ignore.

Better yet, the physician then stumbled across a computer disk marked *Do Not Release*. Maha placed the disk in his lab coat, returned the file to a nearby drawer, and moved carefully to his office where he locked the door and sat down at his personal computer. After a deep breath and a nod of his head, he placed the disk in the computer and searched its file directory. His attention was immediately drawn to a video file. Having come this far, there was no point in hesitating, so he ran the video to observe its contents.

It was a video taken in Moscow during the space conference. Jensen was seated near the center of six or seven others, presumably Russians. From the expressions on their faces, the participants seemed in no way to acknowledge that they knew the video was being taken.

What caught Maha's attention right off the bat was the young man sitting to Jensen's left. His eyes were an unusually bright blue, and Maha had seen his face before. He was a Russian cosmonaut! The two were carrying on a lively conversation when the cosmonaut handed the senator a small plastic container, which Jensen glanced at and then placed in his coat pocket. Unfortunately, the exchange was too quick for Maha to determine exactly what was in the container.

Soon the video was interrupted for some unknown reason. Maha quickly made a copy of the disk with all its files and moved back to Jensen's room where he returned the disk to the medical file after removing any possible fingerprints of his from the disk's surfaces.

Once again the physician returned to his office and slumped down into his desk chair. He knew he had to clear his mind because he had several important appointments that afternoon, but he also knew that he had to talk with someone…but who? Suddenly, the answer popped into his mind, and he picked up the phone and began dialing a long distance number.

16

When You Least Expect It

I can see by your coat that
You're from the other side.
There's just one thing I've got to know.
Can you tell me please who won?

Wooden Ships
Jefferson Airplane

Somewhere in Northern California

The room was dark…pitch black would be a more accurate description. The lone prisoner sat slumped over in a wooden chair. He was totally exhausted from struggling against the bonds on his hands and feet. Duct tape loosely covered his mouth and both of his eyes. His hands were cuffed together behind him and his arms were bound to the chair by ropes at each elbow. As he slowly regained complete consciousness, the prisoner could hear a mild and not unfriendly voice asking him a simple question.

"What is your name?" were the words he heard repeated several times by his male interrogator.

The prisoner tried to organize his thoughts, but only with great difficulty. Where was he? Who…was speaking to him? Why was he so unceremoniously bound and gagged? And who drugged him and with what foreign substance? He decided to play the game. As far as he was concerned, he had absolutely nothing to lose. He needed to find out what this was all about.

"My name…my name is Pence," he stammered through the duct tape, purposely freezing his jaw and lips so that the tape would be removed by his captors. In seconds the tape was gently pulled from his mouth and then, surprisingly, from his eyes. As he blinked his eyes in the darkness, a small light was turned on across the room, and he could immediately detect the presence of three figures standing around him. They stood silently obviously waiting for his response to question.

"Dr. Dallas Pence is my name!" he exclaimed firmly and with a flash of personal pride to his captors.

His answer seemed to satisfy his captors, and in seconds the normal room lights were turned on. Without any further words, one of the men standing near him approached his chair from the rear and began gently releasing his bindings. Soon, he was rubbing his wrists to revive the circulation in his hands and accepting a paper cup of cold water, which he drank quickly. As he did this, he wondered what had caused the sudden change in his prisoner status. Why had his captors relaxed so quickly once they knew who he was?

"Dr. Pence…we apologize for the unceremonious manner in which you were brought to this meeting. However, we have a rather significant problem, and we couldn't take any chances just in case we had the wrong man. Had you been someone else, we would have taken you back and released you but not identified ourselves. We mean no harm to anyone and definitely not to you.

"As it turns out, you may be able to help us as well as your fellow Americans and probably the whole world with a rather significant and serious problem. Please remain seated and look straight ahead while we have this conversation. Things will be explained in due course of our discussion. You may doubt this now, but we are actually your friends."

Pence couldn't see the face of the man who was speaking because he was standing behind the chair. He started his response with a conclusion.

"You're with the CIA or the FBI and you are investigating Professor Laurie for some reason! Right?'

"Very close, but it's more complicated than that," his host replied.

"More complicated? No one is more complicated than Victor!"

Pence did detect a slight accent in the man's speech, but he couldn't identify the speaker's country of origin. But as he thought about it, it was definitely not the United States. His voice had a definite European lilt to it.

"What…how…? Please explain in more detail. I'm very, very confused! I really have nothing to hide from anyone," Pence mumbled. "Tell me how I can help…and specifically who I can help?"

The man patted Dallas on his shoulder.

"I understand completely. You may call me Roger for the time being. That's not my real name as I'm sure you will guess very soon, but who I am is not at all important as you will come to see. I have personally read all of your research publications on viral research. I personally know several scientists who are working on a similar problem in another place...half way round the world at that. It is not our intention or their intention to steal any of your work; however, we have encountered a serious problem which... could threaten the existence of all of mankind. I am not exaggerating at all when I say those words!"

Roger paused to allow his allegations to reach their full effect, but the prisoner interrupted the silence immediately.

"How do you know about my research, and I don't know you? Scientists don't go around kidnapping each other...do they? I don't think I know a scientist or graduate student by the name of Roger. Wait...there's Roger Christianson, but you're not him. You're definitely not him. He's too chicken to pull off something as complicated as this operation."

Dallas paused as a cynical grin crossed his face and brow. He began laughing at himself as he considered the situation more abstractly. Unexpectedly, this was starting to be fun for him.

"That's it!" he shouted, causing the other men in the room to jump back in varying degrees. "This is a movie, and you wanted a realistic portrayal of the character I'm playing. Why didn't you just tell me? I'm not very expensive. We have a storage room in the old chemistry building that's something straight out of *The Count of Monte Cristo*! You know, the old jail the Count escapes from! That would work perfectly for...whatever your film is about?"

Roger held up his hand to silence Dallas for a moment.

"Let me explain, Dr. Pence, and believe me when I tell you that I admire your sense of humor, especially under the circumstances. We know a lot about your research with viral colonies. In particular, most interesting is the seemingly instantaneous communications between those colonies at a significant distance. Maybe I should mention your tachyon experiments, too? I'm not an expert in that area, but I know several people who are quite interested in that area of endeavor and with good cause."

Pence seemed stunned by his captor's knowledge especially since he had not yet mentioned tachyons in any of his publications.

"How...? Actually, I wish my students would pay as much attention to me as you seemingly have! But, I don't really understand completely.

If you're…spies, why would you spy on a little fish like me? You must be with the CIA? Seriously!"

"We have our ways of keeping up, Dr. Pence. But, let's stick with the subject…the problem…our problem. Everything will become clear in a short time. I promise you that much."

Pence nodded his head and sat back in the chair as he tried to relax. "This is almost as bad as going to the dentist!" he mumbled under his breath.

Roger gave his prisoner a moment and then continued.

"We have a viral research program of our own. Unfortunately, up to now our scientists never considered the possibility of communication between viral colonies. I know that you don't call them colonies, but we find that reference convenient. I hope that you don't mind me taking liberties with the nomenclature?"

Pence shook his head and shrugged his shoulders in agreement.

"One of our…their recent experiments seems to have run amok. The sample virus seems to have taken over complete control of its human host, and it seems to be communicating with an external source that we assume is also a virus. In layman's terms, they are talking to each other over a great distance."

"You're using a human host?" muttered Pence under his breath in disbelief. "That's really dangerous, isn't it? I mean, Victor Laurie's viral experiments are being conducted on Spacelab in orbit just so humans would not become a host! At least not willingly!"

Roger shrugged his shoulders sympathetically.

"I can only agree with your analysis of the situation. They didn't call me…or you, for that matter, in on this particular aspect until there was an actual problem. So, it seems that we're in the same boat…together. We have someone else's instigated science problem to solve…before it becomes our collective problem here on earth."

Something in what Roger said triggered Dallas' next response.

"Ah ha! There is only one way this can be happening. Laurie…Victor Laurie put you up to it. He's got a problem in Houston and didn't have the guts to just come out and ask me for help. That figures, all right. And he loves *Spy Game*…the movie! You come in here acting like a bunch of foreign agents…Russians? Cubans? Who cares! You pull a theatrical kidnapping, first class, I must admit. Then, you make it look like I'm the only one available who can save the world! Wow…this could be a movie!"

Pence started laughing again and put his head in his hands as he paused for a brief moment.

"Hell, yes! I'll do it! I'll kick Victor's ass later. Exactly how much did he promise to pay you for this theatre?"

Roger extended his hand, and they shook vigorously, but Roger did not confirm Pence's conclusion about his former professor.

"One thing, Dallas. You don't mind if I call you Dallas, do you?"

"Not at all," Pence replied. "After all, it is my name. Just don't call me Texas or Cowboy!"

"We have to keep this whole thing to ourselves for a while. Don't even admit to Laurie that you're involved with us or it might just queer the deal. You know how unpredictable he is at times. If this gets out to the public anywhere, we will have a full-scale panic on our hands on at least two continents."

Roger paused as another man handed the two men glasses of diet soda. Dallas was happy about that. He was hungry and thirsty to say the least.

"You weren't really at the bowling alley just before we picked you up… were you?" Roger asked with a smirk on his face.

That comment caught Pence before he could completely relax and his defense shields popped back up. Something was very wrong here. How did Roger know that detail about the phone conversation.

"Were you tapping Laurie's phone? Don't lie to me. You were, weren't you?" asked Pence calmly. "And all the time I thought he was just super paranoid. This explains quite a bit."

"I apologize, Dallas, but we have to take certain precautions as I said. It turns out that we have reason to believe that Professor Laurie may possibly have been infected by a test virus on his recent journey into space. The particular virus in question is relatively benign…we believe it is benign, and our people tell me it can't easily be passed along. Still, it is our obligation to watch the good professor until we can examine and treat him properly if we are right about the situation.

"Of course, when you spoke with him, we were listening to every word. I'm sorry about that. I thought that mentioning the bowling alley was a good way to introduce the subject of Laurie's surveillance. I wanted you to be fully aware of our presence and purpose. In a matter of days this will be all over…I hope, and it will have a happy ending as Hollywood would say!"

"I appreciate that," said Pence, although deep inside his shaky trust in these men who seemed to be working for the United States began slipping.

He told himself not to pass on any of his recent experimental results until he was alone with Laurie…really alone with him.

"What else do we need to do here?" Pence asked. "I'll be glad to help in any way I can, particularly if it means protecting the public. But I also have a life and things to do, believe it or not."

"Thanks for your understanding," Roger replied. "Fred here will drive you to the local library where two of our chief scientists are waiting to speak with you in private. They will explain the technical situation more fully and much better than I could ever describe it. Afterwards, we will drop you off wherever you want to go. Fred has been instructed to buy you and the two science guys dinner and drinks if you are hungry. It's the least we can do after all of this weird and unannounced activity."

After shaking hands again with Roger, Dallas stretched his arms and legs, and was then escorted out to a waiting car to begin the next part of his adventure. Once Roger was certain that the car had left, he turned to a man who was standing in the shadows behind him.

"Yuri, I believe he thinks we're CIA. I tried my best to make my accent sound phony. As long as this illusion holds, Moscow won't crush our asses! But, his cooperation is essential to the success of this mission. With Yengoyan on the loose with that virus in his head, it is impossible to tell just how long it will be before we have a major outbreak on our hands or worse.

"And, to make things more complex, our friend, the senator, is missing again! And I do mean again. He's like a slippery loose cannon to say the least. For a supposed ally, he's turned out to be a huge liability to us…to me in particular. I'll be surprised if we all get out of this thing alive!"

17

Where is Sherlock?

Here we are now going to the west side,
weapons in hand as we go for a ride.
Some may come and some may stay,
watching out for a sunny day,
where there's love and darkness and my sidearm!

South Side
Moby

Somewhere Near London, England

His eyes wouldn't focus at first, and he had what is sometimes referred to as double vision that attempted blinking couldn't overcome immediately. He remembered an old song with that title by a group called Foreigner, and he began humming it while he pondered the irony of his situation. The images he perceived were blurry and meaningless. Worse yet, his eyelids wouldn't open all the way. There were blobs of darkness and shafts of light everywhere in his jumbled mind.

He felt certain that he could feel his feet bearing the weight of his thin body, yet he wasn't standing. His hands were cold and numb from a lack of circulation, and his left arm was completely asleep. He could move the fingers on his right hand a bit but not in a normal way. He tried to make a fist with that hand, but that failed, too.

Slowly, he dragged his arms over his lap and shook them trying to revive his feelings. His arms quivered at first and after a few minutes of effort some control returned to his limbs. He was finally able to correctly sense that he was sitting down...almost lying down on something uneven and soft.

He decided to start over from the very beginning. It was the best he could do under the circumstances. First, he took a long deep breath. That seemed to help quite a bit. Then and very slowly over a few minutes, first the left and then the right eyelids rolled back to their normal position so that he could actually see. To his great surprise he found that he was looking straight up at what looked like an early evening sky. It was definitely getting dark, but his awareness of sight caused him to calm down and relax slightly. At least he seemed to be in one piece, as far as he could tell. One deep steady breath continued to follow another.

But, the obvious questions kept coming into his thoughts. Exactly where in the world was he? And how did he get here in the first place… wherever he was?

All he could clearly remember from his recent past was an ominous vibration that seemed to perturb his body and his mind. It was a slow shaking that increased in frequency and magnitude accompanied by a rumbling noise and then it slowed to a stop again without explanation. He had experienced this phenomenon more than once before…but where, and when and what did it mean?

He knew that he had to relax and think carefully about everything he remembered as he allowed his body to recover. He had to put all the pieces together somehow and in the proper order if that was possible. He knew it wouldn't be easy, but somehow he sensed that his very mortal existence…his life depended on it. And he also somehow knew that time was running out! He rolled his head back and forth and stared up into the darkening sky.

Then he saw it! A flickering half-moon shone dimly in the distance just above the shadowy trees. There were no sources of light on the ground, just in the sky. He was in a forest…but where?

Suddenly, he wanted to leap up and run; unbelievably, at the same time he wanted to go back to sleep as an escape. Confusion reigned supreme in his scrambled mind. His thoughts…his mind's occupants were jumbled… disorganized as they fought amongst themselves for attention. The streaks of light became muffled sounds as if someone were playing a big bass drum in the distance. Next, amongst the clatter there was a single voice there inside his head, a voice that sounded familiar as if he had heard it before. The voice was whispering a question that he could barely hear, but he did understand.

What is your name?

He searched his confused mind for the answer, but there was no clear response from his memory. *How could I not have a name?* he wondered to himself. The voice did not respond.

"Where am I?" he mumbled aloud and with a touch of anger through frozen lips. He waited, but there was no response from the voice inside his head. Why wouldn't it answer him? Why was he being treated like this? He knew he had committed no crime, but he felt like a fugitive.

Slowly but surely, he tried to lift his body off of the ground. Unfortunately, his efforts failed and after six or seven serious tries, he slumped back down against the tree that had become his only support, banging his head against it for good measure. Gravity was much too powerful a force for him to overcome. He was lost and trapped with no way to accomplish an escape and no one to rescue him!

Just as he was about to give up, that's when it happened! His last fall back against the hard unyielding bark of the tree that was his support must have jarred something loose in his confused mind. Suddenly and without explanation, two names simultaneously popped into his memory.

Rosenkrantz and *Guildenstern*!

For some reason the names immediately seemed very familiar to him. Somehow over the succeeding moments, he remembered their story as if it were a movie playing in his head. He could see their faces…the faces of the actors Gary Oldman and Tim Roth in the old movie. His first reaction was to cry out for help…for them. Their fate awaited them much as his own fate awaited him…unknown!

At that very moment not thirty yards away, a boisterous group of students from a local university was making its way through the underbrush in the park. The students were on their way to a local pub where they knew they could get served without restriction. They were laughing, singing and jumping up and down because they had just completed a rigorous set of final examinations. It was certainly a time to celebrate and they were bound and determined to do so!

Suddenly, one of their number named Alex turned toward the group and stopped short, threw his hands up into the air and requested silence. A strange sound was coming from the nearby vegetation.

"Listen!" he shouted. "Do you hear it? There's a voice out there coming from the wood!"

Of the nine students only one continued his loud celebration, which was soon halted by the rest. Moments later Alex turned to his left and pointed into the woods toward the spot where the sounds were coming from.

"There! It's…I believe that he's saying *Help me, Rosenkrantz*! By God, this is straight out of Shakespeare! Can we be drunk this far from the bar and having had absolutely nothing to drink?"

After a few more seconds, there it was again for all to hear loud and clear.

Help me, Rosenkrantz!

"Watch out!" yelled a student named Fred. "It could be my nutty literature professor, Dr. Orville, setting a trap for us. He's just the type to pull a prank like this after we've completed our finals just so he could get some free alcohol…from us, of course. They say that when he was on sabbatical a few years back, he got three traffic tickets for driving under the influence in a single month. So, he's a dangerous fellow."

Alex grabbed Fred by the shoulder, and they jumped into the bushes together to find the source of the cries. In seconds they encountered the form of a man propped up against a rather large tree. Quickly, matches were struck so that they could see the man's face. He appeared to be quite unconscious.

"Let's get him out of here…to the road," Gretchen commanded after she saw the stranger's condition. "We can call an ambulance from the pub! He must be alive, but he seems totally out cold. He's probably just a drunk who lost his way. We should let this be a lesson to us."

As they struggled to pick him up, the man's eyes popped wide open, and he tried to smile at his rescuers. Slowly, he started to speak in a loud whisper.

"I knew you would come for me, Rosenkrantz!" he muttered with a noticeable accent. "Hold me and let me try to walk on my own if I can. I'm able to feel my feet and legs again. I'm just a little wobbly for sure. And I'm very thirsty, too. Would you have a drink of water on you by any chance? It would help strengthen my resolve."

Alex nodded as he brushed the man's hair out of his face.

"We can fix that in a reasonably short time," said Alex as the man took his first steps through the underbrush with Fred and George propping up his shoulders. Soon the group was back on the main path and headed toward the pub. Little was said during the journey as the students took turns holding the man upright. With each step he became more steady and sure-footed.

Soon, to everyone's satisfaction, the Wooster Pub was in sight. The man from the forest had regained a lot of his mobility and was now able to walk with the aid of the arm of just one student. After negotiating the doorway and finding a large unoccupied table on the north wall of the building, the party of ten took its place. Alex and Gretchen sat on either side of their newly found guest.

"Are you up for a beer, sir?" asked Alex. The man nodded, but then he apologetically stated that he thought he had no money on him with which to pay for the libation.

"That's not a problem," Gretchen replied with a friendly smile. "You're our special guest for the evening. We are celebrating the end of final exams, and we would welcome your help in that celebration."

"Pardon me," Alex interjected, "but we don't even know your name yet. I'm Alex and the pretty lady is Gretchen. What should we call you?"

The man stared at Alex and began shaking his head.

"I know this is very crazy, but I don't exactly...remember my name right at this minute. Ah...okay, I'm Guildenstern...right? That's the best I can do. I know that I must have a real name, but my mind is a complete blank in that area right now!"

At that point the man started to frantically search through his pockets. Suddenly, he stopped and took a deep breath. Slowly but surely, he began to place items he had pulled from his pockets on the table in front of him as if he was not exactly sure what he had in his possession. His new friends watched with great interest.

A folded piece of paper, some money but it wasn't English currency, an unused airline ticket, a passport, a plastic bottle with pills in it, and a compass followed by a watch and the stub of a pencil, placed neatly in front of him for all to see. Alex hesitated and then slowly unfolded the paper, which bore the title *Saint Petersburg Military Hospital*. To his obvious surprise the words on the sheet were written in Russian which he had no trouble understanding.

"Here's your name," said Gretchen as she pointed to the center of the page. "I've had a little Russian so I can read some of this. Your first name is Leon! I can't quite make out the last name. Let me take a look at the passport to see if your last name is clearer there."

The mention of the name rolled across the man's brain like a tornado! He threw up his arms and his face suddenly wore a broad smile.

"I'm not Guildenstern after all...I'm Leon Yengoyan! I'm...I was a Russian spy in Germany and Holland some time in the past. Then I served

Mother Russia as a jet pilot and a cosmonaut. Then one day the Central Command called me to Saint Petersburg, and they…drugged me as my reward for services rendered. They drugged me! I can't remember anything else right now except a lot of shaking and strange voices rolling around in my head.

"Where am I? How did I get here? If I might ask, who are you? You all have English accents…I think? Please do not be afraid of me. I am just very confused to say the least!"

A serious quiet fell over the nine friendly faces as they realized, one by one, that their guest was serious in his uncertainty and cries for help. He had convinced them that he wasn't just a wayward drunk who got lost in the woods after a binge. His mystery was now their mystery.

"Leon…you're in…near London," whispered Alex. "Are you Russian by any chance? That's what your passport indicates, and you are able to read Russian."

"More or less," mumbled Leon as he continued to search his pockets. "As I said, I feel very alone and confused right now. Ah…I don't mean alone at all. You have helped me very much with your friendship. But, I'm very confused."

"Your English is good, too," Gretchen offered in a sympathetic and calming tone. "I would have guessed that you were an American or a Canadian except for the pronunciation of a few words you spoke out there."

"Thanks, I've had a lot of language training…I think. I must admit that English is easier to communicate in than Russian. Well, at least for me anyway. But I don't recall how I learned the language or why I learned the language. I can speak a little French and German, too, but not a lot. I don't think I've ever been to England before, but I remember a little of Paris and Berlin and Frankfurt. How could I not know where I am or where I've been or how I got here?"

Leon began to feel more secure as he sipped some beer from his glass and slowly participated in several rounds of shots with his newfound friends. The equivalent of a jukebox was busy cranking out classic rock music, mostly by the Rolling Stones and the Dave Matthews Band. Chips and salsa were the main snack provided by the bar. Leon realized that he was indeed very hungry!

After about forty-five minutes of relaxing, Gretchen walked over to Leon who was now sitting at a small table and made a suggestion.

"We've got a couple joints, Leon. The back room is open and safe. The owner lets us use it, no questions asked. Would you like to join us for a toke or two? You might really enjoy it."

Suddenly, the voice in Leon's head gasped an ominous command.

"No more alcohol, Leon! And no cannabis either! Leave this place now! You do not belong here!"

The voice was not as forceful as usual, and its words were slurred in a somewhat comical manner. Leon noticed this immediately.

Can't take a drink, can you! thought Leon to himself, knowing that the voice would hear his thoughts. *Let's see how a little bit of Mary Jane works on you, Mister Voice!*

Leon literally jumped from his seat and was on his way to the back room with Alex and Gretchen before his subconscious visitor could react to his threat. Quickly, a joint was passed to Leon who vaguely recalled doing this same thing before over across the English Channel in Holland. The voice kept trying to intervene, but it was unsuccessful and soon faded away as the drug took its effect. Leon's body and mind both relaxed and soon his memory started to return. He was now alone with himself inside his head. The voice in his head had somehow been blocking his long term memory.

"I know that you'll think that I'm crazy, but I'm certain that I'm part of some strange experiment," he whispered to his companions. "I'm not kidding. The grass has cleared my brain and part of my memory has returned, but I still don't know how I got here...got to England from wherever I was. I do remember being on a spaceship...an American spacecraft up in earth orbit. Somehow, they...someone planted a virus in my head. It took control of my mind. But the alcohol and the reefer must counteract its effects. The voice...there was a voice in my head telling me what to do...the voice is gone for now. I don't know if I'm permanently in the clear or not. I probably owe you my life for helping me."

Alex turned to Gretchen and asked her if she had any more joints. He wanted to give Leon several for future protection from the voice inside his head.

"I'm afraid that those were the last ones. We won't see Phillippe or Jasper until the weekend. They're on the continent right now."

Alex shrugged his shoulders and patted Leon on the back.

"Don't worry," whispered Leon. "Now I know what to do should the little bastards creep into my head again. How about a round of beer on me, and then I'd better get going. There are a couple of American bills in that cash I had in my pocket."

Gretchen looked carefully at Leon's face as she posed a question.

"I've seen you somewhere before, haven't I. It was on the TV I believe. Do you have a brother who is also a cosmonaut? As I remember, you are twins. That's probably why I remember you."

Leon slowly began nodding his head.

"I think you are correct. My brother is named…Tomas, but I have trouble seeing his face. My memories of him are coming back but only slowly. He has disappeared, but I'm not sure of that. Command…the Russian government has denied it…to me. I remember asking where he was. They had no answers for me. They're the ones who put the voices in my head. I must get to the embassy tomorrow and demand that they tell me the truth. We were training for a space mission together…to the moon, but they cancelled it or at least they told me I wasn't going on the mission. They wouldn't tell me why! I performed all of the test procedures with no faults.

"I got the feeling that they didn't trust me for some unknown reason. I must confront them and find my brother."

Leon sipped more of his beer trying to relax himself.

"Do you have a place to stay?" asked Alex. "Our friend Allen left for home right after the tests were over. His room is open for tonight for sure. You can get some rest and a fresh start tomorrow."

Leon thought for a moment, then nodded his agreement.

"I accept your kindness, Alex. Besides, the embassy won't be open… for me at least, until tomorrow. Let's get that beer and let tomorrow take care of itself!"

18

Brothers in Arms

*Through these fields of destruction, baptisms of
fire, I've witnessed your suffering as the battles
raged higher. And though they hurt me so bad
in the fear and alarm, you did not desert me.*

Brothers in Arms
Dire Straits

Saint Catherine's Hospital
Washington, D.C.

The black limousine slowly pulled up through the rain near the emergency
room entrance to the hospital. The driver dutifully parked the vehicle and
opened a large black umbrella just before he reached for the rear door
handle. After the door was opened, a man dressed in a dark suit adorned
with an impressive congressional badge stepped from the vehicle carrying
a briefcase and a sheath of freshly cut roses. A gold-lined card was attached
to the flowers; the outer envelope was addressed to Senator Emil Jensen.

The man in the suit staggered several times before regaining his balance
with the help of the driver who seemed to expect the instability. Then, after
a short hesitation, he strode confidently under the umbrella held by the
driver toward a side door marked 'Staff and Official Visitors Only'. After
entering the door on his own the official visitor approached the security
guard stationed at the front desk and handed her his badge while laying
the briefcase and roses on the desk.

"I'm here to see Senator Emil Jensen. I'm currently his advisor on
foreign affairs. Several urgent matters have come up in his absence from

the capitol, and I need to discuss these matters with him in private…if that's possible. Some items are…for his eyes only."

Having been through this many times before, the guard smiled, checked the photo on the visitor's security badge and ran a photocopy of the badge on a small copier to her left. Then she accessed a database on her desktop terminal to locate the senator.

"He's in the fourth floor post-op recovery area, Sir. You should first go to room 340, which is Dr. Mahadavan's office. He is the treating physician. He will determine if the senator has recovered sufficiently to have visitors. I've sent him an alert, Mr. Constantine, notifying him that you will be up there to consult with him in several minutes. Here, take this floor map, which shows how to get to his office. Just take the elevator to the third floor and exit to your left. Room 340 is straight ahead from that point. Dr. Mahadavan will be looking for your arrival."

The visitor thanked the security guard with a few mumbled words, accepted the paperwork, picked up the briefcase and flowers, and began to head for the elevator. Suddenly, he stopped dead in his tracks.

"Did you want to inspect my briefcase before I go upstairs?" he asked politely over his shoulder.

"Oh, no, but thank you for your consideration. You were scanned when you walked through the door. With government officials often in this hospital, we have to be very careful so our surveillance is automatic and quite advanced technically. Thank you for your concern."

Constantine nodded that he understood and headed for the main elevator although his strides were somewhat wobbly. Soon, he was on the third floor headed straight for Mahadavan's office. As he walked, he softly patted his briefcase as a smile broke out on his face. Upon approaching Mahadavan's office, he could see the doctor standing outside the door conversing with another man. Soon, they both spotted his approach and waved him on.

"Mister Constantine, I'm Dr. Mahadavan and this is Ollie, one of the senator's aides…well, almost an aide," the physician said as he chuckled and patted Ollie on the back. The visitor responded in a friendly manner.

"It's my pleasure to meet you. I'm with NASA stationed at Redstone Arsenal in Northern Alabama. I'm the senator's eyes and ears down there. As you might know, the senator is quite an activist when it comes to our space programs and particularly when a project involves our foreign allies and even more so when it involves someone who's not particularly an ally of ours. Well, in a nutshell, the latter is the reason why I'm here. Is he conscious and coherent?"

Mahadavan smile and nodded.

"Come in and have a cup of coffee," offered the doctor. "The senator has had a rough morning and is just recovering from several injections that were necessary, yet quite unpleasant for him. This delay will give him some much needed time to clear his mind and re-orient himself to the real world and his responsibilities. I feel like I should warn you that he's not in a real good mood after what he's been through prior to arriving here in an ambulance."

Constantine gladly accepted the doctor's offer, and the three men took seats around a conference table inside the office. After some small talk, Mahadavan posed some basic questions to the visitor.

"If I might ask, how well do you know Senator Jensen? I guess I should have asked how well you are acquainted with him on a personal level. The reason I ask is that it would be nice to administer some tests to him with a friendly face in the room. He might relax his defenses and give some honest answers if someone he trusted were present. It's for his own good with regard to his treatment regime and could save him weeks of rehabilitation."

Constantine shrugged his shoulders and pursed his lips. The answer was not what Mahadavan expected.

"We've actually never met...in person. He hates the field. That is, he requires that we come to him as opposed to having him visit our station. He hasn't visited Redstone once during my tenure there, and he has never requested my presence in Washington up to now. We keep most of our projects out of his sight just to keep him from ranting and raving. All his operatives will tell you the same general story.

"But, he'll know me by name because I always give him a lot of...crap when he vetoes our stuff. But it's been phone and mostly email. He won't do anything like internet conferencing. And, in particular, I think he hates me if it's possible to personally despise someone you've never met?"

Mahadavan smiled at Ollie who was shaking his head in agreement. All of Ollie's interactions with Jensen had been quite negative.

"We're definitely talking about the same man here. I think you might as well talk to him alone, at first at least. He doesn't particularly like physicians either. I'll walk you to the door of his room and point you in. From there, you're on your own. All I can say is *Good Luck and Godspeed!*"

They finished their coffee, and the doctor took his visitor to the door of Jensen's room.

"Let me check briefly to make sure he's okay," whispered Mahadavan. "I don't want him pulling any surprises on you."

Mahadavan slipped into the room and found the patient fast asleep. The doctor quietly left the room noting to himself that it might be advantageous to have the visitor awaken Jensen.

After some encouraging words, Mahadavan departed leaving Constantine alone to encounter the slumbering Senator Jensen. Quietly, the visitor shut the door behind him and sat down next to the bed where Jensen was reposed. Almost immediately Jensen sensed the presence of another person next to his bed. This was not due to his actual physical presence. No, it was a voice in the senator's head talking to someone else that awakened him.

Jensen's eyes popped open as if on command. He immediately recognized the face of his visitor.

"Yengoyan! What are you...you're not Yengoyan! But, you look just like him except...except for the tattoo!"

"Very observant, Senator" responded the visitor. "My twin brother, Leon, has a birthmark right here on his neck. I have this tattoo instead. But, you are wrong about me. My real name actually is Yengoyan. You should know this from your visit. The only difference is that my first name is Tomas. Leon and I are twins...maybe I should say *were* twins. But that's a story for another time. I don't want to overload you with information considering your condition.

"You haven't seen Leon lately, have you Senator? Even now some of his best friends and some of his worst enemies are frantically looking for him. As I recall from our childhood, that boy could never stay out of trouble."

Jensen just shook his head negatively as he began to mumble to himself in a gruff and hollow voice.

"And, which are you, my strange visitor? Are you friend or foe? Get out of my head right now, will you! Get out now!" he cried. Jensen calmed down only when his visitor placed the palm of his left hand on the patient's forehead. The hand was cold yet comforting.

"Let's get down to business. Where is the package we sent you, Senator? That's why I'm here. This is no joke. It would take me too long to explain the gory details. That package is very important to say the least. You will not be able to perform your tasks for us without the contents. And, if you cannot perform your chosen tasks, you become very expendable!"

Jensen held up his right hand to stop Tomas before he could finish. With his left hand he pointed toward the drawer of a small dresser next to his bed. That drawer contained what his visitor was looking for.

"Take it! Take the whole thing! By the way, it was empty...completely empty. The voice kept screaming for it, but the package was empty! There were witnesses when it was opened. They have no reason to lie. I have no reason to lie."

Tomas carefully opened the drawer and pulled the pieces of shredded wrapping paper and cardboard out, placing them on the patient's empty food-tray for examination. He methodically leafed through and studied each of the pieces one by one. At one point he put the cardboard up to his nose for a good smell.

"It was here, Senator. Someone removed the contents before they gave the package to you. I know it wasn't you. Do you believe that this fellow Ollie did it?"

Before Jensen could answer, Tomas continued.

"Of course, not! Well, probably not. He wouldn't be here...so relaxed, if he had the compound in his possession. The only other person who knew that I mailed the pills to you was...my brother. I wonder...?"

Tomas stood still for ten seconds pondering the possibilities.

"Well, I've got to find those contents and quickly so I'm going to be leaving you for now. First, let me give you a little present from our mutual friends. This will relax you and relieve some of the strain."

Tomas took a paper cup filled with water and added some crystals hidden in the handle of his briefcase. As Jensen began sipping the liquid, his guest began singing the words to his favorite Lynyrd Skynyrd song.

Angel of Darkness is upon you. Stuck a needle in your arm. So take another toke, have a blow for your nose. One more drink, fool, will drown you. Now they call you Prince Charming. Can't speak a word when you're full of ludes. Say you'll be all right come tomorrow, but tomorrow might not be here for you. Oh, that smell! Can't you smell that smell? The smell of death surrounds you!

"You can't leave me, Tomas," whispered Jensen. "I need you! We need you! Earth needs you...! Our friends..."

Senator Jensen slumped back on the bed...seemingly unconscious.

19

Missing in Action

When I was younger, I was hard to hold;
seems like I was always going whichever
way the wind would blow. Now that
traveling spirit calls me again, calling
me back to where it all begins.

Back Where It All Begins
Allman Brothers Band

Siberian Listening Post

Time seemed to slow down to a crawl for Vlady and Zeg as the routine of their repetitive assignments set in following their enjoyable evening of heavy drinking at the local pub. The very much needed relaxation did both of them a world of good. At least there seemed to be no more voices running around in Vlady's head. What made these men relax even more was the fact that message traffic with Moscow made no more mention of either of the missing cosmonauts. This was quite a relief for both Zeg and Vlady. All seemed to be settling down to the usual boredom of a bureaucratic job in the middle of nowhere.

Vlady's primary interest was still the orbiting American space laboratory and its mechanical passengers. Activity aboard Spacelab was slow and predictable as the robots went about their business like...robots. The essential presence of the secret Russian transmitter remained undetected by the Americans and all seemed to be rolling along without hitch. However, Koslov had made an interesting yet disturbing observation and thought it was time to tell Zeg all about it. The incident was something he had mentioned before but just in passing. During a lull in their conversation, Vlady brought the subject up for review.

"Our weather satellite…ah, spy satellite, has been photographing the American Spacelab as you already know, Zeg. Some strange things seem to be happening up there…not on the inside, but externally. I mean outside on the surface of the orbiting American laboratory. First, the space vehicle started wobbling…for no apparent reason during one of the photographic sequences. And I do mean that the vibration was quite visible."

"Wobbling?" countered Zeg shaking his empty left hand just as he was about to sit down to translate some coded transmissions from headquarters.

"Yes, as if it had just docked itself with something of considerable mass, but there were no other craft in the area at the time. At least nothing we or the cameras could see. But, that's not the very best thing about this anomaly."

"Oh, Vlad, old friend, go ahead. I can take it," countered Zeg jokingly as he slapped Vlady on the back.

Koslov nodded as he pointed to a group of photos on his desk and began his explanation..

There are two sets of stars just over the aft aileron of Spacelab. *Sirius Major* is on the left of *Sirius Minor*, at least from the satellite's perspective, which doesn't change with each orbit. By the way, I just made up those names for these two star clusters. I have no idea what they really are, but that doesn't really matter here, trust me. I left my astronomy book in Petersburg on a small sailboat I acquired recently so you have no choice unless you can come up with better names for them.

"However, in these two photographs that I've got right here…right here on the desk, they've suddenly reversed positions on me, and the micro-image is distorted just a little as if there were something like a lens between them and the satellite. Then, in the next photo and in subsequent ones, it's back to normal for the star clusters. I'd say I was drinking too much vodka and seeing things except that it's recorded on film and time-stamped, too! Our cameras do not drink vodka as far as I know."

Zeg didn't seem too impressed at first, but then it happened when Zeg strolled over toward his desk.

Zeg could be seen mumbling to himself as he stood by the desk and then sat down. He even slammed his fist down hard enough for Vlady to notice. Slowly, Zeg again rose from his chair and made a beeline straight to where Vlady was working before he spoke.

"Remember that communication I showed you last week, Vlady? Cosmonaut Yengoyan was missing, the second one…the twin, and then supposedly sighted aboard Spacelab by the Americans even though our sensors showed nothing at all? Well, it showed the little star reversal you just mentioned, but nothing really ominous. Then, everything quieted down real nice as it should. No more ghosts. No more voices. Nothing else suspicious?

"Well, guess what?"

Vlady shrugged his shoulders and prepared for the worst not knowing where Zeg's outburst was leading.

"I guess we were too lucky for it to last very long. I just translated the latest message from the boys back in Saint Petersburg. You remember… the missing cosmonaut…Yengoyan…? Don't ask me which one! He just popped up on the radar screen…in London of all places! Well, near London anyway. He's alive, too. No ghostly entrails. No fearless phantom of our… their imaginations."

Vlady was surprised by this turn of events even though he shouldn't have been and immediately tried to figure out what had happened. He still didn't understand how this information related to the star reversal.

"So the viral detection system they accidentally mentioned in the message actually worked?" Vlady responded. "That's a first. The little guys they must have put in this cosmonaut's head squealed on him? Now, that's news, at least for the scientists! But how does that effect us?"

Zeg shook his head.

"Not quite. He stopped in at the embassy…our embassy. They're still trying to figure out how he got there. What I mean is how he got to London. And, of course, he slipped away from the embassy before they realized that Command was frantically looking for him."

Vlady yawned and stretched his arms over his head and smiled.

"Well, anyway, it's not our problem anymore…is it? As long as he's not onboard the American spacecraft…we're in the clear!"

Zeg stood there shaking his head negatively.

"Wrong again, Comrade Vlady! Something took him up into space and brought him back again. Something no one has seen with eyes or cameras.

"As a result of these events, we have been selected by the powers that be to save the day. I mean you and me! You're not going to believe this.

"We're supposed go to England as soon as possible…the English word is 'pronto', and find this elusive soul and drag him back to Saint Petersburg in one piece without anyone else noticing. Sounds simple, doesn't it? Have you done your laundry recently?"

Vlady couldn't believe what he was hearing from his partner. How could he and Zeg, good engineers at best, be qualified by Command for this type of cloak and dagger operation? And, they were almost a third of the way around the world from their apparent objective to boot. It was almost impossible for him to imagine.

"How can this be…we're a million miles away, and I'm not a spy, or at least I don't think I'm a spy!"

"Well," said Zeg, "first of all, you have a prestigious degree from Oxford University. Meanwhile, I just completed a comprehensive English language speech course. It's a no-brainer for Command! We're practically Shakespearean actors as far as they are concerned. We're all that Command has got, and we work real cheap. Dammit, I want my salary to double for this and be paid in pounds!"

Koslov slumped back in his chair to attempt to settle himself down; however, the thought of leaving this rather uninhabited part of Russia for a hip city like London began to appeal to him despite the impossibility of the assignment. In a few seconds he wanted to put on his dancing shoes! That's when he heard it again. It was weaker than before, but he recognized the voice in his head immediately.

Go to London, it whispered to him. *Yen awaits us.*

Yen? Vlady thought to himself. *The voice in my stupid head is calling the missing cosmonaut by the name Yen? I wonder…is it Yen I or Yen II?*

Zeg could see that Vlady seemed to be having a debate with himself over the situation. He immediately realized that there was nothing unusual about this under the circumstances.

"Vlady, Baby! We're in this together. Hand in hand! Neck and neck! Tell me what you're thinking about right now. We have to trust each other ahead of anyone else…no exceptions! We are definitely 'best buddies' forever. Our lives depend on it! And you have to show me where the good looking women hang out near Oxford and London!"

Koslov looked Zeg straight in the eyes as he answered.

"Zeg, remember when I mentioned to you that I thought I was hearing things that weren't there?"

Zeg nodded cautiously but didn't speak.

"What did we do just after I told you that? Do you remember?"

"Vodka and lots of it," answered Zeg without hesitation as a huge grin spread across his face.

A big smile exploded on Koslov's face, too.

"I need another treatment and right now. Put the transceiver on automatic…we're going into town for a few shots and maybe more. Then, I'll tell you some interesting details to consider. I just don't want them to hear what we're saying."

Zeg knew better than to hesitate or ask any questions, so in less than a minute the two men were headed for Zeg's car for the trip into town, which was only twenty minutes away. Once past the security fence and guard post, Zeg took a deep breath as he considered the strange situation that was unfolding before him and his partner. He knew that he never could have predicted something like this.

"Vlady, we have a few problems the likes of which most people luckily will never encounter no matter how long they live. But, let me feel a glass of vodka between my fingertips before you completely spill the beans. Did you like that? *Spill the beans!* How about *Spill your guts!* That's why those bureaucrats in Moscow and Saint Petersburg are sending me to England! I know exactly what those colloquial things mean, and they have no damn idea!"

Vlady smiled in approval, but he was still very worried about something. He didn't know Zeg that well, but he trusted him completely nevertheless. He had considered the possibility that Zeg was a plant by Command, yet that didn't make any sense. Until recently, he knew that he had no secrets anyone else would want to know except maybe the one about the hidden transmitter. Zeg could certainly be trusted.

Soon, the two Russians were seated in the local bar at a booth near the front window where they could keep an eye on the surroundings. Vlady watched the locals move up and down the main street as Zeg got up and retrieved the vodka for them from the bar. In a minute or so the two men were seated across from each other toasting their still undefined future. After the first round of drinks Zeg proposed a question to his partner.

"Have you ever met Doctor Alexi Karpov? He's currently working in Saint Petersburg."

Vlady hadn't expected this question, but he searched his memory. The name seemed somewhat familiar.

"I used to work for the man in Moscow," Zeg whispered. "He got me promoted to this position with a nice bump in pay. He's a physician, but he also has a degree in biochemistry. But best of all he was always straight with me. That's why I'm so worried about his communication we received!"

Vlady was all ears. He motioned for Zeg to continue as he sipped his drink and kept his eyes on the street.

"Doctor…Alexi and I have a little code we use between us when we don't want Big Brother to know what we're thinking. I've read his latest note at least ten times. I'd show it to you, but it wouldn't make any sense at all. That's what's neat about his code. When I read between the lines, it is definitely a warning…for us, you and me alike. Command intends to use us as guinea pigs when we get to England! That's exactly what Alexi called us in his note…Guinea Pigs!"

Vlady began to picture himself and Zeg as small stout-bodied short-eared nearly tailless domesticated rodents living inside a metal cage against their will waiting to be injected with a toxic fluid. He didn't like what he saw and was having trouble erasing it from his mind.

"Does all this stuff have to do with this…cosmonaut thing…this Yengoyan fellow that's turned up missing? How are we all related, and why? There must be a pattern here somewhere, but I don't see it."

Zeg didn't say a word at first. He just nodded and smiled a sheepish grin.

"Can you be more specific, Zeg? I'm lost here. Totally confused! I need help understanding what's going on. Did he hint as to exactly who was going to do us in when we got to England and how they were going to do it?"

Zeg thought for a moment, then he answered.

"Well, Vlady, you and I are supposed to take off for London to round up this Yengoyan fellow, right? That's pretty clear no matter how you look at it. Command's reasoning…ah, I mean excuse, is that we know each other and are good with English. Also, you are familiar with the place having lived there while you were in school. No reason to suspect them choosing us for those reasons.

"Next, there's our friend, the cosmonaut. He's had a virus injected into his head…"

Vlady held up his hand to interrupt Zeg.

"Wait right there…a virus in his head…injected? Who would do something like that to a fellow Russian?"

Zeg's eyes were cast down at the table as he replied.

"Vlady, believe it or not, we did it to ourselves. The work on Spacelab, the American orbital laboratory, is viral research. And here we are busily spying on the Americans trying to steal their research in the same area.

For all we know, they probably have spies in Saint Petersburg trying to steal our work.

"Meanwhile, under the great city of Saint Petersburg, Alexi and associates are busy doing similar viral research on subjects like Yengoyan. Now, it appears, according to Alexi, that you and I have become fair game."

Vlady slammed down his drink and told Zeg to hold his thoughts while Vlady got their drinks refilled. As Vlady walked away, Zeg surveyed the other townspeople seated near them.

I sure hope none of these bastards are following us. I'll slit their throats if they are…before they can slit ours!

Zeg's eyes fell on a man in working clothes who entered the bar just after he and Vlady did.

That's got to be him over there. Cheap beer and a glassy look in his eyes. We'll find out just whose side he's on when we leave!

Vlady was deep in thought when he returned with the drinks. He had calmed down considerably, but he noticed how deep in thought Zeg seemed to be. It was that look of paranoia he had seen many times before.

"Zeg, did you get a physical before you came out here?"

The question jarred Zeg out of his trance.

"I did, but not from Command. Alexi gave me the physical. I probably shouldn't tell you this, but you've been injected with what they call a read virus. Alexi said that it's fairly benign and that I shouldn't tell you unless you started experiencing side effects…like hearing voices. But, anyone around here might imagine voices in their head once in a while."

"Fairly benign?" mumbled Vlady in complete disbelief. "The only thing that shuts these voices down seems to be the vodka."

A smile spread across Zeg's face.

"That's it! Alexi indicated to me that alcohol could be a suppressant. When we went drinking the other night…you said you felt better. Right? Well, we seem to have at least a short-term cure working here. Anyway, Alexi said the read virus will go away in six months or so with no adverse effects on your brain. He asked me to let him know how well alcohol does as a suppressant. He deserves that from us."

"Absolutely!" whispered Vlady. "Let's do our own little experiment on me right here, right now. If tonight doesn't kill the little bastards in my head, I'll lay on a really big one…in London. Then, we'll see where it takes us."

"A great idea, but there's something I want to try out first. Don't... do not look over your shoulder, but I believe we have a tail! Did you like my choice of words? I think someone from Command might be following us."

Vlady grinned, but soon was whispering a question.

"What's the plan? I didn't notice any cars following behind us...but then where else would we go but here?"

Zeg covered his mouth with his hand as he replied.

"As soon as you finish your drink, get up and go to the restroom. But, when you get there, slip out of the back door instead. Then...carefully, go over to Petrov's liquor store and wait for me there. It might be fifteen or twenty minutes, but be patient. I've got the car keys."

Koslov nodded and took one last stiff drink of his vodka.

"What if he's not...a tail?" asked Vlady.

"No harm, no foul," Zeg replied, very proud of his use of colloquial English. "We'll come right back here and get you blind drunk from the beginning!"

After a minute or so, Vlady excused himself, leaving a third of his vodka in the glass where it could easily be seen by anyone who was interested. Zeg kept his eyes on the bar and the hallway leading to the restroom, but his good peripheral vision told him what the suspected government agent was doing. The man watched Vlady make his way down the hall and then he turned toward Zeg again.

Let's see which fish he wants more! said Zeg to himself as he finished his drink, laid a tip on the table and started to get up to head for the front door. That's when he saw the other man's face in more detail and also the face of a man sitting nearby.

Help me! Do my eyes deceive me? It's the cosmonaut...one of them in civilian clothes. It's Yengoyan! He's sitting two stools to the left of the man we suspect is following us. But, which Yengoyan is he...or is he just a look-alike? Maybe all of this is just my paranoia? I don't want to make a fool out of myself just yet.

The man who looked like Yengoyan stared straight at Zeg. His eyes were a bright blue. Inside his head, Zeg could almost hear him speaking.

Go on your way. I will take care of this man for you. We will talk in London. Find my brother!

Zeg hesitated for a moment and then assuming that Vladi was already out of the building, he turned toward the front door to leave. But, once outside he quickly turned and glanced back into the bar through a window.

As he watched, both men got up off of their barstools and turned toward the door. Zeg quickly sprinted to the side of the building and took cover around the corner.

After a few seconds the man presumably from Command exited the door almost running and began visually searching the street for something or someone. Zeg knew it was him the man was after. As the tail reached the center of the street, the cosmonaut emerged from the bar and quickly they stood confronting each other. After a verbal exchange, which Zeg couldn't make out, the Command agent reached for his gun. But it was too late. The cosmonaut shot him with a device that appeared to be a small sophisticated and noiseless laser weapon. The man crumpled to the ground and was motionless. After inspecting the man's body, the man Zeg assumed was Yengoyan turned around and reentered the bar as if nothing had happened.

Slowly, Zeg turned and made his way up the street on his way to Petrov's liquor store to find Koslov. He tried, but he couldn't come up with a rational explanation for what had just happened right in front of his eyes.

20

How Far Is It To Scotland?

Took a look down a westbound road,
right away I made my choice.
Headed out to my big two-wheeler,
I was tired of my own voice.

Roll Me Away
Bob Seger

The Russian Embassy
London, England

Somehow he knew this wasn't going to be his day. And it wasn't anything he'd done to initiate all the commotion. It all began when that very polite but strange man wandered into his office. Now, as a result of that visit, the phone on his desk kept buzzing and buzzing relentlessly, but he had no intention of answering it. Only when he was in deep trouble were the rings so persistent and ominous.

Sergei searched in vain for the camera he had used to photograph the elusive visitor he had recently interviewed. It was always resting on top of his small file cabinet waiting faithfully for him, but now, just when he needed it so very badly, it was missing…gone!

He mumbled to himself as his hands parsed through the piles of disorganized papers in front of him. Somehow, he couldn't remember exactly where he'd placed the camera after the interview. He even searched his cluttered wastebasket but without any success. His greatest fear was that the visitor had taken the camera with him when he departed. Sergei began talking aloud to himself as his search continued.

"Damn it to Hell! It's not here where it should be, and I've searched every place it could be. It couldn't have walked off by itself. Did he take it when I wasn't looking? Kucinich will surely have my head for this; I am certain of that. At least I still have the audio tape…somewhere…I hope?

"What was his name again? Leon…yes, Leon whatever. He said his brother was a Russian cosmonaut and that he was searching for him. Does he expect a Russian cosmonaut to be in England of all places? Maybe his brother is visiting the Queen? I should call the palace, maybe?"

Sergei couldn't stop laughing at his own monologue. At least the humor made him relax somewhat, but not enough.

"He mentioned that he was Armeniam of all things. Or did he say Arminian? I remember my teacher telling me that those were followers of Jacob Arminius and his doctrines opposing the absolute predestination of pure Calvinism. I just can't remember the timeframe…probably about 1600 when he was stomping around Europe.

"I wonder whether any of those religious Calvinist nutcases are still running around England these days. Predestination in a universe ruled by Quantum Theory and uncertainty? I heard about crazy and stupid people, but they must have beat all! Put your faith…belief in something that is completely wrong, provably wrong, and see where it gets you? Sort of like working for this embassy! By implication, that's makes me stupid, too… doesn't it?

"How was I supposed to know that Command was looking for this particular fellow out of all the lost souls who wander in here? Supposedly, he's a cosmonaut, of all things, wandering the earth in search of another cosmonaut who is his twin brother. Two space travelers lost on the surface of the earth! There is some irony in that to be sure. But what does it say about our space program? You can't make this stuff up!

"Great, but where does all this leave me? Those rocket launches must have affected their brains…permanently. What brains? All he did was stare at me during the entire interview like I was a movie star or maybe Sherlock Holmes.

"No one ever tells me anything about what's going on around here so why should he? His passport…he didn't have a passport or at least he said he didn't have a passport. How the hell did he get here…get this far from Moscow without a damn passport? He had his military identification papers but no passport on him and no luggage and no idea where he was or how he got here. This has got to be a first of some kind?"

Sergei paused as he considered his last thought.

"The military must have snuck him into England on one of those training flights of theirs! Could be...it wouldn't be the first time they tried that."

Suddenly, Sergei's worst fears were realized. There was a creaking of the door to his office and in front of his desk there stood Rad Kucinich, his boss and first assistant to the Russian ambassador. The look on his face was ominous. Surely, there would be hell to pay!

"Relax, Sergei. We checked the surveillance videos, and our man must still be in the embassy. There was no sign of him leaving the building. Stay put here in your office until the military unit has completed a thorough search of the premises. If you don't mind, I might just stay here with you until the search is finished. In the meantime while your memory is still fresh, we should carefully review the information you gleaned from your interview with this man. I have no idea what Command was expecting so proceed carefully on this."

This situation was exactly what Sergei had feared most, but he also realized that if he did his job right and presented the data he had as clearly as possible, blame might not fall completely on him because of the visitor's sudden disappearance.

"It will be my distinct pleasure, Sir," Sergei replied politely as he returned to his chair. "Would you like me to begin now? I can get a tablet for you should you want to take notes."

Rad thought for a few seconds, then responded.

"Wait a moment while I get us both a drink from the kitchen," Rad mumbled as he walked back out of the office door. This gave Sergei a chance to take the deep breath he really needed. He immediately wondered why his boss was being so civil with him, especially in this situation. That just wasn't Rad's style at all. Maybe this was just going to be Sergei's lucky day!

Soon, his boss returned with two large glasses of ale and some napkins and took a seat opposite Sergei. Sergei noticed that the expression of antagonism that Rad usually wore on his face had disappeared. Another moment of silence preceded Sergei's next words.

"He was a quiet, middle-aged, thin person from the Ukraine, I believe, but he also mentioned Armenia in passing. His only identification papers consisted of orders issued by Command in Saint Petersburg. His existing paperwork seemed to be in order as far as that goes. The documents mentioned participation in some sort of classified scientific experiment, which was, of course, undefined. The photograph was blurred but sufficient to match him for identification. His name was listed as Leon Yengoyan, and he has served as a cosmonaut in the Russian space program and for a time in the Russian intelligence services."

Rad scratched his chin as he pondered things. He wanted to be sure that he had a complete picture of the visitor's mental state.

"Fits so far, Sergei. Did he say anything at all about being aboard the American Spacelab or any other American space vehicle for that matter? This is very important. The smallest clue might be essential to our understanding."

Sergei shook his head negatively, but he thought it might be time for some needed clarification.

"Let me find the audio tape, Sir. That way you can hear exactly what he said during our discussion."

Sergei had just remembered where he put the tape so he reached behind several books standing on his desk and retrieved it. He emitted a big sigh of relief when his fingers actually touched the tape. His hands were shaking as he installed the audiotape into the player on his desk, but he was lucky and in thirty seconds the tape was beginning to play with no problems. He fast-forwarded to the point where he believed his guest began speaking about his space travel experiences and was again in good fortune. Rad seemed pleased by his apparent efficiency. Now the men settled back to listen to the voice of their visitor.

"I must have fallen asleep, and when I awakened, I was in a strange place. I don't remember putting on a space suit, but there I was in a small room, all white with no windows, experiencing what is best described as weightlessness. I know how that feels because I've been on several Russian space missions in earth orbit. But this spaceship, if that's what it was, was definitely not Russian."

Sergei could be heard asking Leon how he got there.

"I have no idea! All I remember is the voice in my head telling me to go to sleep. I was certainly dreaming, but I'm not sure about what. On earth I dream about my space missions, and this was more or less the same kind of dream…I think? Then, I remember vibration, but that's about all. Nothing visual. A slow vibration began and increased in intensity until it stopped short and all was quiet. For some reason this all seemed familiar to me, but I can't explain why.

"My English is fair so I was able to read various signs on the doors and walls. There were numerous warnings about canisters containing chemical samples. Somehow I knew that these also contained viruses. As I began to move around in an attempt to discover exactly where I was, I encountered the first of several robotic elements. The robot recognized my presence and led me out into a narrow passageway. It even opened the sliding door for me. At the time I thought nothing of it.

"It…the robot obviously wanted me to follow it, so I proceeded down the passageway to another room. Just before we reached the door, another robot came up to me and handed me a small cylindrical plastic container. Out of curiosity, I looked inside…there were several small pills. They looked like salicylic acid…aspirin is what the Americans call them. Then, as if there was a voice in my head, I was urged to enter the room pills in hand.

"There in a medical lab was a patient…a man I assumed could be my brother, Tomas. I hoped against hope that it was him, but instead he turned out to be an American. At least I believe he was an American. We didn't really speak. I just handed him the pills. He thanked me, and I made my exit. I don't know where I thought I was going, but soon I was seated at a table and…I guess I fell asleep again.

"When I awoke, I decided to find the American and ask him some questions, but as I entered the medical room, I was suddenly confronted by the American I had encountered before and two other…astronauts. That's when I passed out cold. The next thing I knew I was here in England somewhere in the woods not too far from here. I encountered some students in the woods. They rescued me and gave me food and directions to our embassy. And so here I am."

At this moment Rad received a call from within the embassy. He told Sergei to wait for a few minutes until he returned. With Kucinich absent, Sergei stretched out and relaxed for a while. He began to consider the possibilities.

Maybe they've found old Leon, wherever he was hiding. I can't help but feel sorry for him. Imagine imagining being in a spacecraft and not knowing how you got there and how you got out of there. That boy will have some serious mental problems at the end of all of this. If he survives, that is! Whatever they are, the voices and the problems, I hope they're not catching, at least for me! My mother would not be pleased.

It was quite a while before Rad returned to the room where Sergei was relaxing. Unfortunately for Sergei, his rest period was definitely over for some time to come! As Rad entered the door and purposely slammed it behind him, Sergei shot straight up in his chair expecting the worst.

"All hell is breaking loose in Saint Petersburg and Moscow and all because of a missing cosmonaut who has eluded us…has eluded you, Sergei! Now there are two cosmonauts on the loose. Command is going to be descending upon us like a pack of bloodthirsty wolves…and sooner than we'd wish.

"They want us…they want you to contact two scientists in Saint Petersburg and arrange transport for them to London. Prepare two guest rooms, too. All you can tell them over the phone is that we've been visited by one of the missing cosmonauts. Here are the names and the number of their laboratory. Get on it now before anything else goes wrong!"

Rad handed several papers to Sergei and then left the room in a huff without entertaining any questions from his assistant.

I'm in big trouble now! thought Sergei to himself as he glanced through the scribbled notes. *Doctor Pavel Malkin and Doctor Alexi Karpov. I hope they're friendly and understanding! Well, I might as well get it over with.*

Suddenly, Sergei stopped short. The names of the Russian scientists rang a bell, and Sergei began mumbling to himself.

These two men were already scheduled to come to England to attend a scientific meeting at Oxford University. And Command was unaware of this? That figures.

Sergei wandered over to the window behind his desk. From the third floor of the embassy building it gave him a restful view of a residential part of the city. He loved living in London, but he needed to find a less stressful job in some place like a library. His primary hobby was reading and how great it would be to be surrounded your best friends…the books and the normal people who enjoyed reading. As his mind wandered off, he heard a mild tapping on the door to his office. It definitely wasn't Rad.

He bade the person who was knocking to come in and slowly the doorknob turned revealing a thin, middle-aged man with bright eyes and brown hair. That's when Sergei almost passed out!

"Leon! Is it you? You're back. But you look…different somehow. Everyone is looking for you! How did you get…"

"My name is…Tomas. I seek my brother…Leon. Do you know where he is? I must find him before…"

The man's knees began to crumple as he fell slowly to the floor. Sergei raced around his desk and caught the man before his head could hit the floor. Carefully, he dragged Tomas over to the couch where he laid him down and took his shoes off. He used one of the cushions as a pillow and stepped back as Tomas appeared to fall into a deep sleep while at the same time his eyelids were fluttering. Sergei fished a small washcloth out of his desk and after dumping some water on the cloth, he placed it on the man's forehead.

This is Leon's brother? His missing...the missing cosmonaut? They do look much the same...except for the eyes. He could easily pass for Leon at a distance. Command has been looking for him for weeks, too. Should I inform them or wait until he comes around? If I tell Rad now, they'll just come and carry him off into the darkness never to be seen again. He deserves better than that, and he did pick me out as the one to visit here in the embassy. I want him to tell me as much as possible about what's going on here...straight from the horse's mouth!

In a minute or so, Sergei's phone buzzed. It was Rad, and he wanted Sergei downstairs immediately along with some intelligence files under Sergei's care. He also commanded Sergei to lock the door to his office because one of the staff members reported that he had seen Leon heading up the main staircase. Sergei kept his word to himself and told Rad he would be downstairs in a minute with an armful of requested reports. He didn't mention Tomas, and immediately hung up the phone before he could change his mind and spill the beans.

He's out cold, so I should be able to leave him. I'll lock the door just to be sure he doesn't start wandering around the building again. Hopefully, I'll be able to get back here before he recovers completely.

With a click of the lock, Sergei was gone downstairs while Tomas continued to doze on the couch. In a few minutes his eyes began to flutter, and he sat up rigidly on the couch. The distant voice in his head told him to go to the window and open it. The building began to shake slightly as he opened the window and crawled out on the windowsill some three stories from the ground.

"Jump!" the voice commanded and without hesitation Tomas obeyed. He started to fall, but he didn't reach the ground.

Meanwhile, on the first floor of the embassy the vibration was obvious to all the embassy personnel. Dust could be seen rising from the vacant lot next door. Without a word, Rad grabbed Sergei and pushed him up the stairs toward his office. They were stopped by the locked office door, which Rad kicked in rather than wait for the key. He left Sergei in the hallway as he picked his way past the shatter door. The office was exactly as when Rad had left it minutes ago except for one small detail. The window over the vacant lot was wide open!

21

Duty Calls

Although Yale has always favored the violet's dark blue.
And the many sons of Harvard to the crimson rose are true.
We will own the lilies slender, nor honor shall they lack,
While the Tiger stands defender of the Orange and the Black.

The Orange and the Black
Clarence Mitchell

Princeton Faculty Club
Princeton, New Jersey

This was one of his most favorite places on earth after the Stanford University campus and the City of Montreal. He liked Montreal because everyone there was a hockey fan and everyone had a friend or relative living in or visiting South Florida where he grew up. So, all he had to do was wear his favorite hockey jersey, which was a Florida Panthers' jersey, and complete strangers would stop him on the street to talk about Florida and the next game or, if he was in a bar, they'd buy him drinks and come over to talk about their friends and relatives in South Florida.

On the Princeton campus he liked the quiet beauty and friendly people he found there each time he visited. Princeton was far enough from New York City to keep its relaxed nature intact and his blood pressure down. Besides, he hated the Yankees and the Jets.

He now found himself standing just outside an elegant building that he had visited many times before. The European architecture swam through his mind and quietly and warmly invited him inside. Every time he viewed the exterior of this particular building, his mind shot back to world history class in high school and the stories and tales of ancient Greece which he loved the most. He was definitely on Athen's side in its fights with Sparta. And he loved the interesting and diverse group of gods they worshipped in those historic days.

Dallas Pence quietly entered the old oaken door and proceeded through a stone archway to the information desk. There the receptionist, Michelle, recognized him immediately. She knew exactly what he wanted without having to ask. Dallas was obviously in pursuit of his mentor of years past, Victor Laurie, whose favorite hangout when he wasn't working in his office was the campus Faculty Club.

"Guess what? He's taking his usual afternoon nap right now, Dr. Pence. I'm sure you're familiar with that. Do you want me to wake him up for you? I'm sure he'll be glad to see you."

"Oh, no, Michelle" responded Dallas with a smile as he brandished a newspaper. "I'll just have a seat on this comfortable couch over here and catch up on the latest news. I haven't been here in New Jersey for quite a while, and I do need a little rest, too. Victor's probably still recovering from his trip into outer space or at least he's dreaming about it and the notoriety it's brought him. I know he'll tell me every gory detail when he comes to."

"How are things at Stanford?" asked Michelle who had known Dallas for several years. "I noticed that your football team is ranked in the top ten again."

"Same as usual. It's what's going on outside the campus that concerns me right now. One of these times you must let me treat you to dinner so I can tell you the whole story. I'm sure it's worthy of a best-selling novel you could write and then we could do the movie! I get to play the role of Victor, of course. But I guess that I will have to fight with him about that!"

Michelle laughed as Dallas took a seat on the soft and inviting couch. Just as he was getting comfortable, Victor Laurie appeared from around the corner, rubbing his eyes to make sure he wasn't seeing things or still dreaming.

"Pence! What brings you out here this time of year? It's your turn for dinner and drinks you know. I thought you'd never show up to pay off, but here you are. It must be my lucky day!"

Dallas was pleased to find his former teacher in such a good mood for a change. But after a smile and a handshake he sat Victor down for some serious words regarding Victor's near term future.

"Victor, I know you're not going to believe what I'm going to tell you, but…I'm going to tell you anyway. What the hell? We're going to England…to Oxford."

"You mean the American Physical Society meeting there next week. Mahadavan told me to sit tight for a month or so. But he also knows that I need to rub shoulders with some fellow scientists for a change instead of NASA robots in order to maintain my sanity. What's changed all of a sudden?"

Pence smiled and was obviously pleased by Laurie's apparent interest in the trip overseas.

"I just spoke with Maha and explained the current situation to him. He's coming with us because he thinks it's a good idea! How's that for a prescription?"

"What's up?" asked Laurie as he sat down.

"We have what I would call a situation. We're actually going for another reason, too. If you can believe it, we're going to find a missing Russian cosmonaut. Our intelligence sources tell us he's somewhere in the area between London and Oxford."

Laurie couldn't believe what he was hearing from his former student who was now speaking more like a spy than a scientist.

"Pence! I warn you! I'm not in the mood for jokes, especially after what I've been through this last month. Start at the beginning and go very slowly and explain yourself clearly…very clearly. And don't leave out any salient details."

Dallas took a deep breath and looked around the room to be sure their conversation would be private. He trusted Michelle to warn him if they were speaking too loudly, which Victor was known to do. Once he was satisfied with the environment, he began his explanation for better or for worse. At this point in time he really had no other choice.

"I need to describe several seemingly unrelated situations, so you'll have to give me the benefit of the doubt for a while. But, trust me, these things all come together in the end or at least they should."

Laurie nodded his head as he sat back on the couch with his arms folded. He motioned with his left hand in a professorial way indicating that he was ready for Pence to proceed with his explanation.

"Do you remember an American astronaut, a Major Robert Vostry, who was aboard Spacelab by himself at one point?"

Dallas didn't wait for an answer, but began to fill in the verbal picture he was drawing for Victor.

"Well, two astronauts were sent up to Spacelab after you returned to earth to retrieve the Major who was in quarantine at the time. During the retrieval mission, all three astronauts report that they encountered a Russian cosmonaut onboard Spacelab. Not just one, but all three confirm the sighting and their descriptions match. We can rule out mass hysteria here."

Laurie's eyes popped wide open, but he didn't interrupt. His former student certainly had his attention now.

"At about the same time, believe it or not, I was kidnapped by people I believed to be working for the CIA, but now I believe that they were actually agents of the Russian government."

Now Victor lurched forward on the couch in total disbelief, but Dallas snapped his right hand quickly into the air indicating that questions and reactions must come later in the discussion.

"Actually, considering the situation, I was very well treated, and it turned out to be a good thing in the end...well, it's not over yet. These guys even bought me dinner, desert and drinks. They told me that they...I read that as *Russia*, were having problems with their own viral research here on the planet, and that one of the vital pieces to that research, a Russian cosmonaut, had come up missing. I am not sure what role this man plays in this story, but I...we can guess.

"Primarily, without going public with this thing, they want your help and cooperation. They specifically mentioned you by name. I'm not exaggerating when I say that they believe that the future not only of Russia but of the entire human race depends upon solving their problem!"

Dallas paused to let his words sink in. Laurie's head was slowly shaking back and forth in apparent disbelief as he mumbled a reply.

"You mean to tell me that just because I went up to Spacelab and got back in one piece, more or less, that that qualifies me to hunt down and capture a missing Russian cosmonaut here on earth?"

Dallas smiled as he remembered something.

"Guess what?" Dallas said hopefully.

"After this...so far...I'd say they want me to play Santa Claus in a Broadway play!" Laurie mumbled in response.

"Almost... You've been given the American Physicist of the Year award by the Physical Review for your work. The award and your thirty-minute acceptance speech are to be given at Oxford University next week. You can wow them with your stories on folding space and space travel.

"Besides, it's perfect cover for our trip to England. I'll be there with you all the way, you lucky dog! So you won't have to do everything yourself except brag. You'll just get all the credit…as usual!"

Just as Laurie began to spring from his seat in disbelief, Michelle came over and pointed at the phone on the end table.

"You have a call, Professor Laurie. Line 3."

Laurie thanked the receptionist and slowly picked up the receiver. Laurie spoke calmly, uttering a string of 'Yes' and 'No' answers interspersed with an 'I might' and an "I could' and terminated with a final 'Goodbye'.

"Let me guess," whispered Dallas. "It was Maha calling to congratulate you on your award and your trip to Oxford!"

Laurie knew better than to fight his former student who always seemed a step or two ahead of him.

"Pence, I just want to know how he knew you would be here…how I would be here at the club this very hour for that matter. Conspiracy, that's what it is! Then, there's the matter of being kidnapped by Russians? Who's going to believe an obvious fairy tale like that? You're just trying to out do me in weirdness."

Pence smiled and answered Victor's questions.

"Maha set the whole thing up after he heard about the missing cosmonaut and my kidnapping and a few other things. He's coming with us because he wants you to come through this in one piece. Actually, believe it or not, he thinks that there are two missing cosmonauts instead of one which might complicate things a bit. These guys are twin brothers of all things."

Laurie grudgingly nodded in the affirmative. It was pretty clear that he had little choice in the matter.

American Physicist of the Year! thought Laurie to himself. *That's not too bad! I deserve it after that trip into deep, dark space. Maybe this will be fun? While Pence and his friends search for the Russians, I'll promote my ideas on space travel…now that I've actually been there and back. And I'll have a few dinners and drinks! Not a bad way to spend a week on the house…they better be picking up the tab!*

Pence realized that his former mentor was discussing things with himself so he didn't interrupt the conversation. It was time to pack some clothes and get Victor to the airport.

"Exactly when are we leaving and do we have flight reservations?" asked Laurie just at the right moment.

Pence paused and with the flourish of an accomplished magician he pulled two airline tickets out of his suit coat.

"All we need is your passport and your toothbrush and some underwear...clean underwear. But, I want to ask you about something else first. Now, this could be important so give it your best shot. During the... incident on Spacelab, did you take off your helmet? I just need to know."

Laurie's face screwed up for a moment, but then he remembered the fun trip that stood ahead so he decided to tell all without further hesitation.

"There was a lurch in Spacelab...followed by some vibration. I have no idea what it was. I lost my balance and fell to the floor...to the deck to be perfectly correct. I believe that's when the dewars and canisters fell over in the lab and my helmet came off. The air pressure was good, but there was a distinct odor, and then in seconds I must have passed out. Nobody at NASA mentioned it so I decided to keep that to myself for the time being."

Pence seemed very interested in what his mentor had to say.

"Victor, I don't remember when you first mentioned the...voices. Did they start after or before that fall on Spacelab."

Laurie did not hesitate in giving his answer.

"Definitely after the fall. Do you think...?"

Dallas shrugged his shoulders. After some reflection, Dallas had a confession of his own.

"You know that Swanson and I have been conducting communications experiments with your viral family. We've had some positive results inside the lab. It's very encouraging. Well, you know how our lab faces west, and we have those sliding glass doors out to that second story porch of ours?"

Laurie nodded.

"Well, we were moving some of the samples while they were still wired up and Terry noticed something very strange. Now, we verified what I'm going to tell you several times. It's weird, but reproducible. One of the viral samples was apparently communicating with a source outside our laboratory...something that definitely wasn't ours!"

Victor couldn't believe what he was hearing from his former student.

"You're trying to tell me that one of your samples escaped out onto the porch and was calling its friends for help?"

A big smile broke out on Pence's face as he got ready with the punch line to his story.

"Well, not quite. Apparently, the other virus appears to be very far away...on the moon!"

"You mean that what we have here is an inter-planetary version of Facebook for viruses?" laughed Victor as he slapped his sides. "Or did the astronauts leave some viral samples up on the moon on their last trip?"

"We both laughed, too…at first. Call Swanson if you doubt what I'm telling you. We still have to do some anaerobic testing on the samples, but the results are confirmed beyond any doubt."

Laurie couldn't believe what he was hearing from his former student. He wiped some perspiration from his brow as he formulated a conclusion.

"Do you know what this means, Dallas? As far as we know, there are only two groups of scientists in possession of these classes of artificial viruses, which seem to be capable of communicating over considerable distances between themselves. You have samples in your lab, and I have samples inside Spacelab. We know…we can assume that the Russians in Saint Petersburg are similarly situated. We didn't place any samples on the moon so who's left? It must be the Russians…except that they haven't done a detectable moon landing in over seven years! Seven years in this business is a long time! Nothing we or anyone else could detect. Do they have some sort of super-stealth technology we are unaware of?

"And don't haul out your alien spacecraft theories. That's much too obvious an answer, and we haven't seen any aliens on the moon lately, have we?"

"Have we even looked yet?" Pence responded in a serious voice. "I wouldn't rule out anything yet until we have a valid answer."

Laurie became very quiet, but his mind was abuzz with conflicting thoughts and unanswered questions. He wanted to go to the moon and search for…whatever it was that was corresponding with the earthbound viral samples in Palo Alto. But England would probably be as far as he would get.

22

Which Way Did He Go?

Well, John the Baptist after torturing a thief,
Looks up at his hero, the Commander-in-Chief.
The Commander-in-Chief answers him while chasing a fly,
Saying, "Death to all those who would whimper and cry!"
Saying, "The sun's not yellow, it's chicken!"

Tombstone Blues
Bob Dylan

The Houston NASA Space Center

It was an exceptionally slow day as Phil sat at his desk wondering why he was still in his office when lunchtime had almost passed. He had accomplished absolutely nothing so far, and, for some unexplained reason he wasn't the least bit hungry either. The latter was a very unusual situation for him. As he thought about going out to the nearby diner for some dessert, the phone on his desk buzzed, so he picked up the receiver and listened to some words from the other side of the line as his head slowly began to shake back and forth.

Phil slowly lowered the phone and shook his head even more vigorously. He couldn't believe what he had just heard. It was none other than Senator Emil Jensen from Oklahoma on the other end of the phone. In person! He was down in the lobby requesting an immediate audience with Phil and Frank. Phil felt trapped like a rat.

That wasn't all. Astronaut Major Robert Vostry was down there with the senator from Oklahoma. As he looked around the room trying to guess what to do next, Phil realized that Frank was still out to lunch. It was the best and worst timing he could ever imagine.

Frank, that lucky bastard! He picked today of all days to get his haircut, not that he has much up there to worry about. The barber spends most of his time trimming his nose and his eyebrows. Well, it's not my fault that Jensen popped up just now. Frank can't pin this one on me just because he's missing in action. I'll just grit my teeth and wade in and see what happens. I can't be expected to know everything about Spacelab anyway. I've never actually been aboard. So, bring them on!

Good thing that Doctor Mahadavan warned me about the senator and his nasty habits. I remember what he told me...'This man is not all there, most if not all of the time!' First of all, he's a screaming alcoholic. And where there's that much alcohol, drugs can't be far behind. Actually, my mother told me that fact now that I think about it. Senator Jensen wanders off without warning. He's had some very strange visitors when he's been in the hospital. Even the C.I.A. is taking notice of that. I hope that his kind of insanity isn't catching!

As I remember, Maha also said that they have film of him talking to himself in what sounded like a foreign language. Maybe he was just practicing his Russian or Chinese? Maha probably shouldn't have divulged that kind of medical data to Frank and me, but what are friends in high places for anyway? I'm curious as to what the conversations are about and who he was talking to. And he always carries a considerable roll of cash on his person. Very strange thing for a senator to be doing, indeed! Well, it's strange behavior for anyone, but he seems to have strangeness down to an art. That doesn't say much for the voters in Oklahoma who keep reelecting him, does it?

And, how did he get here...in Houston in the first place? He was supposedly hospitalized in Washington according to what everyone said. I should have listened more closely. And, I thought the major was still across town undergoing medical tests and a second round of debriefings on Spacelab? What's he got to do with Jensen anyway? This whole thing doesn't make any sense at all no matter how I look at it. Nothing around here adds up any more. I need a vacation real bad!

Phil sat down while pondering whether he should call his supervisor and warn him of what was sure to be a total disaster or let it be a complete surprise. He quickly decided not to disturb Frank based on the feeling Phil had that he would not want his small modicum of free time swallowed up by work related crap. Later, after first blowing his top, Frank would thank him for it.

Without a knock, the door opened and there stood a smartly dressed senator and a major in full uniform. Neither was smiling back at Phil.

"Where's your boss, Dr. Blair?" were Jensen's expected first words. "He might want to hear what we have to say. After all, we do pay him for services rendered out of the federal budget."

Blair paused, realizing that his worst course of action would be to let the Senator manipulate him. He knew that Frank would agree completely. Phil decided to take the offensive right off the bat.

"To get Frank Hurbert into an important official meeting of this kind it's always best to phone ahead and make an appointment," was Phil's response, which wasn't particularly appreciated by the congressman. "He's pretty much booked up today and now that I think about it, pretty much booked up tomorrow, too. He didn't take his cell phone to lunch with him so contacting him now is not in the cards. We'll just have to wait and hope that he returns to his office."

Phil felt very good about his opening salvo in this battle. Frank would indeed be proud.

"Well, then, you're the one I really wanted to speak to," countered Jensen in a sarcastic tone. It was a much preferred response to conducting a lunchtime search for his boss.

Phil offered both men a seat and some coffee. From the look on Vostry's face, Phil guessed that the major had no idea why this meeting was called by Jensen or why he was in attendance in the first place. He still seemed a little wobbly presumably from his recent trip into space.

"Let me just lay this out for you as simply as I can," the senator began. "I firmly and truly believe that we've encountered our first real…space aliens. And by space aliens I mean alien beings from outer space."

Silence fell over the room just as Jensen had hoped. Finally, Phil asked the obvious follow up question.

"Why do you…propose that scenario, Senator?" asked Blair seriously. "It is certainly an interesting proposition, but we are unaware of any evidence suggesting the existence of said aliens."

Jensen retrieved a torn envelope from Major Vostry and waved it in the air in front of Phil as if it were a flag.

"They mailed me a warning in this very envelope that I hold in my hand! Major, please retrieve the senate page so that he can verify my story. He should be outside in the hallway waiting for you to summon him."

At that moment Phil reminded himself that his cousin Ollie worked in the senate as a page.

"Is his name Ollie?" asked Blair casually.

The senator leaped up from his chair as he shouted his question back at Phil. His face had turned beet-red.

"How did you know that information, Doctor Blair? You are holding out on me in defiance of my office! Nobody…no one is…"

Phil now knew the answer to his question. He relaxed back into his chair and explained in a very quiet tone.

"Just a wild guess on my part, Sir. My cousin Ollie works the senate floor these days, and I figured that with my luck and the way things have been going lately, it would be him! I'm actually as surprised as you are should Ollie walk in through that door with the major! But, actually, it would be nice to see him face to face. We don't get to visit with each other very often, and he's a great kid with a bright future. We have a lot of things to talk over."

Blair took the envelope from Jensen's hand and searched through it looking for the any contents.

"It's quite empty, Sir, as you can see. Exactly what were the contents that they should point to the existence of aliens from outer space?"

Senator Jensen pointed an accusing but shaking finger at Blair as he gathered his jumbled thoughts.

"So, you're one of them, too, you are! I thought that they might have infiltrated NASA! Aliens of any form cannot be trusted at any time. Especially these particular aliens with their high technology and chemical sorcery! They get right into your head and tell you what to do. They're in my head right now. I hear their voices all the time, telling me what to do and where to go. They're in Professor Laurie's head, too. They mean to seize the earth and enslave us all with their viral technology! I wouldn't be surprised if they aren't working with the Russians! They want the anti-virus Professor Laurie is developing out in space. With that we can stop them cold! The future of the entire human race is at stake here!"

Jensen stopped cold and grabbed his head as if he was suffering from a sudden massive headache. He staggered and reached out for a nearby chair.

At that moment Ollie stepped through the door and saw Phil holding the package in his hands while the Senator was bobbing his head. He was surprisingly calm.

"Hi, Cousin Phil! That's what's left of Senator Jensen's package you're holding there in your hands. I had it in my possession for quite a while as I was trying to deliver it to the senator. Nobody messed with it after I received it from the congressional mail system. It was just as you see it when it was opened…empty! I have two other very reliable witnesses to that fact no matter what the senator alleges. If something was removed, that happened before I delivered the envelope to the senator."

Phil temporarily disregarded Ollie's remarks and shook his cousin's hand and smiled, telling him how good it was to see him again. Next he offered Ollie a chair and served him a cup of coffee. He made a strong effort to ignore the senator's writhing behavior.

"I was just looking for a return address on this thing, Ollie. There doesn't seem to be one anywhere on this envelope. Something here on the back appears to have been torn off, but I can't be certain. That's a little strange, isn't it?"

Ollie pointed at the back leaf of the envelope where it did appear as though something had been ripped off the surface.

"When they handed it to me in chambers, what I assume was a return address label had already been removed. There is a postmark, but I haven't tried to determine its origin yet. You can see that it's a bit smudged, and the red ink makes it hard to read. Maybe that's something we can do now that we have some time. I'm very curious as to who sent this thing to the senator and what was supposed to be inside it."

"Time?" shouted Jensen. "We've got to go to London and pronto… now! The Spacelab is in danger from those aliens. NASA will try to destroy it, and the aliens will try to steal it and then destroy it after they have what they want. There's something onboard that they really want, really bad! The Russian cosmonaut told me that it's a lethal defense to their viral colonies growing on the moon! He wouldn't lie to me about something like that!"

About this time Phil Blair began wishing that his boss were actually present to deflect and absorb some of the craziness stirring throughout the room. His next tactic became an obvious stall for time.

"Frank will be here in a few minutes. Make yourselves comfortable while I retrieve some files I know he'll want to show to you. And let's ponder what might have been in this package…if anything, and we should make a list of possibilities no matter how remote or absurd. We may have to drop in on Sherlock Holmes when we arrive in London…if we go to London."

Phil paused for a moment then asked a question.

"Are we really going to London?"

The timing couldn't have been more perfect. At just that moment Frank Hurbert entered the room carrying an envelope that he waved at Phil.

"Phil! Pack up your duds. We're going to England!"

23
Happy Hour

I'm getting drunk; I'm feeling mellow. I'm drinkin' bourbon,
I'm drinkin' scotch, I'm drinkin' beer! Looked down the bar,
Here come the bartender. I said, 'Look man, come down here!'
So what do you want? One bourbon, one scotch, one beer.

1 Bourbon, 1 Scotch, 1 Beer
George Thorogood

O'Malley's Pub
Oxford, England

A small round table in the rear of the bar had been reserved for several foreign visitors attending the upcoming American Physical Society meeting at Oxford University. It was just past 4 PM local time and two men were already seated at the table conversing and sampling the local beer supply when Vlady and Zeg entered through the front door. As the Russians approached the table, it became obvious that all four men knew each other very well. Dr. Karpov and Dr. Malkin leaped to their feet and were greeted with handshakes and hugs.

"It's been a long time," whispered Zeg with obvious relief in his voice as he and Vlady took their seats. "Nothing could make Vlady and I happier than seeing the two of you here, especially this far from home. It gets pretty lonely out there in Siberia…almost as lonely as working in that cave under St. Petersburg! We Russians have to get out a little more! The English and French are having all of the fun."

Vlady glanced around the table and noticed that there was still an empty chair ready to be occupied.

"Are we expecting anyone else at this get together?" asked Koslov of the two Russian scientists. Simultaneously, they both nodded their heads in the affirmative and smiled.

"A very special guest...an American at that," whispered Karpov. "He's one of Professor Victor Laurie's former students. Laurie is the American scientist heading up the viral research on their spacecraft...on Spacelab.

"His name is Professor Dallas Pence. We've gotten to know him pretty well for being half a world away. Some of our concerns seem to be mutual. Command has already talked to him indirectly about cooperating with us, and apparently, he has his government's approval. At least that's what he told us...told our agents when they interviewed him.

"In any case we want to discuss Spacelab and some unusual data we've come across related to it. From what we know this isn't a Russian-American thing. We need to work together regardless of what our governments say about each other. As you will learn from this discussion, we believe that a third party is interfering with our research. And here I mean interfering with both the Americans and us with equal distain.

"So there is some risk to this...to joining this particular project. You can leave now, and we won't think the lesser of either of you. It's complicated to say the least, and it's very unofficial. But your help is essential to say the least."

Koslov slumped back in his chair and tried to relax as the bartender brought over a pitcher of beer and some clean glasses. He had always loved being in England, especially near Oxford and London, yet he was now worried about factors that were far beyond his control.

"Does this all lead to a certain missing cosmonaut or two by any chance?" asked Zeg. "You know, like the one the Americans reportedly encountered apparently staggering around on Spacelab with no apparent means of transportation. Don't worry about how we know of the sighting... Vlady and I just know about these things! It's our job.

"I'd like to learn just how he got there...and got back again...without a spacecraft. A cosmonaut traveling from earth to orbit and back without a spacecraft of his own! Now, there's a Nobel Prize winner if I ever saw one.

"But that's where Vlady might be able to help. He's observed some anomalies I'm sure he'll tell you about in great detail. They just might explain everything that we're missing here."

Dr. Malkin cleared his throat as he rubbed his eyes and shook his head. He also had something to say.

"As we sit here, gentlemen, absent one of our number, it is possible…just possible, that between our three points of view from three separate locations spaced around the world as they are, we might be able to hypothesize a solution to this riddle? What we can't do is leave out anything that we've seen or thought or felt just because it seems implausible or stupid or it might have been classified by some well-meaning bureaucrat. That's the only way we will succeed in this matter. Please lay everything on the table and make no assumptions. We all promise to respect each other after this is all over. All your ideas are welcome."

Zeg and Koslov both agreed by nodding their heads. A brief smile swept across Malkin's face as he glanced toward the door of the bar. The missing guest was on his way to join the party.

"Unless I'm mistaken, I believe that our American friend has just arrived! I believe that you will like this man. He's friendly, a straight talker and an excellent scientist."

Malkin waved his hand toward the man standing in the doorway and soon Dr. Dallas Pence took his seat at the table after introductions and handshakes and the ordering of a drink. Dallas apologized for not speaking Russian but Malkin assured him that there was no problem. Every one at the table spoke and understood English quite well and as Koslov pointed out, after all this was an English pub!

"Dallas, I haven't told our friends Zeg and Vlady much about you, nor have I told you much about them; however, we have plenty of time this evening to make up for that deficiency."

Dallas agreed as he sipped his beer.

"It should be interesting to say the least, and let me tell you that I appreciate your skills in English because my Russian is almost nil. There was a point in graduate school where I had to be able to read in two languages out of either French, German, Russian or Japanese."

Smiles broke out on all the Russians faces.

"Well," Pence continued, "I had some undergraduate French and German so I began brushing up on them, and I started auditing a beginning Russian class. The German test was given by Herr Professor Otto Koenig who drove a diesel Mercedes to the chemistry department each day. Even in the basement lab where my desk was, I could hear him coming to work at least a block away.

"Now, I went to Koenig for the German test but failed to pass on my first attempt. He told me to study some more and come back. So, naturally, I fired up my French studies, and after a few weeks I went to make an appointment with Professor Pierre van Rysselberge to take the test, but he was in Europe attending an international committee meeting of some sort. I had received an A from Pierre in his statistical mechanics class so I felt good about this.

"But, guess what? Professor Koenig was now giving the French test! Well, I went for it anyway, and the professor told me that I could probably read scientific French if my life depended on it. He passed me!

"As I literally danced down the hallway toward the departmental office to file the document proving that I had passed the French language exam, I noticed something very peculiar. Professor Koenig was so used to giving the German test that he had written 'German' on the language line instead of 'French'!

"Wow! I froze. A little angel popped up on my right shoulder and told me to take the form back to Koenig and tell him of the error. The little devil that simultaneously appeared on my left shoulder made much more sense. Did I really want to take the German test over again and again and again? No way!

"So, I turned in the German form to the office and waited for Pierre to come back to campus so that I could take the French test again. Guess what? I passed! I've loved everything French ever since!"

The four Russians sitting at the table were laughing hysterically. Pence had managed to break down any barriers between himself and these four men in a matter of a few minutes. After some small talk and another round of drinks Malkin decided to get the meeting down to business, particularly to a discussion of the observations of Koslov and Pence.

"Each of us has a different perspective on the viral research and strange incidents being conducted aboard Spacelab as well as in Saint Petersburg. I am embarrassed to admit that Alexi and I have conducted extensive research on human subjects in our Saint Petersburg lab as required by our government. We had no choice, but that didn't make it right!

"Our last subject...well, next to last one, was Leon Yengoyan. That would be the first of the twin Yengoyans if you are keeping score, and you should be. It can get confusing to say the least. We believe that he is the cosmonaut the Americans sighted onboard Spacelab recently and who has recently appeared at the Russian Embassy here in London. This is a well-traveled cosmonaut to say the least. He and his means of transportation are the main reasons we are all here.

"Zeg and Vlady here have been monitoring Spacelab electronically, and they have observed some very strange incidents, once again to say the least, incidents that can only be explained by some form of third party intervention! And according to what Dr. Pence indicated to…his friendly kidnappers back in California, he has received transmissions directed toward Spacelab from…dare I say it…the moon! The rumor mill has it that Dr. Laurie is hearing voices inside his head…caused by the virus he's been working on or was exposed to on his trip to Spacelab.

"Personally, I don't need any virus…my head is ringing from all these weird happenings and occurrences we've collected here! We've got to try to figure this out once and for all!"

Malkin let his words sink into the group. Soon, Pence decided to open the questioning.

"Zeg, exactly what strange phenomena did you and Vlady observe related to Spacelab?"

"Actually, it was Vlady who saw what I probably would have missed had he not been there next to me. But now that I've learned of these other perspectives, there were a few things that didn't fit the way they should. Let me describe what I saw and then, more importantly, we may be able to use Vlady's insights to explain these things.

"Several times during this last week or so in Siberia, the Spacelab seemed to vibrate as if it were docking with another vehicle of some size. But nothing normal was visible to our equipment as far as a docking module or ship is concerned. At first, I assumed, probably incorrectly, that our transmitter was loose and that a robot probably bumped the panel thereby shaking it and causing this vibration. I've seen similar signals when we were testing the semiconductors, but these were of much lower frequency. I apologize because I should have realized it from the beginning. A robot or human collision wouldn't have created these more intense low-frequency vibrations, which require considerable mass. At least from the physics aspect of it, I don't think so. Spacelab itself was being shaken by something much more massive than itself!"

Koslov nodded his head in agreement. Dr. Pence and the two Russians from Saint Petersburg were frozen as if they'd just seen a ghost.

"Vlady, tell us what you observed," whispered Dr. Karpov. "I'm almost afraid to ask!"

"Well," Koslov began as he cleared his throat, "I was going over some photographs of Spacelab taken by one of our surveillance satellites some days ago. I must confess that I know little or nothing about astronomy. I'm sure it's fun, but I've always been too busy trying to figure out what's going on down here…at least until I was assigned to my current project.

"As I glanced at the many seemingly identical profiles of Spacelab, something peculiar caught my eye. Like I said, I don't know a constellation from a star cluster or a galaxy. They are...were all just stars to me. Well, on almost every shot a set of stars that I call Sirius or something like that can be seen to the left of the hull. There is one bright star next to a group of lesser lights. In almost every case the bright star is between the cluster and the hull. That's because our satellite takes these photos from roughly the same position relative to Spacelab's orbit every time it comes around. Of course, we take other sets of photos too, but this set is the interesting one for our problem."

Koslov reached into his briefcase and removed a set of photographs, which he passed around with the exception of two that he kept in front of him. The other men at the table scanned the photos with great interest. Zeg, who had reviewed these photos many times, helped point out the features his partner was talking about. Soon, Koslov continued.

"Now, I hold in my hand two interesting photos of exactly the same objects. After you've digested the initial set, take a look at these two and tell me if you see anything unusual."

Pence was the first to be handed one of the comparison photos. Koslov watched the American's eyes widen as the difference became obvious.

"They're reversed!" Pence exclaimed. He immediately became somewhat embarrassed by the high-pitched nature of his voice caused by the excitement of his discovery. "The lone star is on the outside here, just the reverse of all those others. It's almost as if someone inserted a lens between the stars and the camera."

Soon, the rest of the men were in complete agreement. Something was literally reversing the positions of the stars viewed near the hull. Every other star in the photos was normal in that their positions did not change! Koslov had indeed introduced an interesting variable into the problem.

Now it was Pence's turn. He now fully realized the importance of his meeting with four Russians he had never met in person before. And his contribution to the riddle facing them was probably the strangest and hardest to understand of all.

"I've been working," he began, "on communication between physically separate viral strands...distant communications. Strictly by accident we discovered that two viral samples ten yards...okay, eight meters apart, were literally talking to each other. By we, I mean with Professor Terry Swanson. I wish he were present now with us to hear this discussion.

"One of Professor Laurie's viral samples was divided in two and each half placed at opposite ends of our lab. Keeping it simple, when a hot glass rod was poked into one sample, the other heated up, too! Just off the top of my head I proposed the implausible...that the viral samples had the means to transmit and detect tachyons...faster than light particles similar to photons.

"But, that's not what's most interesting and important, at least for now. What is strange is that these samples seemed to be receiving extra-terrestrial signals. And they seemed to respond to them as if they somehow understood them. We seemed to have found a correlation between the communication and the medium's temperature. Eventually, the source or sources of these signals was determined with the help of my friends in the electrical engineering department. At first, it was definitely the moon! Then, correlated with the vibrations you've noted, communications were being conducted with Spacelab...by the virus, presumably with a viral sample near or aboard Spacelab."

Dr. Malkin was staring up at the ceiling of the bar as if he were looking for the moon. A suspicious smile was spreading across his face.

"So, we've reduced the problem down to one or more viruses in the head of a cosmonaut or at least onboard the American laboratory communicating with...viruses on the moon? I don't know about the rest of you, but for me, it's time for another drink. We might possibly have a Hollywood movie here! Aliens have got to be involved in this one for sure!"

The other men waited for Malkin to proceed, but Karpov seemed to read his mind before the others did.

"We have to find our friend Yengoyan. Is he an alien, or have we just stuffed his head with too many viral components that have permitted the aliens to take over his mind and body...if, in fact, there are aliens up there on the moon? Is the other Yengoyan...the second cosmonaut that's on the loose, his twin or a clone or what? Nothing about this situation would surprise me any more!"

"There's another cosmonaut? Two missing cosmonauts?" whispered Pence. "Oh, the Russian space twins! I remember now...sorry."

Karpov just shrugged his shoulders and smiled.

"That's not all," said Koslov. "I never thought I'd admit this to anyone except Zeg, but lately...ever since I left Saint Petersburg, I've been hearing very strange things...voices in my head every once in a while. I'm not kidding about this. I've heard the rumors about Professor Laurie hearing things that shouldn't be there. I think I have a mild case of the same disease he has.

"But…there is hope, if you want to call it that. Every time I have a drink or two, the voices fade away and stay gone for hours and sometimes days. I think the alcohol messes up the cerebral environment the virus is hiding in. Seriously. At least this could be a defense, if only a temporary one. Dr. Pence, I suggest you give your samples a shot and a beer and see how they do for the next twenty-four hours."

Suddenly, Pence pounded his fist on the table and jumped up.

"I know where I've seen this type of thing before! The stealth bomber project! There was a lens effect involved there, too, very similar to what you've observed, Vlady! What if this strange spacecraft is using stealth technology to stay…try to stay invisible so we don't detect its presence? If so, they…it must want something Spacelab has?

"And whose spacecraft is it anyway? Is it Russian? Is it American? Is it someone else from earth…China or Brazil? Or, is it alien? It would be nice to find that out somehow! And Leon is the one person who should know all about it because, presumably, he's been inside the stealth vehicle with its owners and operators!

"He's messed up for sure, but he must have seen and remembered something if we assume that this stealth spacecraft has been his means of transportation into orbit and back to earth again. If we can corner him and use the read viruses we have, maybe he'll tell us all about these things. And, we probably shouldn't spread this theory of ours around until we can pinpoint ownership of the mystery craft…if one exists. If it turns out to be American or Russian, we'd be in big trouble!"

24

Back at the Bar

Once I had a little game.
I liked to crawl back in my brain.
I think you know the game I mean.
I mean the game called 'go insane'.

Go Insane
The Doors

The Wooster Pub

Leon wasn't exactly sure how he made it all the way from the Russian Embassy to the park and then over to the Wooster Pub in one piece. But with each step his paranoia grew stronger causing him to constantly look over his shoulders, first one side, and then the other, like one of those twisting bobble-head dolls he'd seen somewhere in the past. He was certain that *they* were following him every step of the way. Leon just wasn't at all exactly sure just who *they* were. But he was absolutely certain that he was the target.

He searched his fragmented memory for clues as to his past and what he might have done to place himself in this precarious position. There were no answers coming to him, just confusion and disorder. His mind hurt and throbbed, but it wasn't a physical pain. It was the anguish of not knowing what he was doing and why he was here.

In this strange, unfamiliar land he knew that his only real hope was to find his new English friends, particularly Alex and Gretchen. And his memory told him that his best shot was the Wooster Pub, if he could find it again. With any luck this time of day they would be inside the establishment having a drink or two. There was no one else on earth he knew that he could trust right now, and the voices in his head were getting stronger by the minute as the alcohol from his last drank wore off. There was more than one voice present, and they did not sound happy about the situation. From the tone of their voices he knew that their problems were quickly becoming his problems.

After several errors in direction he finally came across a street and some buildings he recognized. Hope sprang into his step, and he almost ran the last two blocks to his objective.

As he stumbled into the front doorway of the pub, he couldn't believe his eyes and his good luck. There at the bar right where he needed them sat Alex and Gretchen talking to each other! Without hesitation Leon hurriedly made his way toward the place where they sat. Before he could say a word, they both spotted him and were all smiles, much to his relief.

"Leon!" shouted Alex with sincere enthusiasm. "You're back with us again! That's incredible! Did everything turn out okay at the embassy? We were wondering how you were doing. We have so many questions for you! We were hoping that we would see you again soon.

"Sit down and have a beer. Let us treat you this time. My dad just sent me some spending cash just for this purpose, which was perfect timing because I was absolutely broke when I last saw you. Everyone will be very pleased when they hear that you're okay."

Leon tried to smile as he gladly shook hands with his college student friends. After some small talk, Leon expressed his main concern.

"I know you won't believe me, but I have to tell someone what's going on in my head. I hope you don't mind if I impose upon you? I have no one else to turn to whom I can trust. You are the only people I know, and you and your friends have been so good to me. And, believe me, I'm not making any of his up. This is not a joke!"

Alex and Gretchen exchanged confused glances as they recalled what Leon had divulged about himself during their first meeting. Then Gretchen touched Leon's arm, which was quivering nervously and tried to reassure him that they wanted to help him in any way they could.

"Leon, we don't know you very well because we just met, but we like you a lot, and we'll try our best to help you with any problems you have… if we can. We'll do our very best. So, feel free to let absolutely everything go. Tell us the way it is, and we'll attack your problems with you.

"But first, please try to calm down a little and relax. You are safe here with us. Take some deep breaths and have a few sips from your drink to help things along. We'll do the same."

"Thanks," whispered Leon as he exhaled strongly and began to relax just a bit. "Please don't think I'm absolutely crazy when I tell you about my strange experiences. I don't fully understand what's happened to me so what I tell you will sound a little disconnected and nutty even for me. But I will not lie to either of you. You have my word on that!"

"Not a problem," replied Alex as he patted Leon on the back. "Have a drink and go right ahead. We're all ears, as we English often love to say!"

Leon took several sips from the beer that had been placed in front of him and decided to proceed with his confession immediately.

"I think that…I might be some sort of alien."

The words seemed to hang in the air over the bar. Alex briefly pictured a space alien, but immediately remembered where Leon was from. It made sense if the word 'alien' meant foreigner.

"Of course, you're Russian, right? You could call anyone in the room who is not from Great Britain an alien, that's for sure. My father often refers to his mother-in-law, my grandmother to be sure, as an alien! But, of course, he pictures her as being from outer space."

Gretchen, who was frozen in her seat by Leon's opening words, quickly relaxed. A big smile broke out on her face as she spoke.

"Leon, there are times when I'm visiting Scotland and Ireland that I am sure I'm an alien from another planet. I remember that when we first met, you thought you were Guildenstern! Do you remember that? Then, you said you were a Russian spy and that you've been in outer space… as a cosmonaut? My head was spinning all the while when you left for the…Russian embassy? You were starting to look like a cross between James Bond and that space pioneer, Yuri Gagarin! That's actually not bad company to be in at all."

Leon realized that his new friends were just trying to help and encourage him, but he also knew that he had to disclose more about himself so that they would understand the whole picture. This was no time to hold back because he couldn't be sure when those voices in his head would try to stop his confession.

"I should clarify what I seem to know about myself a little bit more. This alcohol and the pot we had together seem to have neutralized, at least for a while, the virus someone planted in my head. How do I know it was a virus? Believe it or not, it told me when I asked! The voice or voices in my head always respond to my questions…when they are there. And it seems honest about things I ask about. I'll have to give it that. But, like I said, the voices don't seem to like alcohol or grass. That is certainly a lucky break for me.

"But let's go back to when I first met you two and your friends…over there in the park. Ever since, I've been asking myself a very interesting question. How did I get out there in the woods in the first place? As you remember, we came here to this pub for a drink. The alcohol obviously did something for my memory. Over the next day or two my memory began to come back in little pieces. I remembered being strapped into a seat in some sort of vehicle about the size of a car. Only this thing was almost perfectly rectangular if that's the way to say it. I remember some vibration and then going up vertically but about that time I must have passed out. Or I went back to sleep if it was really a dream.

"Next thing I knew some sort of machine was lifting me out of the seat and putting me up against a tree. That was the tree you found me leaning against when I thought I was Guildenstern. Speaking of Guildenstern, I also remember sitting on a couch and watching a movie…the one with Rosenkrantz and Guildenstern and Hamlet. I was in a rather nice house, and I remember seeing snow outside on the lawn. Several uniformed Russian soldiers were watching over me. They didn't do anything to me, but just watched and waited for something.

"Then, everything went blank again…except for the rat!"

"You saw a rat?" mused Gretchen as she sipped her beer. "That must have been scary!".

"You'd better believe it! One of the biggest, fattest rodents I've ever seen in my entire life. We were in some sort of dark tunnel, and I was on some sort of cart. It was like a coal mine although, fortunately, I've never knowingly been in a coal mine so how would I know that? I recall that my hands were tied to the cart because I couldn't move them. The rat fell off the ceiling right onto my stomach. We both looked at each other. I don't know who was more afraid, me or the rat? I remember feeling sorry for the poor thing because he seemed more surprised than I was.

"Well, it wasn't tied down like I was, so it scampered away into the darkness as fast as it could before we could become friends. It was the first and last time we saw each other."

Both Gretchen and Alex were now laughing aloud. Neither had ever encountered a rat that was viewed so favorably.

"Then, I found myself tied down in another chair while I faced a large television screen. A voice was instructing me from out of the darkness. The funny thing was that it first spoke in Russian and then in English. Anyway, that's what I heard. I recall that both languages were spoken very badly. My English is so-so as you've been able to tell from our conversations, but my Russian is good to excellent according to my teachers. I even wrote a short screenplay when I was in college.

"What was wrong was what I call colloquialisms in English. Every few sentences the voice would use the wrong words. A Russian in Moscow describes Red Square in a certain way. I would bet that the person behind this voice had never seen Red Square ever before. The same was true in English when he…the voice sounded male…told me about where to go in London. I can't remember the exact words he used in his instructions, but take my word for it. He had never been in London.

"A spy must be good at these things, or he'll get caught for sure. Well, then came my instructions on whom to contact in the United States. The voice said that I was to seek out Trebor Yrtsov! Sounds a little Russian at first, doesn't it? Well, when the time came, I searched one end of Houston to the other. No Yrtsov. There wasn't a Yrtsov anywhere in the western hemisphere for that matter. You're not going to believe how I unraveled this one. I still chuckle to myself every time I think about it.

"I was taken up to the American Spacelab in some sort of spacecraft. That's obvious. Don't even ask me who it was that provided the transportation. I don't…didn't know at the time. But there was a presence controlling me and my movements, a presence which I couldn't see or identify.

"Now, I was able to see through several portals as we made our way to the rendezvous. Suddenly, the view of the earth shifted…reversed. Everything out there was backwards from the way it was. Well, for some reason the backwards thing hit my brain and when I asked these voices about this person, Trebor Yrtsov, they came back with the name Robert Vostry.

"As I discovered later, this craft I was in had certain stealth features. It was not easily visible on the outside. How? I don't know. It seems that the stealth device in the spacecraft affected the viral…memory? It had reversed the spelling of the contact for the virus…somehow. Next I realize that this Robert Vostry is an American and that he's an astronaut!

"What this meant is that if I couldn't figure out who he was, neither could the virus. When we were on Spacelab with Vostry, it didn't know who he was. It stopped looking and retreated! The technology used by these…aliens beat itself! And for some reason, it didn't realize the error when I figured it out.

"I've got to warn him…the American! He's supposed to be here in London quite soon. I've got to drink and do some pot quickly to keep the voices in my head from communicating with their 'friends' on the moon. Oh, yes, they slipped up and told me that they were up on the moon of all places!

"I may need your help with this. Believe me, it's going to be fun for us, but it's almost most important for all of mankind! I stole several bottles of liquor from the embassy and I've been sipping them ever since. Maybe that's why they couldn't read my mind."

Leon slumped forward on his elbows as his friends caught the attention of the bartender. Soon, several shots and two beers sat in front of the cosmonaut as he pondered his fate and that of his fellow man.

"There is one more question that needs to be answered," whispered Leon. "And I believe that it contains the reason why all of this is happening. What is it on Spacelab that these…creatures want from the earth? We must figure this out and soon. It must be something viral. Is it a threat to the other viruses or is it a new advanced virus or is it something that will protect humans and their brains against these fellows inside my head? I don't know."

25
Why Am I Here?

Hold your head up high. You know you've come a long way. Tainted as a fugitive with nothing left to say. Temptation may come! Hope your vision doesn't stray. In the name of God, you may be forced away.

Endless Dream
Yes

Heathrow Airport
London, England

As the sleek unmarked jet came to a smooth halt near the terminal for private aircraft, Senator Jensen slowly emerged from a deep sleep. After liftoff from Houston and a stop in Atlanta followed by a ham sandwich and a glass of wine, he had dozed off in his comfortable seat and missed most of the sights available to someone crossing the Atlantic Ocean by air. However he was exhausted and had flown this route several times before.

It had been quite a while since he had slept so well. There were no dreams or voices as far as he could remember; everything just faded to black for a welcome change. For the first time in a while, his mind felt free and unchallenged by external forces.

After staggering to his feet and grabbing his personal briefcase, the American legislator exited the craft and was immediately greeted by two representatives from the American embassy. Inside the briefcase was the mysterious shredded wrapping from the even more mysterious apparently empty package that had been delivered to him at the hospital in Washington.

"Where...the hell is Blair...are Blair and Hurbert?" was his first garbled attempt at a complete sentence.

"They were on a separate flight, Senator," responded one of his escorts named Harold. My brother Ray has the flight number back at the embassy. We shall be having dinner with them back at our embassy tonight after they arrive. Ray said that you were also inquiring about a Major Vostry. He checked and the major should be there with two other astronauts, Lundgren and Goldsmith."

"Fine," mumbled Jensen under his breath. "I need to have a private talk with Major Vostry...alone when he arrives for dinner. It's very important and a matter of national security. Whatever you do, do not warn him about this. I need to get his honest reaction to some important questions, and I don't want him to have any time to come up with a cover story."

"Yes, Senator," responded Harold. "We will direct him to one of our conference rooms at the embassy where you can wait for him. Our lips are definitely sealed on this matter."

Jensen seemed satisfied with the representative's response. Now it was time for some Scotch whisky...or is it whiskey? The embassy was replete with its own private bar maintained to entertain visitors on occasions just like this so Jensen wasted no time jumping into the waiting limousine.

"A couple'a shots and a short nap for me, and I'll be perfectly ready for the little bastards!"

Across Heathrow Airport another international flight carrying Phil Blair and Frank Hurbert had just landed, and the two Americans were making their way through customs. As they waited to retrieve their luggage, Frank expressed some of his many recent fears and concerns.

"Phil, are you certain that Jensen won't be able to snatch the astronauts from us while we're busy talking with Laurie and the Russians? We need them to find and locate and also to understand this Leon fellow if everything I've seen and heard remains true. Well, if anyone ever actually does find him...if he exists, that is. We need their insights and ideas to solve this."

Phil smiled reassuringly at his boss who always seemed to need some bolstering of his backbone at moments like these.

"Positively, Frank. They're on a regular MATS flight...you know, military air transport service...or something like that. I can never keep all of these acronyms straight. They are listed as three American embassy guard replacements just in case anyone looks. Not bad cover, if I should say so myself. And they're dressed in civilian clothes for the flight so they should be okay.

"They've also been briefed to keep a low profile until we pick them up which should be within the next hour or two if nothing goes wrong."

"Phil, with the egos these men carry, I really doubt the low profile bit you mentioned. And then, when they're with us…there's no hope at all. Everyone will guess who they are immediately!"

"That's the whole point, Frank. We want them to attract attention once we're with them. We need Leon to show his face! I just have a hunch that our cosmonaut Leon is somehow programmed to seek them out… especially Vostry. He gave Vostry those pills when he was aboard Spacelab. Those things were anything but aspirin according to the NASA lab guys. They told me they've never seen anything like the chelating action of that chemical…whatever it is."

"Chelating?" whispered Hurbert. "I'm going back to folding space! It's a lot simpler, for sure."

"Just look at it as a rather large molecule with a rather large claw; two fingers will suffice." Phil held up his right hand and made a pinching motion with his thumb and forefinger. Next he produced a small napkin from a nearby table.

"Now imagine that this balled-up napkin is an iron atom…an iron ion would be better I think. Ions are charged. Oh, well, that's not important for our purposes."

Next he grabbed the napkin with his imaginary molecular claw.

"Wha…la! A chelate! At least I think so."

"I don't want anything like that near me, my friend!" laughed Frank. "No, sir. I'm keeping my distance."

"What about your blood, Frank? You have hemoglobin in here! Chelating is how it transports oxygen from your lungs to your body's cells…I think? Never mind. At least now you have an idea of what Leon gave Vostry up there in Spacelab. Why? I have no idea. And I'll just bet that the same stuff was supposed to be in the Senator's package, but someone heisted it. I think I can safely say that someone out there is doing some serious chemistry on us!"

Frank shook his head and pointed toward a tram that could take them to the other side of Heathrow where the MATS flights land. Their luggage and documentation were waiting for them in the hands of a guide from the embassy.

"Let's get the boys and start this analysis all over. They were up there. They've seen Leon on the hoof. He'll probably talk to them without freaking out. At least it's worth a try."

Phil agreed, and they were on their way. Soon, they were standing outside the gate leading to the MATS terminal. Their guide grabbed some paperwork out of his briefcase and entered the area leaving Phil and Frank sitting at a small café sipping coffee. In twenty minutes they were joined by the three astronauts. After handshakes, Vostry was the first to speak.

"Okay, where is the little bastard? We wouldn't all be sitting here unless NASA or the CIA or the FBI had him under wraps."

Frank just shrugged his shoulders and shook his head.

"You saw him last, Major," whispered Hurbert trying not to laugh. "We were going to ask you the same question, but you beat us to it."

Vostry got up and whispered something into the guide's ear. The guide nodded and walked away.

"Okay," mumbled Vostry as he sat back down. "I might as well come clean with what I know. The four of you are the only people I can trust, and I have to trust somebody if I want to live much longer."

Frank and Phil were caught off guard but let Vostry continue.

"Leon and I have spoken. Don't ask me how. He calls me Trebor Yrtsov and thinks I'm a Russian. It took me a while to figure it out. That's my name spelled backwards. He thinks I'm a Russian spy. The Russians do have a transponder hidden aboard Spacelab somewhere; he told me as much without hesitation thinking I knew about it.

"But I'm not a spy. Still, I let him think so to find out what he knows. That way he might tell me more. Somehow he got into my mind. I could hear and understand him, and I don't know a lick of Russian. What I don't know is whether he could read my thoughts about him.

"Then, he gave me some pills. He told me that these would *protect* me! At first I thought I only needed protection from him. You can understand that; just put yourself in my position. He indicated that my job was to destroy Spacelab, but not just yet. I was to wait for the signal. The spacecraft has the means to leave orbit and then blow itself up. I don't know the procedure or the passwords. But he said that a voice from the moon would tell me what to do.

"Why destroy Spacelab? That was what I kept asking him. Why? Finally, he broke down and told me what he knew or was told. Of course, he could have just been trying to calm me down."

"Keep going, Major. This should be really interesting!"

Vostry paused and took another sip from his cup of coffee.

"Apparently, Professor Laurie's experiments aboard Spacelab have been successful beyond anyone's expectations. He...I can't remember the exact words, but he said something like the virus on Spacelab could protect us against...*the aliens.*"

"Aliens?" blurted Frank before he could stop himself. His eyes rolled back and his arms shot up over his head.

"That's right! Call me crazy..." whispered Vostry.

"You're crazy!" yelled Phil with a smile.

Vostry took a deep breath after laughing along with Phil. Then he continued.

"Just bear with me on this alien thing. 'Alien' is what I heard, but maybe he didn't mean an alien or aliens from outer space. Maybe he meant another country like...Russia or China or... But since I heard him call them aliens, I'm sticking with Mars and beyond until something or someone proves otherwise."

Everyone seemed to agree so Vostry continued.

"I just wish that Leon was here so you could...verify this for us."

Suddenly, the major froze with his eyes glued on the entrance to the coffee shop. There, standing between a young man and a young woman was...Leon! Without any words, a waiter brought three additional chairs to the large table and the three visitors sat down.

"Trebor...ah, Robert, this is Gretchen on my left and Alex on my right. They are students who rescued me...well, that's another story."

Leon's English was perfect especially considering he was essentially Russian, but it was obvious that he'd been drinking.

"I have come to warn you, something I should have done when we were on Spacelab, but I didn't understand what was going on then. Did you take the pill I gave you?"

Major Vostry nodded in the affirmative.

"Excellent! I was able to hear most of your conversation. Please don't ask me to explain that process just yet. Time is of the essence. But first my friends and I need a drink to fortify our defenses."

After some libation was passed to Leon and his friends he continued to tell his incredible story.

"Professor Laurie doesn't know it yet, but he has discovered a defense against the cerebral virus these...aliens have been testing on me. Oh, they were well-meaning Russian scientists who injected test samples into me, and they didn't know that their research program was being controlled from somewhere else. It was by pure chance that I got my hands on samples originally intended to be given only to a Senator Jensen who, by the way, is working for Moscow on the side. But, worst of all, he's being used as a pawn by the aliens. I don't know who injected the senator or what he was given, but he takes orders from the same…people…that might not be the right word…anyway, people who try to give orders to me. His job is to slow down Laurie and Spacelab and mine was to destroy Spacelab before the working virus could be transferred to earth. Confused?

"But understand this. The Russians do not know what is controlling them. They are unwilling victims just as we are. And with their help mankind can win this battle for survival."

Frank and Phil couldn't believe what they were hearing.

"So, what do we do now, I ask you? From what you've said, we need to get up to Spacelab and fast." asked Phil as he scratched his head. His last comment was obviously directed to the astronauts present.

Leon smiled but only briefly.

"It took me a while to figure that out. I'll do the hard part. You and Mr. Hurbert need to keep Professor Laurie from divulging what he has discovered at this meeting at Oxford. The…aliens will be watching and listening!"

Leon hesitated, then pulled on the backs of Alex's and Gretchen's chairs.

"We've got to go…now! Hurry. There's no time to lose!"

The students jumped up on queue and without any further words, the three left by a side door.

"What was that about?" said Frank in a bewildered voice.

No one offered an answer to his question. They were all wondering what Leon concluded, and they quickly realized that he had slipped through their fingers.

"I need another drink," whispered Phil and those remaining at the table agreed wholeheartedly. It was going to be a long day.

After about five minutes of small talk, Phil's eyes focused through the front window on a man approaching the door. At first, Phil just smiled and tapped Frank on the shoulder.

"Look! He's back…and all by himself."

Frank looked up and seemed to agree. But it did seem strange when the guest looked around the room at all the tables as if he wasn't sure where his new friends were sitting.

"He's spotted us," whispered Frank. "You'd think he'd remember where we were sitting…?"

Suddenly Phil grabbed Frank's arm.

"It's not…not him. Look at his eyes! His eyes almost glow…bluish. "

The man approached slowly, looking straight at Phil.

"Has anyone seen my twin brother, Leon?"

26
Facing the Music

People running everywhere,
Don't know where to go.
Don't know where I am?
Can't see past the next step!

Does Anyone Really Know What Time It Is?
Chicago

Physics Department Lecture Hall
Oxford University

The time for his talk before the world's physics community had finally arrived. Comments to Victor during the informal cocktail hour, which preceded the meeting, suggested what the audience hoped to hear from the world-renowned scientist and space traveler.

Tell us what it's like to conduct research in orbit with robots as lab assistants! Tell us about your theories on folding space as a means of traveling great distances without moving! Tell us about your discoveries concerning viral communications and how mankind can take advantage of the technology!

The physical chemist's prepared paper included very little if anything on these topics, but was restricted to some new spectroscopic work done at his Princeton lab by current graduate students. He had decided to save the 'fun research', as he called it, for the inevitable questions that would come after his main talk. It would be much safer that way, or so he thought.

As he sat in his seat in the first row of the lecture hall waiting for his introduction to the assembled audience, he pondered his other pressing problem…the voices he had been hearing inside his head. These strange entities had been absent now for quite awhile, actually, since he left the

United States. Even his former student, Dallas Pence, had commented on his remarkable calmness under the circumstances, especially since he had arrived in England. Victor's blood pressure always seemed to double when he had to face questions from his colleagues, but that hopefully was now a thing of the past.

But where was Dallas now? It was just a few crucial minutes before the beginning of the session in which Laurie was to give his honorary talk, and Pence was nowhere to be found. As the professor nervously scanned the lecture hall, an attractive college-aged woman sat down next to him and began by introducing herself.

"Professor Laurie," she said softly, "my name is Alice Jackson. I work for the American Embassy here in London. There is someone of importance here to speak with you. He tells me that it is a sensitive matter involving your research and that time is of the essence. I have been instructed to tell you to please go to the first conference room on the right in the adjoining hallway. I will tell the scientist at the podium that your appearance will be delayed for a few minutes by a matter of importance. The assembled audience will understand."

Subconsciously, Laurie was eager to seize upon any reasonable excuse to delay the commencement of his speech, so without a word, he carefully rose from his seat and made his way toward the conference room which was only a few short steps away. As he entered the doorway to the conference room, he saw a single man whom he didn't recognize immediately sitting at the table in the center of the room. However, he knew that he had seen this face before...somewhere.

"Good afternoon, Professor Laurie. Please forgive me for the untimely intrusion, but I have some...interesting information for you."

Laurie stared at the man for a few seconds, then he took a seat. The voices in his head were weak, but they were definitely back.

"Director Hurbert, it's good to see you again," mumbled Laurie who couldn't hide his surprise. "I hope all is well with Spacelab and NASA."

"That's why I'm here, Victor. As is usually the case, there is both good news and bad news."

The voices in the professor's head were almost screaming now. Much to Laurie's surprise and pleasure, a third person entered the room carrying a tray with several glasses. A drink was exactly what he needed right now!

"I hope you're into Captain Morgan?" asked Phil Blair as he handed a glass of liquor to Victor. "This should shut down those voices that are messing with your head for quite a while!"

Victor didn't question the medicine and downed the large shot glass of liquid with one gulp.

"What's the bad news, Frank?" Laurie mumbled as the voices began to fade into the background.

"We have positive confirmation that several of the robotic elements onboard Spacelab have been reprogrammed. They are not responding to their required protocol as they should. The lab at Langley ordered an inventory of your lab samples, and the two robots charged with that task failed to respond properly. In fact, they began to move the samples around as if...they were hiding them!"

"Who are they hiding them from...us?" asked Laurie with some disbelief in his voice.

"We're not exactly sure yet," Frank responded.

"What about malfunctions?" asked Laurie. "A couple of those robots assigned to the laboratory area seemed a little spastic to me when I was up there, especially after the vibration incident occurred."

Frank just shrugged his shoulders as he responded.

"As you know, we have software onboard that checks these things every thirty minutes. Several chips have been replaced, but the serial numbers don't seem to match our records. What was in effect our password system has somehow been overridden. This is not a mere equipment malfunction or an accident. Someone or some thing has overtly and purposely seized control of these units for their own purposes...whatever those might be?"

"So, what do we do now to counter this?" asked the professor quietly. He didn't expect the answer he received.

"We have to send a mission up there and fix it...or blow that sucker up if they fail!"

Silence fell over the three men for a few moments as each pondered the situation. Laurie thought for sure that he was going to be asked to go back up into orbit, and he started shaking his head negatively to express his feelings. Phil decided that it was time to lay all of the cards on the table.

"I can't tell you how we know this, but your experiments on Spacelab may have...probably have succeeded beyond our wildest hopes and dreams. The origin virus you established for control is now communicating with another viral entity...this one is definitely on the moon! And our read virus is perfectly able to completely decipher the communications between these entities."

"There's a virus on the moon that someone is feeding data into?" gasped Laurie before he could stop himself. "Now you're talking like that nutcase former student of mine...Dallas Pence." Laurie paused and thought for a moment. "How did he get the sample off the Spacelab in the first place? Have you been doing this behind my back...as usual?"

"That's what we're trying to figure out for ourselves," whispered Frank as he looked around the room to make sure that their conversation was secure. "Our satellites and ground based telescopic systems are all coming up negative. We don't see any moon men up there dancing around just yet, and the Russians have been nowhere near the place for quite a while... five years and probably a lot longer! We asked them, and they verified our data without hesitation."

"Then, you're telling me that these viruses are making up the messages themselves...in English or whatever human language?"

Laurie paused and decided to update his friends from NASA about the voices in his head, which were currently quite silent.

"I know about the rumors...the jokes about the voices in my head. But, they are actually there. I'm not crazy! When they are active, I can hear them...in English! I must have exposed myself to one or more of these viral entities when I was up on Spacelab. They tell me to do things...to go places, but I ignore them as best I can. When I was sitting out there in the conference room waiting, they were jabbering away telling me to return to Princeton on the double. I've created a virus that's aware of Princeton...or someone else has? What's next? The Chicago Cubs!

"And Dr. Pence at Stanford. As you must know, he was my student. He has established that viral colonies can communicate over considerable distances with each other...how far away can they be? Who knows? His tachyon theory makes the moon seem just a hop and a skip away!

"And, why not the moon? But the little boogers couldn't get all the way up there by themselves...could they? So, did someone else create their own variety and put them up there just to help us out? I don't necessarily mean the Russians here. What about...aliens? I mean real aliens!"

Then Laurie stopped short as if he were assessing the situation from a different angle. He had always ruled out the close proximity of advanced alien life forms because of the vast distances between stars and the severe speed of travel limitation set by the speed of light. But what if Pence's thoughts about tachyons were actually correct. Or what if some species had successfully folded space? Suddenly all the known limitations to travel would be off and all was possible.

"But, you know, as soon as I drank that shot you gave me, Phil, they were gone! The voices clammed right up and took off. They must like liquor or dislike it a lot. Hey, give me another glass just in case. It's so nice when they shut up for a while. I might have to become an alcoholic! It would be a double enjoyment for me for sure!"

Phil Blair gladly refilled the professor's glass, and Victor downed the alcohol just as quickly as a smile widened on his face.

"This could be great fun!" shouted Victor as he slammed his glass down on the table and waited for Phil to pour him another.

"So, what do you want me to do for you?" whispered Laurie. It took a few seconds before an answer came from Frank Hurbert.

"We need your approval to immediately destroy Spacelab before things get any worse!"

Laurie's jaw dropped open in complete surprise. It was a possibility he didn't want to entertain.

"What? Why do you need my approval? I'm a mere college professor with a mobility problem."

"It's political, Victor. If we want to conduct any project of this magnitude ever again, this solution has to go smoothly. We need you to announce to the scientific community that your Spacelab research has been successfully completed, but because of the rather dangerous viral remnants still onboard, it was decided to destroy the lab and replace it with a new, more modern version which is already designed and under construction. Of course, you can hint that destruction was our plan all along so as not to risk any infection of the human race down on the planet surface. We were ahead of the game all the time.

"Tell them that the details of your research will be released as soon as they are declassified. This way we all win and no one gets in a hurry or a frenzy."

Laurie wanted to object, but he saw the brilliance in the plan. Credit for him without having to return to orbit. And then there was the inevitable additional funding he would receive when the second Spacelab was ready to go into orbit. He quickly decided to play along.

"I'll do it," he said quietly. "After that, it's…the blow up is up to you to do. I'm washing my hands of Spacelab One and viral research forever, but that will be our little secret. Pence can take over. He's much better at it."

Once more the professor's empty glass was filled with alcohol by Phil Blair who was simultaneously dialing his cell phone as he poured the drink.

"Bulls-eye is a go," Phil whispered into the phone calmly. "Call me upon completion."

Phil put his phone down on the nearby end table and then retrieved his own glass.

"An hour or so after she leaves orbit should do it, Victor. You should probably wait for confirmation before you address the public on the actual destruction. We shouldn't let the cat out of the bag until she's gone away for good. But you can tell them our plans now."

Victor was in no hurry, and the look on Frank's face told the others that he was quite relieved by this turn of events. Just then, a strange thought flashed across Frank's mind.

"I wonder what old Senator Jensen is up to these days? We haven't heard from that little bastard in quite a while. You never know...he might just be out in the audience today spying on us."

Phil just shrugged his shoulders as he slowly sipped his drink. He offered a glass to Frank, but the latter declined for the time being. The next ten minutes passed slowly and uneventfully until Phil's phone began buzzing. He picked it up anticipating good news about Spacelab leaving its orbit. Unfortunately, after a few seconds, his jaw dropped.

"Jensen!" he shouted. "How...? Both of them? And it's...what? Working and not working? Are you sure? I need to think! Frank and I will call you back."

Hurbert jumped up from his seat and demanded an immediate explanation.

"The automatic self-destruct system aboard Spacelab is down for some reason! They ran a preliminary test sequence and it failed.

"And, we've got some surprise visitors aboard Spacelab...again! We were discussing Senator Jensen a moment ago. He is now onboard Spacelab! Don't ask me how he got there or who took him there or what he's doing there. The lab guys picked him up coming in from the docking port area, but our satellite surveillance showed no docking vehicles whatsoever. He has NASA gear on, too. I thought he hated NASA? How he came by that will be interesting. And guess what! Now he's in the main recovery area taking a nap!"

Frank Hurbert pounded his fist on the table in anger and surprise as he jumped up and down.

"Russians, dumb-ass senators...who'll be next? Santa Claus and his reindeer? I want to blow that sucker out of the sky and fast. Jensen got there without our help. Let him get himself back the same way. Phil, tell the lab guys to keep trying while we come up with an alternate plan."

"Who's the other visitor…if I dare to ask?" whispered Professor Laurie in a hesitant tone.

"They said it was that Russian cosmonaut we've run across before… either Leon or his twin brother, Tomas, I believe?"

Laurie was shaking his head negatively in disbelief as he wondered how the Russians got Jensen up into orbit so easily and quickly. But, as he looked up, another question sprang from his lips.

"Then, Phil, if all this is true, would you mind telling me who that is standing in the doorway over there?"

Blair whirled around and to his wonderment, there stood Leon Yengoyan and his two Oxford friends, Gretchen and Alex. Without any prompting, Leon stepped forward and offered an explanation.

"He's what you might call my twin brother, but now he is more my clone. They call him Leon II, but he has a regular human name…Tomas, which isn't really important right now.

"He's been…he's posed as my twin brother ever since our birth. He's not really human any longer if he ever was. But I still certainly am. That's the important difference between us. Now he belongs to certain aliens who have been monitoring your viral experiments for quite a while from their ship and their base on the far side…the dark side of the moon.

"I've been in one of their space ships several times…involuntarily. That's how I got onto the American Spacelab and got back here again. They zapped my head with a virus they have, and it pretty much controlled me until my two friends Gretchen and Alex found the flaw in their methods. Believe it or not, that would be alcohol and possibly what they call recreational drugs. They saved me…saved my life because I'm sure our alien friends will dispose of me once my usefulness is in the past! And that time has probably come."

"But we've seen no other spacecraft nearby Spacelab," offered Hurbert with an obviously nervous voice.

"It's cloaked. It could be hanging right next to Spacelab, and you wouldn't see it. The aliens are about to steal Spacelab, lock, stock and barrel! Right now, I'll bet, they're busy pushing Spacelab toward the other side of the moon and none of your regular onboard instrumentation senses it or can prevent it."

Phil held up his hand to silence everyone for a moment.

"He's correct. Spacelab is already out of orbit...heading toward the moon. We have no control over it whatsoever. The Houston lab just thinks it's obeying that part of its destruct protocol. But the current trajectory of the lab is way off of a proper destruct trajectory according to our tracking data."

"We've got to do something...to destroy Spacelab and fast, or the human race as we know it is screwed!" muttered Frank as he looked from face to face for an answer.

Quiet settled over the room for a few moments.

"I think I've got an idea on how we can accomplish that," said Leon quietly. "Do you know the two Russian fellows, Zeg and Vlady? I believe they have the answer we need."

"How can you say that...Leon? What do you mean?" mumbled Frank in desperation.

Right at that moment as if on cue, Dallas Pence entered the room. After handshakes and hellos, Pence sat down next to Laurie.

"You fellows seem deep in thought. I hope I didn't interrupt anything important when I came in."

"Not at all,' said Frank with some relief in his voice. "Do you know the two Russians?"

"Two? I just met four Russians. Nice fellows, I must admit, and their English is a thousand times better than my Russian. The guys from Siberia have been running electronic surveillance on Spacelab. Seems like they've detected an...alien presence out there that keeps visiting Spacelab. How's that for excitement?"

Frank glanced at Leon and nodded.

"Spacelab has left orbit," added Phil quietly, "and we have lost control of its systems. The aliens' ship is hijacking Spacelab right under our noses, and there's nothing we can do about it!"

Pence was truly surprised. He looked to Laurie who just shrugged his shoulders and shook his head. But Pence had an idea.

"Koslov and Zeg...one of the Russian technicians and his partner, described a scenario like this during our conversation at dinner. They told me that they were going to the Oxford physics labs to take a look at Spacelab to check out what's happening. We'd better get right over to Oxford as quickly as possible! They may be able to save the bacon for us!"

27
Teamwork

Blinded by science, I'm on the run.
Blinded by science, where do I belong?
What's in the future, has it just begun?
Blinded by science, I'm on the run.

Blinded by Science
Foreigner

Oxford University

In less than half an hour the team of Russian and American scientists, astronauts and administrators found themselves assembled at the Oxford University physics laboratories. Only Victor Laurie was left behind to complete his speech before the American Physical Society meeting. He wanted to go to Oxford, too, but the group decided that this was no time for a panic.

Vlady Koslov and his partner Zeg manned a pair of computer consoles in the center of the room. With the proper software and passwords, the group was able to view most of the internal areas of the Spacelab. There was no activity to speak of. Senator Jensen was still out cold in a recovery room and the alien referred to as Leon II sat in the main control room. Several of the robots could also seen, but they were also relatively inactive.

"We're ready to give it a try," said Koslov quietly.

"Let her rip," said Dallas Pence who was sitting next to Koslov. Phil and Frank were still pretty much in the dark. As Koslov was entering some data, Pence leaned over to explain.

"The Russians compromised one of our robots…on Spacelab. So, we should be able to control it…get it to initiate the destructive sequence before the others can react to our plan."

At that moment Koslov smiled and patted Dallas on the back.

"It's working so far. I'll move him over to the left side of the console so Leon II can't see him at work. Then we'll initiate a malfunction in the lab on the other side of the ship. The robot can do this by cutting three wires in the console and then when the attention of our enemies is focused elsewhere, accomplish our goal by reconnecting them differently. With that the ship should self-destruct when it comes to a halt, wherever and whenever that is. Let's hope that they don't change their minds and bring it back to earth."

"How do you know so much about our…?" muttered Hurbert.

"I apologize," said Koslov. "We were…spying on your research. We have a similar…ah, what the hell. We have similar research going on in Saint Petersburg. We are not as far along as you are, and unfortunately, we are responsible for injecting Leon Yengoyan and his so called brother with several new forms of virus. Neither Zeg nor I did that and the two research scientists behind you are innocent, too. It was our Central Command who forced his action. They're still fighting the cold war. I guess they think that their jobs depend on it? But, actually, the aliens made them do it so I shouldn't cast any blame even though I want to.

"Also, we decided not to fight it directly so that we could be nearby and keep an eye on what was going on. If we resisted directly, we'd just get shot, and they'd do it anyway."

Suddenly, there was activity in the command center of Spacelab. The robot with the planted Russian chip in it had successfully cut the wires under the console, but Leon II saw it, and he leaped up and lunged at the robot. In seconds the lab lurched as the alien and the robot rolled across the floor. Obviously, the occupants of the alien spaceship had been monitoring the scene, too.

Leon II grabbed the colored wires from the robot's mechanical arm, and he went back to the console and started replacing the wires. The robot was helpless as it was positioned on its side against the wall. Suddenly, the visual monitor blanked out. All of the observers in the Oxford lab gritted their teeth in frustration as they waited and hoped for the video to return.

They say that at the moment of the explosion in space, Victor Laurie was in the middle of a sentence describing how and why Spacelab was being terminated by NASA, which ,of course, is a subject he thought he wasn't supposed to discuss with anyone just yet. And it is unlikely that anyone on earth actually saw the brief flash of light. Years later, small pieces of metallic shrapnel were found on the moon, but it could never be absolutely proven that these remains were from either Spacelab or an alien craft.

Dr. Dallas Pence continued his viral communication experiments but was never able to reproduce the communication he had observed with a viral entity on the surface of the moon. Senator Jensen wasn't really missed by his associates and colleagues in the government or back in his home state. Zeg and Vlady returned home to Russia as did their two scientist friends although it is said that the latter never continued their viral research underneath Saint Petersburg. The Russian government waited a week and then announced that their former lab had been sealed permanently as a precaution against viral contamination.

Victor Laurie returned to Princeton and focused his future research on millimeter-wave molecular spectroscopy. They say he took up a serious interest in astronomy, but at the same time he seems to have developed a serious drinking problem. Leon Yengoyan decided to stay in England and landed a job at the Russian embassy. He was truly a local hero in England as well as back in his homeland as can be judged by the number of talks he gave and the number of movies created and books written about his life and that of his probable twin brother.

Alex and Gretchen graduated at the top of their class, got married and started a string of very successful bars and restaurants in England and Europe. Of course, Leon was one of their best customers. They even named a favorite vodka drink after Tomas. A youthful photo of Tomas and Leon hung in a place of honor behind the bar. And Ollie Blair gained admission to the United States Air Force Academy and was performing at the head of his class.

Phil and Frank continued their careers at NASA. Somehow the subject of folding space as a means of travel never came up again. Dallas Pence and Terry Swanson successfully continued their careers, more as teachers than researchers.

And the strange voices in the heads of many of these people were never heard from again…as far as we know.